D1464633

05343693

THE SILENT MAN

A HARVEY STONE THRILLER

J.D. WESTON

WESTON MEDIA

THE SILENT MAN

To find the killer, he must lose his mind...

PROLOGUE

Jennifer Standing hadn't shed a single tear.

If her father had been there, he would have been proud. But then, if her father had been there, she wouldn't have anything to cry about. He would have stopped the man with the warm, foul breath, whose sweaty palm had left a bitter a taste on her lips.

It had still been dark when she had heard the man's footsteps trail away and had finally dared to open her eyes.

But she hadn't screamed.

An entire night and day had been and gone, and not a soul had passed her by, so even if she had screamed, nobody would have heard.

She had stayed hidden in that place deep in the forest, with her arms tied around a thick tree trunk, and her face resting on its rough bark.

She was hungry and thirsty, and her knees buckled with fatigue.

But Jennifer Standing hadn't shed a single tear, and she hadn't been afraid.

At least, not until night-time came, when the silent man watched her from the shadows.

PART I

CHAPTER ONE

His hand slammed down onto the steel-clad table and rocked the tea inside the polystyrene cup.

"I'll make you talk even if it kills me," said Detective Inspector Myers.

The suspect stared back at him, expressionless, as if he'd been drugged or was mute.

"I'll run through the facts for the third time. Feel free to join in."

Myers glanced at his watch. His time was nearly up. Twenty-three hours and forty-five minutes had passed since they'd brought the man in, and they were no further along with the case. He hadn't uttered a single word.

"Forty-eight hours ago, a teenage girl was

reported missing by her mother. Jennifer Standing. She was blonde with blue eyes and she was wearing pyjamas. According to her parents' statement, she was on her own downstairs while the pair of them were making the beds upstairs. You know, ordinary day-to-day life. But, when they return, she's gone. They look in all the usual places, but they soon realise she's not there. The back door is open and their pride and joy, their only child, has been taken. Finally, they report their child missing."

He studied the man, searching for any kind of sign that his words were registering, but there was nothing. No empathy. No emotion. Nothing. It was common in Myers' experience that guilt would creep in when the details were narrated. The suspect would change expression, wipe his or her eyes, offer some kind of involuntary signal.

But there was nothing.

"Units were dispatched, dogs dispersed, a helicopter and a search team were sent to search a nature reserve half a mile away. The nature reserve is large, and they found nothing. So, the search team was increased, and I was assigned to the case. This was no longer a child who might have run away or wandered off. This was now an abduction. Serious stuff."

Myers paused.

"Local people helped with the search. More dogs were brought in and the area was widened. But still, we couldn't find her. One hundred and fifty people in total, a helicopter, and six dogs couldn't find one single girl."

The man said nothing.

"Fast forward twenty-six hours. Faisal Hussein, a man in his early twenties, leaves his house at nine p.m. We know this to be true because his neighbour saw him leave. He heard the front door close."

Myers paced the room back and forth with his hands behind his back, unable to stare too long at the man whose eyes followed him like a tiger's might follow a deer. Myers hated to admit it, but the man gave him the creeps. The whole case was creepy. He'd rather have been dealing with a straightforward murder case than having his name involved in a sordid child abduction case, which were rarely solved after twenty-four hours.

Rarely, but sometimes.

"Hussein walked to the end of his road,

turned left, and crossed the street, where he entered the local nature reserve. He wasn't high, he wasn't drunk, and he didn't smoke. In his pockets, he carried nothing at all. Do you see him? Do you see him in your mind?"

There was no response from the man, only a mild curiosity that grew with Myers' anger.

"He followed a path that dog walkers use. It runs beside a little river for a while then cuts into a forest through a small gap in the bushes. Nobody uses this but him. Nobody even knows it's there. We checked the footprints in the mud and there was only one set. His."

Myers stopped pacing and turned to face the man, suffering his gaze for as long as it took to spit out his next words.

"Inside that little secret place in the trees, that place that nobody but Faisal Hussein and that frightened little girl knew existed, he set to work. Even while the helicopter circled overhead and the dogs barked less than a mile away, he did what he set out to do."

He checked his watch. There were ten minutes left before the suspect walked.

It was time to get graphic.

"A hole was dug in the earth, small enough to be covered with leaves yet deep enough to conceal the body of a child."

There was no change in the man's expression. Not even the arrogant, bored sneer that many adopted while they exercised their right to silence.

There was a knock at the door and it opened enough for DS Fox to lean into the room and shake her head to signify that the tests from the man's fingernails and clothing did not place him at the scene of the crime. Myers had asked the lab to expedite the analysis to make sure they found something to hold him.

But they had found nothing.

"Sorry, boss," said Fox.

The door closed and, once more, Myers checked his watch.

Five minutes.

"Fast forward one hour. The Standing family receive a knock at their door. They answer it, dreading the news that their only child's body has been found, hoping for the torment to be over, but dreading those words, the finality of it all. But who do they find at their door? Not a female detective and a social worker ready to offer support. No. Somehow, out of the darkness that had become their lives, from the train wreck that was their tormented minds, comes an angel. They find their daughter standing there, dressed in filthy pyjamas with tears running down her face."

The man said nothing.

"You might think the case would be over. The girl had been found and the searches called off. But no. You see, at about the time that young Jennifer was found on her doorstep and the nightmare of her parents was coming to an end, a new nightmare revealed itself."

He leaned into the man, keeping his distance, well aware that he was alone in the room with a potential psychopath.

"A police dog found the little place in the trees and wandered inside. His handler followed him and called for backup. Detectives followed the handler. Can you tell me what they found?"

Again, the man said nothing. He maintained his casual stare as if he was waiting for a bus or in the queue at the supermarket.

"Faisal Hussein," said Myers. "They found Faisal Hussein naked, pinned to a tree with six-inch nails, and his chest sliced open like a Sunday roast."

He leaned across the table to get close to the man once more, lowering his voice to a growl.

"Tell me. What kind of man does that? What kind of man could have found that girl when the police with all our resources couldn't? What kind of man can do that to another man, regardless of his crime?"

A single beep from Myers' watch told him the twenty-four hours was up. He stood back, shaking his head.

"Interview finished. Three-fifty a.m.," said Myers, holding the man's stare with disgust.

He hit the stop button on the recording.

"I know it was you. You know it was you. And before long, I'll find a way to prove it."

He unlocked the handcuffs that held the man to the table and watched as he stood and made his way to the door.

"You might think that what you did was good. That somehow everyone here regards you as some kind of hero. But trust me, you're no better than Faisal Hussein, and all you've done is give us another headache."

The man said nothing as he walked toward the door without looking back, until Myers caught him by his jacket sleeve and turned him.

"You haven't won, sunshine. Not by a long shot. I'll find a way, and when I do, I'll break you."

The man glanced down at Myers' hand and then back at his face.

Myers released his grip.

"I'm watching you. I know your face," said Myers. He leaned in close with total disregard for protocol and safety precautions to whisper in his ear so that Fox and the duty officer wouldn't hear him in the control room. "Your cards are marked."

The man didn't reply.

CHAPTER TWO

Warm, yellow hues of the dying summer sun lit the fine edges of long grass that reached Harvey's waist. His bare feet found soft sand and the ocean breeze carried the taunting laughter of the girl he could never reach. The beach seemed endless. The sea met the sky in blurred watercolour strokes, and every time Harvey reached for the girl, she seemed to pull away and his hand clenched nothing but warm sea air.

Three thuds came rolling over the breaking waters.

But still, Harvey ran, unperturbed.

She turned as she ran, smiling back at him and laughing, giving him the chance to catch her again. Yet as his hand reached once more for the flowing tails of her summer dress, three thuds, louder than before, rolled across the breaking waters.

He slowed just a little as he sought the source of the sound.

And the distance between them grew.

His young legs ached, and the sharp grass had cut the soles of his foot for the sand to sting.

Three thuds came again. They were even louder. Like dull hammer blows.

And the distance between him and his sister grew.

Harvey stopped and turned to face the ocean. The yellow strip of sand reached on as far as the eye could see in either direction; behind him, the long grass blocked his view.

Three more thuds. They were harder and fiercer than ever before, like the beating pulse he sometimes felt in his temple.

But there was nothing. Not a thing moved as far as he could see, save for the long grass that danced in the breeze, the breaking waves, and Hannah, whose diminishing silhouette threatened to vanish at any moment.

But it was another round of hammer-like

blows that roused Harvey from the deep slumber. He sat up in bed, feeling his arms slide against his slick, sweat-soaked body, and took in his surroundings.

The morning sun shone through the bedroom window of his small bungalow and Harvey squinted against the light.

Thud, thud, thud.

The dream slipped away, just as it did most times, and Harvey pulled on a t-shirt and grabbed a pair of shorts on his way to the front door.

There was time for one more round of thuds, as Harvey was pulling on his clothes, and he snatched the door open before the third rap of knuckles connected with the wood. The sudden snatch surprised Sergio, whose attention was elsewhere, and his knuckles found thin air.

"Harvey," he said, and stepped back away from the door. It was when he was scared that his Eastern European accent shone through the most. "I'm sorry, I-"

"I was sleeping, Sergio."

"It's John. He said you should come. He said he would like to see you," said Sergio.

A van trundled past one hundred metres

away, but the driver did not see them due to the foliage that had overgrown on Harvey's porch. Harvey watched the van wind along the long, gravel track toward his foster-father's house. The house had been built centuries before and stood in the midst of a three-hundred-acre estate. It was where Harvey had grown up, and he had memories tucked away in each and every corner.

The orchard at the highest point of the property was where he and Hannah used to play when they weren't playing in the stream that ran through the centre of the grounds like a crystal-clear vein. There was a barn in the lower field that his foster-father, John, had converted into a garage and used to store his prized possession: a nineteen-sixties classic E-Type Jaguar. At the front of the property, beside the pair of iron gates and tucked into the trees, was the old groundsman's cottage. There hadn't been a groundsman for many years; John had decided to pay a maintenance company for weekly visits. Harvey had moved into the little house as soon as he had started working for his foster-father, when he was just a teenager.

It was his home. His own little pocket of peace.

The view to the great house was unobstructed, as was the view from John's ground floor study of Harvey's cottage. Manicured lawns stretched out either side of the gravel track to give Harvey a view of serenity and peace.

But the day that Sergio had banged on his door was different.

The driveway was clogged with vans and small lorries. The centre lawn that overlooked the village of Theydon Bois was filled with white chairs all facing an arch that somebody had built and adorned with white flowers. A small stage was being erected and there was a bandstand, a bar, and an area for children to play.

Still dazed from his dream, Harvey blinked and took in the scene and then stared back at Sergio, who waited with that characteristic fear in his eyes.

"John would like to see you, Harvey. I didn't know you were sleeping. I-"

"I'm going for a run," said Harvey. He had little patience for the man John put so much trust in as to call him his adviser. "When I'm done, I'll go and see John."

"He told me to say that he would like to see you now and that I should not let you disappoint him."

Sergio was in an awkward position and his expression was almost pleading Harvey not to make things difficult for him.

Harvey nodded at the commotion on the lawn.

"If John is throwing a party, tell him thanks but no thanks," said Harvey, and made to shut the door.

But Sergio blocked the door with his foot, a move he regretted as soon as he saw Harvey's expression.

"Today is a big day, Harvey," said Sergio. "Today is Donny's wedding."

CHAPTER THREE

The sound of the old telephone was shrill and harsh, but DI Matthew Myers lay unmoving in his bed. He outstretched his arm to the phone on his bedside table and raised the receiver an inch. Recognising the tinny voice even from afar, he let the handset fall back onto its cradle. The memories of the man who hadn't uttered a single word still rolled around his mind. He hadn't worn the familiar expression of guilt or shame. He hadn't even developed a nervous twitch.

The silent man had been calm, as if he was untouchable. As if nothing Myers had said had even penetrated his skull. As if the ticking clock of the law had been the only sound he could hear.

But Myers would never forget his face. Those stone-cold eyes and the way he had carried himself.

Untouchable.

Myers found himself mouthing the word and had to shake himself from falling into some semblance of admiration for the man's control.

Of all the disturbed, cruel, and heartless men Myers had brought down in his career, whoever that man had been was off the scale. In Myers' experience, sex offenders carried no physical attributes. He'd seen them as young teenage boys, young men in their twenties and thirties, and, of course, middle-aged to senior men who had begun their sordid, sexual deviations before DNA had been discovered, who had relied on the silence of their ashamed victims. They often masqueraded behind a mask of innocence and do-gooders: politicians, community faces, and even the oh-so-cliched men of god.

But the man from the previous day, who had haunted Myers through a night of restless anxiety, had been nothing he'd ever seen before. He wore no stereotype, he fell into no silo, and he carried none of the traits that Myers and countless other detectives looked for in such men.

It wasn't unusual for Myers to be able to imagine the man in the interview room carrying out his deed. As terrible as it was to imagine, Myers found it helpful. To visualise how capable the man was, how sick he was, and what drove him to do such things.

Men like Faisal Hussein often had an inbuilt distaste for female flesh. They despised women and girls and sought to ruin them. Some men were so depraved and socially outcast that to touch a consenting female rarely went further than brushing past one as he squeezed onto a packed bus or a train. Like Derek Young, thought Myers, and he remembered a case he'd worked on two years previously. He remembered the man sitting in that very same interview room and how he had cowered as Myers berated him and broke him into tears of shame. It had been those tears that had opened a world that Myers hadn't been ready for, and one he had never been able to leave since.

It had only been when Young had been

unable to restrain his excitement that he had risked everything. The bus had been packed, he had said, too packed to move without touching anybody. The woman had been wearing a short skirt, shorter than anything Young had seen before, and when the bus leaned into the corners, she too had pressed up against him.

"What did you do, Derek?" Myers had asked, his voice calm now that the confession had begun.

"You know what I did," said Young.

"For the tape," said Myers, and nodded at the two reels that had been spinning for thirty-eight minutes.

Young had stumbled at first, as if he was considering changing direction, but Myers had seen that before and steered him right.

"The bus," said Myers, "the girl, the skirt, and her legs."

"Women don't look at me. I'm one of those men who women seem to look *through* as if I'm not there. Even when they do see me, I can see it in their faces, the repulsion."

He paused and drifted into his own world of misery and relayed his story of depravity and cruelty. How he'd followed the girl and taken her to a quiet place where he could take his time.

Savour the moment.

Myers' eyes flicked open as the psychology presented itself. Young had savoured the moment. He had wanted it to last. Just as Faisal Hussein had savoured the moment.

And the silent man had savoured his own moment.

His feet touched the cold floor and his dressing gown rode the air as Myers pulled it on while walking from the bedroom to the kitchen. He pulled the previous day's coffee filter from the machine and replaced it with a new one. He collected three spoons of ground coffee, poured enough water for two coffees, then slammed the lid shut and hit the power button.

Before the coffee machine had even started its whirring, Myers had grabbed a pen from a small bowl on the kitchen counter and pulled his case file close.

"Savour the moment," he said, speaking out loud to prompt his thoughts. "This guy was savouring the moment. How long had he been there? The whole area was humming with police for hours. How did he get into the forest and out again without being seen? He must have been there waiting. Which means he must have known Hussein was going to take her there in the first place. Which means he must have been following Hussein, watching his every move."

Myers tapped the pen on the file, but he couldn't untangle his thoughts enough to write anything. Instead he wrote two words. *Silent man.*

"He's the killer," he said out loud again. "I know he is."

He poured a coffee, added two sugars, and as he strode through to his bedroom, he caught his reflection in the bathroom mirror and stared at himself. The years had not been kind. Two days' growth covered his chin with more salt than pepper. Beneath his plain, white t-shirt, his paunch peeked into view over the elastic of his shorts. The only clear reminder of the man he used to be was his eyes. Though too many late nights and the horrors of his job had left their scars in the form of heavy lines and darkened bags, they were his eyes, a feature his ex-wife had adored, and countless women before had fallen for.

"Still got it, Myers," he said, unconvincing even to himself. It was something his ex-wife had used to say on the odd occasion they had to dress up for an event, a wedding or the annual ball.

In the bedroom, he set the mug of coffee down and fished his notepad from the pocket of his trousers, which were lying on the floor in a heap with his shirt and jacket from being discarded only a few hours before.

On the back page, he had written Fox's phone number. He had tried too many times to memorise the number. But there was no pattern. He remembered other numbers, but not Fox's. He checked the time and judged if she would be at the office or still at home then decided to call her home number. He didn't want to let DCI Allenby know he was awake if he could help it. But as he reached for the phone, its shrill ring startled him.

He sighed, knowing who it would be, then picked up the handset and waited.

"Matthew?"

He was right.

"Matthew, are you there? Don't you dare drop my call again."

He imagined her with her new life. In days of old at nine o'clock in the morning, she would have been wearing her old threadbare dressing gown and nursing her fifth cup of tea. But her new life commanded much more of her. She would be wearing a pretty summer dress and flip-flops, or maybe a long skirt and an off-the-shoulder top. Whatever it was, she would be dressed and made up. She would be looking good.

"Matthew? Talk to me."

She would smell fantastic too. He remembered the girl at the checkout commenting on her perfume one time. The way Alison attracted even the opposite sex.

"Are you there?"

In fact, he would have bet a month's salary that if she was ever going to leave him, it would have been for another woman.

Can't be right all the time.

"Matthew, don't play games. I don't have time."

"What do you have on today?" he asked.

"What? What do you mean what do I

have on? What I'm wearing is none of your business."

"You said you don't have time for this," said Myers. "What do you have on? What am I keeping you from?"

She sighed, and he heard her change the handset to her other ear. The rattle of an earring gave her away, but her lowered tone confirmed it, that lover boy was still at home.

"You said you'd take Harriet today. You said you'd drop her off."

So that was it. She was waiting for Harriet to go to school so she could have some fun time with Darren. Myers knew all about Darren Hunter. He had called in some favours and had him checked out before he'd moved into the family home. For his daughter's security, and to satiate his own jealousy.

"It's Saturday, Alison."

"She has a study session. She has exams soon. I told you all this last week."

"I'm leaving now," he said.

"You're not even dressed, are you?"

She still knew him.

"I can hear it in your voice. You haven't even finished your first coffee yet."

"I will have by the time I'm dressed," said Myers.

"She's already late. So you need to be here ten minutes ago and get her to school by ten."

"Tell her I'll beep when I'm outside," said Myers, and went to put the phone down. But Alison's voice stopped him. He put the phone back to his ear.

"Matthew?" she said, waiting for him to confirm the call was still live.

"Alison," he said, impatient but playful.

"Is everything okay?"

"I'm sitting in my boxer shorts nursing my first coffee and I've had about two hours sleep."

"No. I mean, are you okay? I hate this."

"I'll beep when I'm outside, Alison."

He'd barely let go of the handset when the phone jumped into life again. He held it there, controlling his temper, and then answered.

"I hate this as much as you hate this, Alison. But it was your choice to-"

"Detective Inspector Myers, I suggest you calm yourself," said a new but all too familiar voice.

There were two women in Myers' life.

One, he adored and was fascinated by to the point that she was in his thoughts at least five times a day and could rouse his ageing hormones with a single teasing bite of her lower lip. The other terrified him to the point of admiration, submission, and defeat.

If either of them ever found out which one they were, he'd be screwed.

CHAPTER FOUR

The grounds of John Cartwright's house were littered with chairs, tables, and pedestals. In the time it had taken for Harvey to run ten miles, shower, and dress, more workers had arrived and had begun ferrying crates and boxes from the vans that were parked in a line along the gravel drive.

Harvey kept to the grass and made his way between them to the big house, aware of the returning glances from some of the girls. He paid them little interest and only turned when he was at the top step of John's grand entrance. He wore his leather jacket, despite the heat of the early morning summer sun, with cargo pants and tan boots. It was his usual attire. Most of John's men wore suits, or at the very least trousers, shoes, and a sports jacket, but Harvey preferred the freedom of movement and the solid, protective feel of boots.

The driveway led away from the steps to the gate and his own small house. To the right, the grass was empty up to the stream that cut through the property and the orchard beyond. To the left, the piles of wedding furniture began where the gravel finished. The workers were carrying the items across the lawn for three hundred yards to where the ground fell into a slope that led down to the barn and the old stables. But at the crest of that fall, John had commissioned an arch of oak and maple for Donny and his bride to stand beneath. With only sparse furniture in place, the arch appeared insignificant against the sky beyond, but Harvey knew it was at that point where the arch had been erected that the view across Epping Forest and the village of Theydon Bois was commanding. He also knew that the village of Theydon Bois would be able to see the wedding in the distance, and admire the opulent ceremony, however distant.

In John's mind, thought Harvey, he was a

lord of old and the villagers lived in envious admiration. But it was doubtful that any would even look up.

Behind Harvey, the two huge, wooden, arched doors opened and, as a butler might, Sergio appeared standing to one side, a silent invitation for Harvey to enter.

Meetings with his foster-father were rarely pleasant or interesting. Harvey remained standing on the step, letting Sergio wait a few moments longer. He considered how the meeting might go and its purpose, and he prepared himself with a few deep breaths. The meeting would concern the wedding, of that there could be no doubt. But the specifics were hard to guess.

There was a polite cough from behind him.

"Harvey?"

Harvey didn't reply.

Instead, he turned and, without meeting Sergio's submissive gaze, strode into the house and stopped. It was usual for the house to be immaculate, but what Harvey saw was spectacular.

The grand entrance was high-ceilinged, and two staircases curved up from the ground

floor to the first-floor landing, like snakes,
Harvey had always thought. Every inch of the
wood had been polished, from the ornate oak
floor to the balustrades that ran alongside the
stairways and the length of the upper landing.
Curtains on the upper floor had been cleaned
and tied back to form neat V-shapes, and
though the summer sun beamed through the
windows, not a speck of dust hung in the
golden beams.

The paintings on the walls of each
stairway bore polished brass frames that
gleamed and the ostentatious chandelier that
hung in the centre of the void between the
two staircases sparkled.

On the left-hand side of the hallway was
a dining room, formal and stiff. When
Harvey had been a boy, it had been a lounge
and he remembered playing with his sister
in there under the watchful and adoring
gaze of Barb, John's ex-wife. Harvey imagined the cleaning effort had seeped through
into that room too. It would be where John
would invite only the most privileged of
guests and his stage from which he would
demonstrate his wealth and power in his
usual show, a leading role in a cast of one

with an audience that varied from the impressed to the oppressed, and even the depressed.

On the right-hand side of the hallway was John's study. Harvey guessed the cleaning crew had, under strict instruction from Sergio, John's puppet, been told not to clean in there.

He stepped through.

He was right.

The space was not dirty. John was a clean man, fastidiously tidy and organised beyond normality. But being one of the most used rooms in the huge house, the wood needed polishing and dust particles hung in the air.

However, the room had hosted conversations and acts that could see the entire Cartwright family behind bars. Although there was no paper evidence of the criminal activity, it wouldn't be too difficult for undercover police or even one of John's long list of enemies to plant a camera or a microphone or even find some kind of incriminating evidence that would link the family to a long list of unsolved crimes. There would be only two men that would not and could not be locked up with evidence found in that room, and that was Julios, Harvey's mentor and John's minder, and Harvey. Neither man existed on paper.

Behind his walnut desk, John cradled a crystal tumbler of brandy. It was typical of him to wear a suit with no tie. His image carried him a long way and nestled his personality into the realms of the rich and famous, where opportunity was frequent, and bonds could be made. But the expensive suit had been discarded and, in its place, John wore a tuxedo. It was new, as Harvey hadn't seen it before. The tailoring concealed his ample weight and, despite Harvey not wanting to, he couldn't help but notice that the old man looked good.

"It's a proud day for me, Harvey," he said, pointing at the guest seat that he knew Harvey wouldn't take. Harvey never sat in John's company. Business was business. "Relax, Harvey. Come on, sit with me."

Harvey didn't reply.

"At least have a drink with me. You wouldn't reject my offer of a drink on my son's wedding day, would you?"

Harvey said nothing but felt Sergio's presence behind him.

"Get him a water, Sergio, for God's sake,"

said John, leaning forward in his chair to talk around Harvey. "And get Julios in here."

Sergio slipped from the room as silently as he'd entered, and John set his drink on his desk. He leaned forward, interlaced his fingers, and stared Harvey in the eye.

"I love you and Donny just the same, Harvey. You know that, right?"

Harvey didn't reply.

"I never thought I'd see Donny marry. He didn't seem to have the guts for it," said John, and Harvey felt an emotional rant heading his way, an effort to get closer to Harvey and then slip him a wild card. He'd seen it before and there was nothing John could hand to Harvey he couldn't handle. "I know you two don't see eye to eye. Even as kids, you never really got on, did you? I can remember hearing you, Hannah, and Donny playing in the lounge one time. I thought to myself that we'd finally cracked it. We'd finally got them playing together. But when I walked in, Harvey, I found you and Hannah playing together and Donny watching. He was excluded."

Harvey knew what John was talking about. He couldn't remember the exact time, but it happened more than once. Whenever

Hannah and Harvey played together, Donny, who was only slightly older than Hannah, would come and ruin their game. Hannah had a particular distaste for him, but whenever John or his ex-wife Barb stepped into view, Donny would make out that it was Hannah and Harvey who were being nasty. It was a cowardly trait that Donny had never been able to shake.

"Today is Donny's day, Harvey. Today marks a change," continued John. "Today, Donny is going to marry his beautiful bride, so that means today is a big day for you too. I want you to put aside your history with Donny. Do you know how much it would mean to him if you shook his hand and wished him a happy future?"

Harvey didn't reply.

"It would mean the world to him, Harvey," said John.

He turned and stared out of his window at the hand-built arch where the ceremony would be taking place, and his chest swelled with pride.

"I want you to shake his hand, Harvey. I want you, in your own words, to give him that boost. He's lived in your shadow for too long and if I'm right, this wedding will mark a significant change in him. It will give him confidence. It'll mature him in a way that only having the love of a beautiful wife can. He'll stop all his stupid ways, and he'll stop knocking around with petty criminals. He'll become more invested in our firm, Harvey. That's where we need him. He spends most of his time with people who don't even work for me. That's not what I'd call invested. Is it, Harvey? No, it's not. Why does he do that? Well, put yourself in his shoes. Imagine you had a brother or a foster-brother who is as capable and reliable as you, and no matter what you do, you can't seem to shine above him. Imagine that your father finds only disappointment in you, Harvey, but sees excellence in your foster-brother."

He left a moment for Harvey to put himself in Donny's position, but Harvey needed no imagination.

"That's why he gets himself into all sorts of bother with small-time hoodlums, Harvey. That's why he's so distant. I'm getting older. I shouldn't be doing what I'm bleeding doing now. I should be retiring and leaving my business in the capable hands of my two boys. But

I can't. One of my sons takes more interest in risking his freedom with petty crime and drugs than in the family business, and the other one is a stone cold killer who hasn't said a bleeding word in the ten minutes he's been standing in front of me. Say something, Harvey. At least acknowledge you understand what I'm asking you to do."

Harvey thought about what he might say. He wasn't a man of words. His skill was with his hands. A battle of words against John Cartwright would end in failure, so Harvey chose to say as little as possible as seldom as possible.

"You want me to make peace with Donny so he can take over from you and you can retire?"

"One day, yes, Harvey. I do."

"You want me to shake his hand so he can start his new life without feeling my shadow over him? Without feeling like a disappointment?"

"Yes," said John, as if Harvey had solved a riddle that had been staring him in the face.

"Okay," said Harvey.

"Okay? Is that it?" said John.

"What do you want me to say? I'll do it. I'll do it for you and that's it."

John nodded. He knew he would get no more than that from Harvey.

"Good. Thank you, Harvey. That means the world to me."

Harvey didn't reply, and behind him came the measured footsteps of Sergio and the slow, methodical steps of Julios. Harvey would recognise the sound of his footsteps anywhere.

Julios came to stand beside Harvey. The big man's shoulders were level with Harvey's face, and despite Harvey's strength and abilities, the shadow *he* lived beneath belonged to Julios.

John, reignited with Harvey's promise, sank his drink, and as Sergio placed Harvey's water on the desk, John offered Sergio his empty glass to refill.

"Right, Julios, Harvey, today is a big day. In less than an hour, this garden will be filled with people. There'll be a band, thirty catering staff, and about two hundred family friends who want to send Donny off. It's going to be the perfect day, and for that to happen, I need my two most trusted and capable men to manage security."

Harvey nodded. He could think of little worse than having to mingle with whoever it was that John had invited. The distraction of work would be a welcome one.

"One last thing," said John, as Julios and Harvey made to leave. They turned as Sergio entered the room carrying two bags.

"What's this?" said Harvey, knowing the answer before John had even opened his mouth.

"Suits," said John. "The finest suits money can buy. Sergio will help you with your ties if you don't know how."

CHAPTER FIVE

Unshaven and yawning, Myers pulled up outside the home that he'd worked so hard for and then given away. The deep lines etched around his eyes and across his forehead were the scars of that hard work and were all that now belonged to him.

He'd rushed out of the house. Of course he'd rushed, and he'd cursed himself for rushing. He cursed at the way she only had to open her mouth and the world seemed to fall into her lap. He wasn't doing it for Alison. That's what he had to tell himself. He was doing it for Harriet. And why wouldn't he? She was his daughter. She didn't belong to

Darren. She belonged to him. She was his flesh and blood.

He honked the horn for the second time and those thoughts of love and affection for his only child began to blur into the ever-ready curses that seemed to breed in his throat.

He thought of the half-empty coffee he'd left on the kitchen side and even contemplated stopping by a coffee shop on the way to Harriet's school, but the detour would take too long, and Harriet would be rushing.

"Where are you?" he whispered to himself, and he was about to honk for a third time when the front door opened. Harriet appeared, and although the front door hid her from view, Alison was there. Her outline was framed in the frosted glass that Myers had paid for, and the colour of her pale flesh showed through. He pictured the short summer dress that he couldn't see but knew she would be wearing.

Harriet ambled down the front path, rummaging in her bag for something, then waved to Myers as she grew closer.

"In your own time, Harriet," Myers whispered. "Just like your mum."

The passenger door opened, and Harriet climbed in.

"I'm late," she said.

"I can sense the urgency," said Myers. "Do I at least get a good morning?"

She leaned over and kissed him on the cheek, then rubbed her lips.

"Don't you shave anymore?"

Myers indicated to pull out and checked his mirror.

"Usually. When I'm not dropping off my ill-mannered daughter, that is."

"What? I'm not ill-mannered."

Myers raised his hand to thank the driver behind and caught a glimpse of Harriet's shoes.

"What happened to the shoes I bought you?"

"Nothing," said Harriet. "I just wanted to wear these."

"They look brand new."

"Darren bought them for me."

"Darren? Why is Darren buying you shoes?"

"He's my stepdad."

"Not yet he's not. He's got my house and

my wife, at least let me hang onto my daughter."

"They're just shoes, Dad."

"Well," said Myers, feeling a molehill swell to the realms of a mountain. "If you need shoes, ask me. If you need anything, ask *me*."

Myers slowed for a red light and rolled to a stop.

"Whatever," she mumbled.

"I mean it, Harriet."

"Okay. Okay."

"I'm sorry. I know I nag. It's hard."

Harriet said nothing. She stared out of the window at the car beside them, waiting for the lights to turn green. Myers followed her gaze and saw the driver, a young Asian man wearing a cap and a hooded sweatshirt.

Harriet's eyes closed as she saw what her father saw.

"Dad, don't-"

"He's not wearing a seat belt."

"It doesn't matter. Please. Not while I'm in the car."

Myers laughed. "Oh, come on. Do you honestly think I'd pull him up with you in the car? Give me a bit more credibility than that."

The lights turned green and the Asian boy accelerated. Myers took his time to release the brake and ease away from the lights, much to the annoyance of the car behind who had initially let him out of the turning.

"Can't we just get on?" he said. "I don't see you often. It would be nice to get on with you when I *do* see you. We used to have fun, didn't we?"

Harriet said nothing. She lifted her bag to her lap and began to rummage around inside. The bag was brown check with gold coloured fasteners and fittings. Myers recognised the brand.

"Where did you get that bag?"

"It was a gift," said Harriet, and dropped it to her feet to get it out of Myers' sight.

"A gift. Is it real?"

"I don't know. Probably not."

"It looks real. Who bought you that?"

Harriet turned, and finally met his stare.

"It was Darren, wasn't it?" said Myers, shaking his head. "Well, to be honest, I'm not surprised he can afford to buy you shoes and bags. I paid for his house so he must have plenty of spare cash."

"Actually, no. It wasn't Darren. A friend

gave it to me."

"A friend? That's a three-hundred-pound bag, Harriet."

"Dad, don't start. This is why it's so hard."

"From now on, Harriet, if you want something, you ask me. Is that understood?"

"Whatever, Dad," said Harriet, and turned her head away to peer out of the window.

"Are you tired, Harriet? Are you sleeping okay?"

"I'm sleeping fine, Dad."

"What about school? How are you dealing with the pressure? Exams are soon. Are you ready? Are you worried?"

"I'm dealing with it, Dad."

"You look tired, sweetheart. There are bags under your eyes."

"I'm okay."

"Are you sure? Maybe you need a weekend away with your old man." He tried to inject a bit of fun into his inquisitive tone.

"I don't need anything, Dad. I just want to be left alone."

"Okay, but if you need to talk or if you need help-"

"Yeah, got it, Dad."

Harriet said nothing more, and with the school ahead, Myers slowed and indicated to pull over.

"I'll pick you up at three thirty," said Myers.

"Don't bother yourself," she replied. "I'm going to a friend's house."

Harriet opened the door and was climbing out when Myers grabbed her arm.

"Aren't you going to say goodbye?" he asked. "Do you need me to come in and explain why you're late?" But Harriet just looked away, snatched her arm back, and just as the door was being slammed, Myers called out, "I love you, Harriet."

She didn't look back. She didn't even look upset.

Myers slammed his hand on the steering wheel. It was nine thirty and the street was void of kids. Harriet disappeared around the corner into the school and Myers buried his face in his hands, frustrated.

"She's just like her mum," he whispered to himself, then laughed. "How the bloody hell am I supposed to get on with my daughter when she's just like her mum?"

He indicated, selected drive, and then

pulled out of the parking space and into the path of an oncoming refuse truck.

CHAPTER SIX

The meeting with John Cartwright had taken less than thirty minutes. In that time, the workforce had doubled, and they now moved as if somebody had taken charge and cracked a few whips. From the top step of the grand entrance, Harvey stood beside Julios, surveying the grounds. The property had a single entrance and exit, and the perimeter fencing was secured with a combination of barbed wire, electric cattle fencing, and, in places of prominence, a few cameras. The cameras had never been used. The one time the electric fence and barbed wire had done their job had been years before when a burglar had found himself trapped on top of the fence, cut to shreds. Harvey had been alerted by the man's screams during the night and by the time he'd found the man in the dark, John had gotten there first.

There was a mean streak inside John and, if Harvey was correct, that was the last time the burglar ever tried to break into a country estate without doing his due diligence. John had helped him down, feigning empathy for the poor man.

Then he'd turned.

He'd forced the man to strip naked at gun point, and then held him against the electric fence until he was sure to wake the villagers a mile away. Then, when John was running out of enthusiasm and was sure he had made his point, he'd forced the man to climb back over the barbed wire fence and find his way home with no clothes.

"We'll put two men on the gate," said Julios, and Harvey wondered if he had re-called the time with the burglar too. The night most likely was lodged in the burglar's mind for eternity. He would never forget the agony of the electric fence and razor wire and most likely still carried the scars.

But for Harvey and Julios, it was a time

they barely considered. It was nothing compared to what they were asked to do on an almost weekly basis.

"Sergio has a guest list," said Harvey. "But what about all these?" He gestured at the workforce, who were busy building the set of what was to be John's proudest moment.

"I asked him the same thing," said Julios. "He would appreciate it if we could gain control of the situation."

"He hasn't got a clue who's here or how many?"

Julios said nothing but his silence spoke volumes.

Harvey spied a man in a suit. He was dressed to impress whoever was paying the bill. But unless that suit was handmade in Saville Row, John would be very much underwhelmed.

"That's the wedding planner."

"The what?" said Julios.

"The wedding planner. The man that plans weddings. He'll be in charge and he'll have a list."

"People pay other people to plan a wedding?" said Julios.

A rare smile washed over Harvey's face

and for a moment, the two met each other's stares.

"Apparently, it's a stressful job," said Harvey, and made off down the few steps. "I'll talk to him. If he hasn't got a list, he will have in thirty minutes."

"Before you go," said Julios, and the tone shifted like dark clouds encroaching on a blue sky.

Harvey stopped on the steps.

"Where were you?" said Julios.

Harvey didn't reply.

"I searched for you yesterday," said Julios, and he shook his head. "Not a sign of you."

They locked stares for a moment. If there was one man who could read Harvey like a book, it was Julios.

"Just out," said Harvey, and Julios' face twitched as he read between the lines.

Harvey turned away and stepped down to the gravel.

"Harvey," another voice called when he had taken just three steps. He recognised the voice and stopped but did not turn. He couldn't face Julios reading him.

"John would like to talk to you again," said Sergio.

"I'll be there in a few minutes, Sergio. I'm just doing your job for you."

"Thank you, Harvey," said Sergio. His weak voice and Eastern European accent grated on Harvey at the best of times. "But he wants to talk to you *now*. He said it is urgent. Perhaps Julios can speak to the wedding planner?"

He turned and found them both staring at him, Julios reading his every move and the aversion of his eyes, and Sergio clinging to the morsel of power he bore from being charged with delivering John's wishes.

Harvey didn't reply.

It was Julios who made the first move, breaking the battle of power.

"I will talk to this wedding planner," said Julios. "Harvey, you go. See what John wants."

"Thank you, Julios," said Sergio, then raised a single eyebrow at Harvey, turned, and disappeared back into the house.

"Just keep John happy," said Julios, as Harvey passed him on the steps. "We'll talk later."

Harvey turned once more and watched the dance of the workers as they carried chairs and boxes around and the set began to take shape. Julios' massive bulk descended the steps and an odd feeling of betrayal clawed at his gut. He didn't enjoy lying to Julios. He was, in Harvey's eyes, Harvey's only true ally.

"I'll come and find you," said Harvey, acknowledging his mentor's words. Then he followed Sergio into the house.

"Close the door," said John, as Harvey walked into the room without knocking. "Take a seat."

Harvey stood in the same spot he had ten minutes before and said nothing.

"I said, take a seat," said John without looking up from signing a pile of papers.

Harvey didn't move.

"You can stand there all day for all I care," said John. "I'm not saying what I have to say without you sitting on your arse in that chair, Harvey."

John handed Sergio the signed paperwork, clicked the lid of his Monte Blanc fountain pen into place, and then placed it in the slim pocket inside his jacket breast that he'd had sewn in especially.

Harvey sighed, dragged the chair back, and dropped into it, watching Sergio try to control the wry grin that grew over his face like the fingers of ivy that penetrated the house.

"Thanks, Sergio," said John. "Can you give me ten minutes, please?"

"I thought I might be a useful-"

"You'd be useful coordinating all those people outside to make sure this day goes as it should."

"But, John, I hired a wedding planner to-"

"I don't pay a wedding planner six figures a year. I pay you. If anything goes wrong, Sergio, it'll be your head on the chopping block, not some wedding planner I've never seen before. So, get outside, talk to him, and make sure nothing goes wrong."

"Yes, John," said Sergio, and the ivy withered.

John waited for the door to close then took a sip of his brandy.

"I just wanted to say something, Harvey. I might not get another chance before the day is up."

Harvey didn't reply.

"I love you both, Harvey. You *and* Donny. I know you and Hannah were adopted, but you're just as special to me. If Hannah was here today, I'd be saying the same thing to her. It's Donny's wedding day. It's my proudest moment, Harvey. But I don't want you to think that I wouldn't be doing the same for you."

Harvey nodded.

"Come on, Harvey, give me a little more than that. I just opened my heart to you. I know I'm hard on you. I know I can be tough to get along with. But I mean well."

"Have you met her?" said Harvey.

"Who? Julia? Yeah, of course I've met her. She's a cracker, Harvey."

"Where's she from?"

"I don't know. Europe somewhere. Donny picked her up at some party with some businessmen he's been getting to know."

"But you had Sergio do some kind of background check on her, right?"

"Relax, Harvey," said John, as he gazed through his office window and admired his plan coming together. "She isn't even bringing her family. Doesn't have any apparently. Every guest on that list is a friend of the family or a friend of Donny's, so the only people you need to concern yourself with are the workers."

"She doesn't have a family?"

"Donny said she was a runaway. He said she lived on the streets. She turned her life around. Wait until you see her, Harvey. Even I was amazed that Donny could end up with her." John raised a fresh cigar, flipped the lid of his silver-plated Zippo, and sparked the flame. He turned the cigar with care, to provide an even burn. Then the final act of the routine was to blow the thick, grey smoke into the air above him. "It's going to be a day to remember, Harvey."

CHAPTER SEVEN

A single photo had been placed in the centre of Myers' desk. There were no accompanying notes, files, or history. Just a single photo of the silent man.

Behind him, the office was brimming with policemen and policewomen. Above the hum of voices, clicking of printers, and tapping keyboards, Myers could hear the whispered chats. He could feel the eyes boring into the back of his head.

"He's losing it."

"Twenty-four hours."

"He should have called it in and passed it on to someone else."

"He's too stubborn."

"He wants the case to himself."

"He's been chasing the guy for months."

"The chief is going to rip him a new arse."

"He didn't even get the guy's name."

The desk phone startled him, and he snatched up the handset without even considering who was calling. His hands were still shaking from the accident he had nearly caused only thirty minutes before and the ensuing argument with the arrogant driver of the refuse truck who had slammed on his brakes.

"DI Myers," he said, praying it wasn't her.

"My office, two minutes."

The room had hushed. Even the tapping of keyboards had stopped. But as Myers slowly replaced the handset, the hum, click, and tap began to grow in volume, as if the noise was coming from an old, glass-topped record player like Myers' dad used to have, with the big volume and tuner dials on the front.

"Sir?" said Fox from the desk opposite.

"Have we had any more lab results back yet?" asked Myers, not wishing to hear her bleating questions so early in the morning. Fox would be a good detective one day. Not yet. She needed to slow down. But if Myers was going to get himself out of the hole he was in, he needed a strong partner, not some girl fresh out of training. He needed results.

"DNA found on Jennifer Standing's clothes belongs to Faisal Hussein, sir. I sent the samples from the unknown suspect back to the lab to be re-analysed. Maybe they made a mistake."

"The silent man," said Myers.

"Is that what you're calling him?"

"Well, we don't have a name. The lab rarely makes mistakes. Even if the lab comes back with positive results, we have no way of finding him. It's a mess, Fox, and Allenby is going to chew my arse."

"Let her chew it. You know you did your best, sir," said Fox, hearing Myers' disenchantment and returning to tap out her report on her keyboard.

"Why don't we know about this guy?" said Myers, more to himself than to Fox. She looked around her screen once more to humour Myers' frustrations and he continued airing his thoughts. "I mean, you saw Faisal Hussein, right?"

"Yes, sir."

"You saw how he was pinned to the tree?"

"I've been seeing it ever since, sir. I can't shake the image."

"That wasn't this guy's first time. The first time is sloppy, it's rushed, and they make mistakes. I've seen it before. It's textbook. But this? No. This was the work of a pro. He was there when Hussein brought the girl in or the choppers would have seen him. He watched and waited."

"Waited, sir?"

"Until Hussein was about to hurt the girl," said Myers, allowing the scene to play out in his mind.

"You mean he watched him..."

"Yes," said Myers, and the scene became more vivid. "He watched. He wanted to see it. He wanted to see the pleasure on Hussein's face. He wanted to see the excitement."

"Why? I mean, why would he wait for that? There were police everywhere."

"What if he had a debt to pay?"

"Money, sir? I don't follow."

"Not money. What if the guy had a debt to pay? What if he's some kind of..."

He stopped, unable to bring himself to say the word.

"Vigilante, sir?"

Myers nodded, knowing how crazy it sounded.

"And he pays that debt to society by bringing people like Hussein down?"

Her tone was mocking, and the last thing Myers wanted was for the rest of the office to hear.

"Just leave it, Fox."

"Sir-"

"Don't say it. I know."

"If you mention that to Allenby, sir, she'll have you signed off and you'll be having daily chats with the psychiatrist."

"Well what do *you* think, Fox? I can't seem to find any other motive," said Myers, and raised a blue file in the air, then slapped it down on his desk. "Six men. All known sex offenders. All linked to one man. And guess what? They're all dead."

"Linked to one man, sir?"

He'd said too much, having prepared himself for Allenby's chat, which would be just as thrilling.

"I've been working on this case for months, Fox. You've been here five minutes."

"But if you have a lead, sir, maybe I can help."

"I don't have a lead. If I had a lead, you'd be researching it. All I have is a gut feeling."

"So, tell me."

He sighed. "When I have something concrete, Allenby will assign me a DS. Maybe that will be you. Maybe it won't. Until then..."

His phone rang again, and he ignored it. He knew who it was.

"So, you think each of the victims-"

"They weren't victims, Fox. They were sex offenders."

She raised her eyebrows in surprise at his tone. "You think that one man killed them all and, because they were all linked to one other man, that it's some kind of sex ring?"

The pieces came together and the motive fit the idea. But to convey that to Allenby would be professional suicide. Proposing a vigilante was like playing the joker card. It was an easy way out and Myers knew it.

"Well," he said as he pushed back his chair, "if you can think of a better idea, I'm all ears."

He left her with the conundrum and carried his file to Allenby's office.

The door to Allenby's office was closed, but Myers heard the order to enter before he'd even knocked, and he saw her straightening a pile of paperwork through a gap in the window blind.

"Close the door, Myers," she said without looking up.

She didn't offer him a seat. Instead, she left him waiting. It was a power play he'd seen at least three other chief inspectors try in the same office and from the same cheap desk. He knew how to ride the wait. He wondered if she used similar techniques at home. She had a husband called Clive. Myers had spoken to him once at a gala dinner. He'd seemed okay on his own but shied in his wife's presence, which emphasised Myers' image of her ruling the household with her trouser suits and neckerchiefs.

Maybe she told Clive when he should enter the bedroom and made *him* wait like a naughty schoolboy?

Myers was professional enough to conceal the smile that was creeping onto his face.

"Twenty-four hours," she said. "Twenty-four hours and not a single word left his lips."

Myers said nothing. He knew it was always better to be invited to speak rather than anger the beast.

"In that twenty-four hours, you didn't let a single other detective question him. Not one. Not even Carver, for God's sake, and he's more experienced than you."

Myers let her rant. It would be over soon, and he could go about his day.

"Talk me through it," she said, and sat back. That was his invitation to speak.

"The suspect was caught walking down Jennifer Standing's street near to her parents' house shortly after she arrived home."

"That's right," said Allenby. "Tell me something that isn't in the report."

"He was brought in on a potential abduction charge before we found Hussein's body."

"And you couldn't charge him for murder?"

"With what evidence?" said Myers. "If we'd have brought him in on a murder charge, we'd have needed something to keep him here. All we have is him being in the same area as an unharmed girl who arrived home safely."

"So why did you keep him for twenty-four hours?"

"We were waiting for the lab results to come back."

"Oh no, don't play the *we* game. This is *your* case. You didn't let anyone else in. This is all you, Myers."

"*I* was waiting. *I* gave Fox the order to wait and *I* held him here. She's new. She doesn't know the lay of the land yet."

"Despite my direct order to go out and find something to keep him here?" said Allenby.

It didn't matter which way Myers spun the story, she would always have a comeback. So he went with it.

"I had Fox check the body. It was a professional job."

"A what?"

"A professional job. Fox is writing up the report as we speak."

"Do you mean it was a professional hit, Myers? Next you'll be telling me the mafia killed a sex offender."

"Not organised crime, ma'am," said Myers. He knew she was trying to get him riled and flustered, another tactic that senior police officers used to test their detectives. "At least I don't think so. But the kill was professional. This wasn't his first time."

"Tell me more."

"There's no trace of him for a start. No fingerprints, no footprints, no DNA."

"Could have been lucky."

"There was no struggle, no skin beneath Hussein's nails, and the kill was precise. Like a surgeon. Hussein didn't stand a chance."

"And what about Jennifer Standing? Did you find-"

"Nothing. He was clean."

"No hair? No DNA of any description? Nothing else?"

"We swabbed him all over."

"And Hussein?"

"Faisal Hussein was found naked. There was no trace of Jennifer Standing on his body. I have reason to believe that our man didn't let him get that far."

"How far did he let him go?"

"Jennifer Standing was physically un-harmed. But only Jennifer knows what he did prior to being stopped."

"What do you think happened?"

"It's common for predators like Hussein to masturbate in front of their victims. They like to show themselves. It excites them. They often have a complex, a hang up about their body that prevents them from seeking sexual partners the way the rest of society does. Showing off their body to their victims forms a kind of release."

"You don't need to preach the psychiatry books to me," said Allenby, maintaining her grasp at the top of the chain. Then she offered him a taste. "Is that why he was naked?"

"I believe so, ma'am. I think Jennifer Standing was tied to a tree. I think she was forced to watch Hussein dig a hole for her body."

"In front of her?"

Myers nodded. "He would have enjoyed her watching him dig her grave."

"So, what's your next move?" asked Allenby.

"Forensics are working the site and the surrounding area. Our man must have left a mark somewhere. When we have it, we'll go after him on a murder charge."

"Talk to DI Carver. He knows the organised crime world better than they do," said Allenby. "And Hussein? What are your plans?"

She eyed the file in his hand.

"Can I see?"

"This is just a theory I'm working on."

Her expression was unmoving. There was no way he was getting out of there without her seeing the entire file and not just the parts he was prepared to share. He opened the file and slid the report on Faisal Hussein out of it.

"Previous offences of Faisal Hussein include-"

"Give me the file, Myers."

He slid Hussein's report back inside the blue folder and passed the file to her. She made a show of pulling her glasses on and reached for her pen from a ridiculous pen pot shaped like a monkey wearing a circus suit and holding a drum.

Her eyebrows raised once or twice. She bit her lower lip and then she slammed the file shut and placed it in front of her on the desk.

"This has to stop, Myers."

"Ma'am-" he said, knowing full well where she was going.

"Rashid Al Sheik is the counsellor for the East London labour party. He is not at the centre of what you note as a *paedophile sex ring*. He is an upstanding member of our community-"

"But, ma'am-"

"Who has already lodged both harassment and racism complaints about you."

"I know-"

"I didn't ask you to speak, Myers."

The entire office would have heard that outburst. Myers sighed and felt his hands wander to his pockets.

"Can't you give me anything else other than Rashid Al Sheik? It's been months." She dropped the file into a plastic container by the wall. From there, it would be taken, scanned, and then destroyed. "I need something else. I need you to stop thinking about Rashid Al Sheik and find who is killing these men."

"Yes, ma'am," said Myers.

"You're better than this, Myers. I know you are. Do you need some time off? I know you've had it rough these past couple of years."

"I don't need time off, ma'am."

Her tone softened. They had known each other long enough for them to know about each other's personal lives, and he had to admit, when he'd separated from Alison, she *had* been supportive.

"Now, I'll ask again. What's your next move? The media will be all over this."

"I think if we play it right, it's an easy PR win. Jennifer Standing was found. Win. Faisal Hussein, a known sex offender, was caught. Win. We don't have to give any more details."

"What about Hussein's family?" asked Allenby, and she pulled a folder close to her, a sign the conversation was drawing to a close. "What if they make a scene?"

"That all depends on Jennifer Standing's statement, ma'am," said Myers, as he reached for the door.

"Excuse me?" said Allenby, and for the first time, her expression weakened. "You're not going to ask Standing for a statement. Not yet."

"Time is of the essence, ma'am. If she's willing to talk, we need to hear what she has to say. She may have seen him. Standing could give us an insight."

"After what she's been through?"

"The only way we're going to catch this guy is by finding out how he operates."

Allenby considered it. "Okay. Clear it first and take DS Fox with you. She could do with the experience and you could do with the support. Consider her your partner from now on."

"Oh, ma'am-"

"Close the door on the way out, Myers," said Allenby. "I want a report this afternoon."

CHAPTER EIGHT

The hive of workers had dispersed, leaving only the serving staff who stood in two lines ready to welcome the first guests. There was no denying it, even with Harvey's limited opinions, he had to admit that the scene was incredible.

Two banks of seats arranged similar to church pews had been placed in an arc around where Donny and his bride would stand. A string quartet had been set up to one side and were playing Bach's Air on the G String. A full swing band had been established on the stage which was set before a large dance floor. The caterers had set out twenty eight-seater tables with white table-

cloths and seat covers. The tables, which overlooked the village below, had been adorned
with lilies and silverware.

But the centrepiece was the wooden arch.
Its pillars had white roses climbing in uniform
and, beneath it, waiting patiently, was the
vicar who looked sombre and serious.

Harvey resumed his place at the top of the
steps. From there, he could survey the entire
scene. He adjusted his suit and pulled his tie
loose. His shoes were uncomfortable, but he
could bear them for a while. It was almost
comedic to see Julios walking from the main
gates where two of John's men were welcoming the arriving guests.

When Julios walked, he commanded the
space. All eyes followed him in a mixture of
awe and fascination. He was a large man, the
largest that Harvey had even seen or known.
But he had a presence that was larger than
even his physical size. He had little cause to
speak, and when he did, his words were
chosen well. He and Harvey had spent hours
together with barely any exchange of words.

From a young age, Harvey had admired
the man. He looked up to him as a mentor and
his opinion meant more to Harvey than any

words John could ever say. But in his tuxedo, Julios was transformed. He was a new man and looked as if he might have stepped off a film set. It was a far cry from his usual rudimental appearance.

A line of cars made their way along the gravel driveway. Sergio had placed another of John's men in charge of parking and he was guiding them into an area beside the stream, away from the ceremony and reception.

Julios handed Harvey a guest list, which he placed in his breast pocket without looking at it. The men on the gates were checking people off the list as they entered. All Harvey and Julios would need to do was ensure the day went to plan.

The guests began to congregate near the bar, where several high tables had been arranged. Hands were shaken, wives were hugged, and glasses were chinked, and all the while, the quartet moved through what Harvey recognised as some of John's favourite pieces of music.

Harvey recognised some of the faces. There were villains of all descriptions. Men who had, over the years, been involved with John in one way or another. A group of men who Harvey did not recognise were greeted by Donny and led to the bar for a quick, last-minute send-off drink. Harvey was fully aware of Donny's taste for drugs, a subject that only embittered John. He could only assume that the men who all raised their glasses to him were his closest friends. Sergio had even taken a break from welcoming guests to stand with Donny and his mates. It was only when the congregation grew to well over one hundred and fifty people that Sergio and Donny's crew began to usher people towards their seats.

But not to be outdone by the sheer magnificence of the scene, it was John who made the grand entrance. He came to stand between Harvey and Julios and raised his arms in the air to a low and subdued applause. He moved through the crowd as naturally as any man could, offering kisses on both cheeks to the wives of old friends and allies, and shaking hands he hadn't shaken for many years, thanking them for coming. He introduced himself to those he didn't know and assured them that Donny's men, who Harvey had learnt to be the ushers and groomsmen, would take care of their every need. There were young women in beautiful dresses, men in their finest suits, and even two Asian men who wore fine, white kurtas.

Time passed slowly and more cars arrived. More hands were shaken, women were hugged, and champagne flowed. Until the men at the gate caught Harvey's attention and gave him the signal that all of the guests were accounted for, except one.

Harvey nodded.

Donny took his place at the arch, and after a final fake laugh with an unknown, Sergio joined him.

"Is Sergio Donny's best man?" asked Harvey, as they looked on from the top of the steps.

"Who else could he ask?" said Julios.

He meant no comedy or insult by the statement. It was a fact that Donny moved through groups of friends like a dose of salts, then moved to the next group as soon as he'd insulted, angered, or ripped them off. It was just Donny's personality. He didn't pick up on the social cues that the rest of society did.

For Sergio though, the honour was apparent by his beaming smile. He had dropped the serious expression, and, for a short period of time, he would be able to enjoy the fruits of wealth and power as a somebody, rather than a man who served the family, as was his job.

The scene was set. The groom and his best man stood at the arch with the sober-looking vicar. The congregation waited patiently for the bride. The catering staff manned the bar and covered the lunch platters. All was still. The only movement was from the quartet who continued to provide soft, atmospheric music to the wedding party.

Then there was the rumble of an engine, deep and throaty, but finely tuned. The two guards on the gate both waved a single hand to Harvey and the wedding planner. The wedding planner in turn nodded to the vicar, who then leaned over to the quartet and muttered a signal.

They stopped playing and between the gates arrived a gleaming, open-topped, white Rolls Royce Silver Ghost. The driver wore leather gloves, a hat, and tails, and in the back-seat, sitting alone, was the bride.

Harvey said nothing, but he felt Julios' eyes and the two exchanged a look of amazement.

The man Sergio had assigned to car

parking directed the driver toward the seating. It was the only car to have turned right off the driveway, and as he stopped and switched the engine off, the quartet began once more. The bride, elegant in her ways, and beautiful beyond anyone else there, stepped down from the vintage Rolls to the tune of Canon in D. Her hair flowed like falling water that had been frozen in time. Her skin was smooth like that of a doll, with shades of pink makeup to accentuate her facial features. She had slender shoulders that she pulled back as if she had attended elocution classes.

She was a picture to behold and every man and woman who stared at her right there and then did so with envy, lust, and admiration.

There were tears and smiles as the bride made her way between the rows of seats. And at the top of the aisle, Donny faced forward with his hands folded before him, and he looked up, as if reciting one last prayer of silent thanks.

He turned as his bride drew close, and even from the distance at which Harvey and Julios were standing, Harvey could see his face melt with emotion.

The soon-to-be-wed couple stood side by side before the vicar while the quartet played out their final bars. And then the vicar began the ceremony. His voice reached Harvey and Julios almost effortlessly.

"Where were you?" said Julios, taking the opportunity to air his thoughts while the ceremony took place.

"When?" said Harvey.

"I looked for you. Yesterday. You were nowhere to be seen."

"Do you mean to say John was watching my house and wondering where I was?" said Harvey, and he remembered Sergio pounding on his door a few hours before. They had known Harvey was inside, which meant that John had been watching.

"Why do you not tell me?" said Julios.

"About what?"

Julios said nothing. He watched the ceremony, as calm as could be. But beneath the question, Harvey felt bitterness.

"There's nothing to tell," said Harvey.

Again, Julios said nothing. He was a tower of strength, both physically and mentally. Just as John could beat Harvey, or anyone, in a battle of words, Julios could overpower

Harvey with his mind. Julios was the man Harvey respected most and to disappoint him would mean failure on his behalf.

"Perhaps you need re-training."

"I don't need re-training, Julios."

"There's something you're not telling me, Harvey. Are you in trouble?"

"No, Julios. I'm not in any trouble."

It was impossible to lie to Julios.

"You were not following the rules."

Harvey said nothing. If he couldn't lie, he wouldn't speak at all.

But Julios' silence added a weight that Harvey couldn't ignore.

"I was arrested. They let me go. Nothing happened. It doesn't matter."

"Of course it matters," said Julios. Then he turned to face Harvey. "This habit of yours must stop. If you were sloppy like this on a job with me and we were both caught..."

"Then what? What if, Julios?"

He met Harvey's stare, looking down at him as a disapproving father might be repulsed by his son's insolence.

"I'd kill you myself," said Julios.

CHAPTER NINE

"Sir?" said Fox, as Myers whipped his jacket from the back of his chair and pulled it on in a whirl of flowing cotton en route to the door.

"Not now, Fox."

Myers was seething. He couldn't stand Allenby's patronising, condescending, and sanctimonious tone. He'd seen her rise through the ranks. If she hadn't been sitting in that seat, either Carver or himself would have been. She knew it and he knew it. And that unspoken statement was the crux of their relationship.

"But, sir-"

"I said, not now, Fox. Whatever it is, you can deal with it."

She looked disappointed, hurt almost, but she was too strong to let emotions stand in the way.

"I'm sorry," said Myers. "I shouldn't have snapped."

"It's Jennifer Standing, sir," she said, and Myers stopped for a brief moment with one hand on the door. "Her father called. She's ready to talk."

Beyond Fox's shoulder, Myers saw the window blind in Allenby's office twitch.

"Get your coat," said Myers, and left the office before Allenby could protest. He called out that Fox should meet him in the car park and pushed through the double doors into the fire escape.

He fired up his old Mercedes and waited for Fox. His reflection stared back at him in the rear-view mirror, reminding him of his age, his lack of sleep, and his high blood pressure. His own mortality and the Standing case reminded him of Harriet. How much of her life had he missed already? How much more would he get to see? He wondered if she would ever be the same around him again, like she used to be. Those times when they would watch a movie as a family, and Harriet would rest her feet on his legs. It was the closeness he missed. There were things that he, as her father, felt privileged to know, privileged that she chose to confide in him. She would ask for his advice if friends were choosing the wrong path or mixing with boys that were less than law abiding.

But that was an age ago. The tired, old man that stared at the bags beneath his eyes in his rear-view mirror kicked himself for not savouring those moments and for letting it all slip away.

The car door opened, and Fox climbed in. Myers had pulled away before she'd pulled on her seat belt, and he slowed for the automatic gates to open. Fox said nothing, but she wanted to. Myers' senses were attuned to those little, unspoken thoughts.

But Fox was a pro. She would go far if she kept her nose clean and learnt how and when to break the rules. Her words were professional and clear and masked the undertone of, 'Is everything alright, sir?' better than he gave her credit for.

"What's this?" she asked, as he pulled out of the station car park onto the main road.

Myers glanced across and saw her

opening the file he kept tucked into the side of the passenger seat.

"Leave that," he said.

"Is that a duplicate file?"

"That's none of your business is what that is."

"I didn't think we were allowed to take files out of the office."

"Look, if we're going to get along, you're going to have to rein in the rules. This isn't college."

"I'm aware of that."

"I've been working on this case for months. It's all I think about, Fox. Do you think when I wake up in the middle of the night that I'd drive into work to pore over some files and reports? You have to understand, Fox, when you get this deep into a case, you don't switch off at five o'clock. It's a twenty-four-seven job and it takes over your life. So, if that means I need to have some kind of intelligence with me and that happens to break a rule, then so be it."

She tucked the file back down into the side of the seat. Myers waited for her to say something.

"I'd like to lead the questioning, sir," said Fox.

It was a welcome surprise that offered Myers a little reprise. He considered it and felt her stare as he checked his rear-view mirror.

"Jennifer Standing has been through a lot, sir. Her parents agreed to her being interviewed on the condition that it was done at their home."

There was something else. A catch, or a supporting reason. And it was coming.

"And I think, if you don't mind me saying, sir, that-"

"Did Allenby put you up to this just now?"

"No, sir," said Fox, doing well not to fluster at Myers' slight aggression. She hesitated. "Well, yes. But I'd like to though, sir. If you don't mind. You can jump in whenever you want, but right now, I think we need a clear account of what happened and if the suspect actually did anything wrong."

"You mean the silent man?"

"Yes, sir."

"He killed a man, Fox. He opened him up-"

"We don't know that it was him and, as far as evidence is concerned, all we have is that Jennifer Standing went missing, Faisal Hussein was killed, and Jennifer was delivered home safe and sound. That's all we have."

"That man we arrested last night was-"

"That man we arrested last night, sir, was arrested for the abduction of Jennifer Standing. Hussein's murder is a whole different case, sir."

Myers licked his lips. He knew he did it but couldn't help it. Fox knew it too. It was his signal that he didn't appreciate the tone of her voice.

It was Allenby talking.

"Look, sir, I'm sorry. But the Standings are good people. Good people that care about their daughter's welfare. If we've got any chance of Jennifer giving evidence, then this is our only chance. We can't keep hitting her with open case questions. We need to close the door on her abduction and let the poor girl move on with her life."

"She was the only witness to a murder, Fox."

"A murder that took place in a forest in

the dark while she was in a state of shock and fear," said Fox. "You know as well as I do that she won't have a clear understanding of what happened. It'll be garbled, and rightly so. Poor thing. All I'm saying is that we've got two open cases and if we mess this up and drag it out, we'll have two open cases tomorrow and the next day. Let's at least close the abduction off so she can get on with her life."

Myers stopped the car.

"It's all yours," he said. "You lead the interview. If it goes well, I'll make sure Allenby knows about it. If it doesn't go as planned..."

He paused and imagined the scene.

"Sir?"

"Well, let's cross that bridge when we come to it."

CHAPTER TEN

Mr and Mrs Cartwright turned to face each other and kissed. Then the blushing bride smiled at the congregation and the newlyweds walked down the aisle hand in hand. The new Mrs Cartwright was beaming, radiant and full of excitement. Donny wore his facade of bravado that he'd inherited from his father. He adopted a proud expression, maintained his composure, and nodded at the guests who sat on both sides, leading his wife to the end of the aisle.

It was there that John Cartwright was waiting. One of the servers stood beside him holding a tray of champagne, towards which John turned, collected two glasses, and handed them to his son and new daughter-in-law.

It was a cheap attempt at control, thought Harvey, that even John would conjure a moment in the wedding to inflict his display of wealth and power on his guests. But his placement was apt at the south end of the aisle, outside of the makeshift, open-air chapel. He spoke loudly enough for everyone to hear but directed his words to Donny and his new bride.

He took a glass for himself and flicked his head for the server to return to the line of girls holding trays and waited for the string quartet to finish and fade away.

"It's a glorious day," he said, and the murmuring crowd hushed in anticipation. "Not only is the sun shining down on us, but I get to welcome this beautiful young lady into our family and call her my daughter-in-law. So, Julia, welcome." He raised his glass to the congregation, who were still standing by their seats, keen to get drinks of their own. "We'll be dining in an hour. In the meantime, please help yourselves to drinks and canapes and enjoy the music."

There was a rushed and muted applause

and John spoke quietly to his son and daughter-in-law as people left the ceremony and approached the line of servers. From where Harvey was standing at the top of the steps, he could not hear what John was saying, but he guessed it would be pretentious, ostentatious, and authoritative, despite the positive intent.

A few children ran between the seats, starting a game amongst themselves while the adults formed groups. Harvey watched as men he'd known John to have worked with in the past had words in the ears of other men and, despite the scene of splendour, bore expressions of distrust and caution as they eyed other familiar faces.

The children brought their game to the steps and were soon running around Harvey and Julios' legs and, for a second, Harvey thought he saw a fond smile creep over Julios' face, but it was masked by the shadow of his focus as movement caught his attention.

It was Donny and his new bride who had managed to escape the crowds for a few moments and were heading towards the steps, hand in hand.

The children saw the newlyweds approaching, stopped, giggled, then ran off towards the stream and the orchard.

Harvey steeled himself to be nice to his foster-brother, as per John's latest instructions.

"Congratulations, Donny," said Harvey, then turned to his wife. "Mrs Cartwright. It's lovely to meet you."

"You must be Harvey," she replied, and gave Donny a look of pleasant surprise. "Please, call me Julia."

"Well, Julia Cartwright, welcome to the family," said Harvey, turning to Julios. "This is-"

"Julios," said Julia, and locked eyes with the big man. "I've heard so much about you that I feel I know you already."

Harvey was surprised at his own ability to make pleasant small talk with Donny and his bride. But Julios surprised him further. He reached down, collected the girl's delicate hand in his own fat fingers, and bent to place a gentle kiss on the back of her hand. He admired the ring for a few seconds, then straightened.

"If there is anything you need, Mrs Cartwright, anything at all, then, please, Harvey and I will be glad to help you."

Donny's eyebrows were raised in astonishment and only settled when Julia returned to his side and pulled herself close to him.

"Why don't you go and show that ring off," said Donny. "I just need a few moments."

She smiled an adorable, playful smile and backed away.

"You'd better not be talking business on our wedding day," she threatened.

"Of course not," said Donny, and glanced at Harvey before returning his attention to her. "Just brotherly stuff. You know?"

"I see," she said. "Well, don't be long, the photographer wants us under the arch."

She was greeted by a group of John's friends who were waiting to capture her and learn more about the girl who had won the heart of the Cartwright heir. Donny watched her with adoration before turning to Harvey.

"Should I go?" asked Julios. "Maybe you both want some time."

"There's no need," said Donny, his tone flat and short, a contrast to just moments before. "I wanted to thank you both, you know, man to men."

Harvey didn't reply and Julios straightened his jacket collar.

"I've known you both for most of my life and you should have been a part of the ceremony."

"There's no need-"

"Just let me finish, Julios. Please. I wanted you both to be a part of it. I really did. But the truth is, and I'm sorry if this is hard to hear, but I've not got many friends. In fact, I have more enemies than friends. Dad offered to have the place swarming with men so that you both could enjoy the ceremony."

He stopped, as if he were choosing his words and taking the time to clear his throat.

"I know we haven't seen eye to eye, Harvey. I know you think little of me. And, Julios, I honestly don't know what you think. But the fact is that I wouldn't feel safe without you two looking after the security. You're the only two men I trust well enough to make sure that Julia and everyone here has the best day of their lives. So, thanks."

"It's nothing, Donny," said Julios.

"But it is. It really is. I don't deserve it. I don't deserve all this," said Donny, sweeping his hand across the scene behind him. "But I'm grateful to have it. And I'm grateful to have you both looking after it, and for looking after Dad."

The words faded to a hum in Harvey's mind. Donny was a cruel man and had been even crueller as a child. He was vindictive, selfish, and above all else, he was a coward. In Harvey's experience, cowards never learn courage. But in all that time, during all those moments when he and Harvey were growing up and Donny would play a cruel trick to land Harvey in trouble, he'd never shared as many words with his foster-brother as he did now. There was a part of him that felt and sounded genuine, a real honesty behind the words. But history had proved Harvey right more often than not, and he couldn't find any solemn truth in the words, despite Donny's efforts at credibility.

"Are you okay with that, Harvey?" said Donny, snapping him back to reality.

Harvey didn't reply.

"You weren't even listening, were you?"

The new solemn, almost likable Donny gave way to the man Harvey knew and recognised in the form of a sneer. But the sounds of the wedding party behind him softened the look and the new Donny emerged once more, all in the space of a second or two.

He was a slight man with slender hands. The hands of a girl, Harvey had always thought. He fidgeted as he spoke, uncomfortable in his own skin, and he pushed his flock of dark hair from his brow, an opportunity to avert his eyes from Harvey.

"I asked if we can draw a line in the sand, Harvey. I'll forget about the past, you forget about the past, and we can all move on. I'm happy now. I'm married. I want to enjoy life and I want our children to have an Uncle Harvey, and I want to be able to come home without..."

He stopped and eyed Harvey, as if daring himself to say the word.

"Without what, Donny?"

There was a silence as the momentum that Donny had built up came to a grinding halt and the pause began to build pressure.

"Without what, Donny?" Harvey said again.

"Fear, Harvey. I want to come home without the fear of bumping into you and feeling your eyes burn into me. What I'm saying is that I'm tired of it all, Harvey. I want a truce."

"So, you'll stop your lies and backstabbing then?" said Harvey.

Donny nodded. "Whatever it takes."

"And you'll stop your dealings with your *druggy* mates?"

"They're not..." He caught himself and sighed. "No more drugs. I'm not a bad person, Harvey. I want you to see that."

Donny held out his hand, ready for Harvey to shake.

Harvey eyed it and felt Julios' eyes burn into him, pressing him to do the right thing. He took the hand and gripped it hard so that Donny couldn't pull away. But Harvey pulled him close enough to lean and whisper into his ear.

"You've got your truce, Donny," said Harvey. "But don't even think about letting me down."

CHAPTER ELEVEN

The Standings' home was an ordinary end-of-terrace house. The front garden was fenced and there were roses around the border that appeared to be well-tended, as did the lawn. A little path led from a small gate to the front door, which was white PVC with three pie-shaped frosted windows that formed a semi-circle.

A distorted figure approached through the frosted glass and stepped back.

It was Mr Standing who answered the door and stood, defensive of his family in the doorway with a long sleepless night etched into the skin around his eyes.

"Mr Standing?" said Myers. "I'm DI

Myers and this is DS Fox. I believe you were expecting us."

Standing glanced up the street, looked both ways, then nodded.

"You'd better come inside," he said, and opened the door further, standing back to let them pass.

The house had been decorated with as much equal care as the front garden. The walls were smooth and white, and the floor was hardwood, expensive and tasteful. It was similar to the flooring Myers had installed in his own family home but could no longer enjoy.

"Go through to the kitchen," said Standing from behind them, and Myers moved in.

The kitchen had been decorated to a higher standard than Myers had expected. There was a large central island with an expensive knife set, a sink, and a huge, wooden chopping board on the functional side. On the side nearest to Myers, there were three comfortable stools for the breakfast bar.

Behind the island was the range cooker, another pair of sinks, and enough work surface to prepare dinner for more than a large family. In the space beyond the island was a lounge area that enjoyed the sun through the glass roof above. Lobelia plants hung from elevated pots on shelves and small tropical trees stood guard on either side of the bi-folding doors that led into the garden.

"You have a beautiful home," said Fox.

"Thank you," said Mr Standing, and held his hand out for them to take a two-seater rattan couch. "Please, make yourself comfortable while I go and find my wife."

While Standing was gone, Myers admired the photos that were on small shelves and had been hung on the walls. Jennifer was in each of them. Alone in her school uniform, with her parents at what looked like a wedding, and as a young child beaming with smiles. Mr Standing bore the confidence of a man who had achieved mild professional success with the support of an incredibly beautiful family. The image stabbed at Myers, reminding him of how he had once been.

Standing's wife was picture perfect and if the families' similarities stretched further than the wooden floors and confident smiles, then it must be Mrs Myers who was the budding interior designer.

Myers remembered a time when his wife was articulating her vision over coffee. They hadn't been in their house for very long and Harriet was yet to be born. She spoke about light and space and colour and contrast to the point that Myers had tuned out, nodding in the gaps where he thought it was appropriate and agreeing with hummed confirmations that rose and fell in pitch to convey enthusiasm.

But despite the huge cost, the disruption of builders and decorators, plumbers and electricians, unforeseen issues that could only be fixed with four figures in a chequebook, the result had been astounding. The house had been transformed. Each day, Myers would go to work and return home to a new change. A wall had been replaced with a steel joist and an archway, an extension had been built and the entire rear side of the house was glazed with bi-folding doors, and just as Alison had said, light bellowed into the open kitchen.

There were footsteps on the wooden floor. Myers looked up and stood to greet Mrs Standing and Jennifer, who also and understandably wore the tired eyes of a girl who had cried herself to sleep and woken to find the nightmare was indeed reality.

She wore a pair of jeans and trainers, the type that Harriet liked to wear. On top, she wore a thick, woollen sweater despite the heat of the morning, and her hands were lost to the sleeves of her arms as she hugged herself.

They sat. Mr Standing took the seat closest to Myers, and Jennifer sat beside him. Mrs Standing sat furthest away and took Jennifer's hand. It was as Myers had thought. They were a close family and although Mr Standing was not a large man and his success had been through good business, he still bore the protective instinct of a father. He was admirable in Myers' eyes. The whole family were, and the scene raised a pang of jealousy within Myers.

"How are you, Jennifer?" asked Myers.

But her expression told him more than her words, which came in a low mumble, indistinguishable through the tears and phlegm.

"I'm Detective Inspector Myers and this is Detective Sergeant Fox. We understand you've been through a terrible ordeal, so we'll keep this as short as we can. Is that okay?"

She nodded but couldn't meet him eye to eye.

"My colleague will ask you a few questions," said Myers. "It might be hard to talk about it, but if you can give us any information at all, we'd be grateful."

She nodded again and looked at her mum, who squeezed her hand and offered her a reassuring, thin-lipped smile that barely raised the corners of her mouth.

"Mr Standing," said Myers, "why don't we leave them to it? Is there somewhere we can talk?"

"I'd rather stay."

"I'm sure you would," said Myers. "But some things are easier told when Daddy isn't around, in my experience, you understand?"

He turned to his daughter. "Do you mind if I go, Jen?"

She looked across to her mum and then to Fox, who, which Myers was grateful for, gave a warm smile that would melt frozen butter.

"I'll be here," said Mrs Standing. "It'll just be the three of us."

Jennifer nodded and Mr Standing rose, letting his hand graze his daughter's shoulder and then smooth her hair.

"If you need me, just call out, okay?"

She nodded again.

Myers followed Mr Standing through the kitchen to the lounge and heard Fox begin her questioning.

"I'd like to see Jennifer's room, if I may," said Myers, before Mr Standing could settle.

"Is that necessary?" he replied, but his protective tone had dropped and had become subservient to Myers' in the space of that short walk. It was as Myers had expected. The man's wife and daughter were being cared for and were in safe hands. It was time for a man to man chat, and Myers' age and experience showed.

"It might," said Myers.

"I'd rather we didn't."

Myers smiled. "As you wish."

"He's dead, isn't he?" said Standing. "The boy. He's dead."

"Yes."

Myers saw no reason to withhold that kind of information from Standing. If anything, it would ease the tension, if only slightly.

"Do you think Jennifer did it?" he asked.

The question took Myers by surprise.

"Your daughter is not a murder suspect, Mr Standing. If she was, we'd be having this conversation in an interview room."

"Am *I* a suspect?" he replied. "Or my wife? I can assure you, we-"

"You're not suspects. Jennifer isn't a suspect. Your wife is not a suspect. You're the victims. Unfortunately, Jennifer is the only witness."

Mr Standing was silent. He was reassured but was processing the information in what Myers could only imagine was a whirlwind of thoughts and emotions.

"Mr Standing, can you tell me what happened? In your own words?"

"Well, we left Jennifer in here and went upstairs for a few minutes. When we came back, she was gone. My wife called for her. She didn't respond. We checked her room and she wasn't there."

"So, you called the police?"

"It wasn't like her. It's strange. We both knew. I don't know how. But we both knew something was wrong. She was acting strange, had been for the past few weeks. She hadn't closed off, but I don't know. We put it down to her age. We thought maybe she had a boyfriend."

"Parent intuition," said Myers. "I'm a dad myself. I know what you mean."

Standing nodded.

"It's hard to describe. As a parent, you have these feelings, these...I don't know what. But they border on paranoia, I guess. But this was different. We knew. I'm sorry. I know that won't stand up in court. It's not tangible."

"You'd be surprised at how understanding a jury can be, Mr Standing. They're parents themselves, some of them anyway. But there won't be any need for you to go to court for Jennifer's abduction."

He nodded. "And the murder?"

"Tell me what happened next."

"The police arrived, and I have to say, they responded very fast."

"Tell me what happened when Jennifer came home."

Myers was keen not to let Standing slip into a story he'd heard before, about how a female officer came to sit with them while the search began and how questions about who might have taken her were weaved into empathetic conversations about friends, family, and neighbours.

"The doorbell rang," said Standing. "The doorbell rang, and the policewoman went to answer it, but I beat her to it. This is still *my* home. Our home."

The defensive male was creeping back.

"And then?" Myers prompted, keen to get Standing back to their mutual parental discussion.

"And she was there. Just standing there with her head bowed."

"She was alone?" asked Myers.

"Yes. But as soon as I got her through the door, I heard a struggle further up the street. There were screeching tyres and car doors slamming."

"And you didn't see the man?"

"I didn't. I was told that whoever it was, he was seen in the area. He watched me open the door then walked away. It was as if he was just out for an evening stroll, the officer said."

The story married up with the arresting officers' accounts.

"It was him, wasn't it?" said Standing. "He did what he did and brought her home and I was just a few feet away from him."

Standing began to pace the room. That possessive masculinity inside him was enraged at how close he had been to the man who had stripped his daughter of her clothes and done God knows what to her.

"Your daughter was unharmed, Mr Standing. I don't need to tell you how much worse things could have been."

"Did he die in custody?" asked Standing. "I heard he was dead. Did he die in custody? You hear about these things happening. Police brutality getting out of control."

"Has Jennifer told you anything?" asked Myers, leading the father away from the silent man.

"She hasn't said a word since she came home. My wife cleaned her and dressed her. She said she hadn't been raped. The medics checked and..." Standing paused and shook his head before altering course. "But Jennifer hasn't said a single word."

The fact that Standing still thought the unknown man was the abductor was favourable to Myers. He would know more than the average public, being the victim's father. And the fewer people who knew about the slaughter in the woods, the better.

Myers said nothing to affirm either way. His expression was grim enough to convey that Standing shouldn't press such matters.

He waited for Standing to talk and, in their silence, Jennifer's sobbing could be heard. The barrier had come down and she would be spilling out the details to Fox and her mother.

The sobbing was too much for Standing who went to head into the kitchen. But Myers stopped him.

"It's better if you don't," said Myers. With his hand on the man's chest, he could feel his racing heart. "Let the story come out. Let her get it off her chest in one go."

Standing was tense and was almost bitter toward Myers, but then relented.

"I can't listen to it. I can't listen to her crying."

Myers watched, waiting for him to open up further. Emotions were like that, he thought. Emotions always bring out the truth.

But Standing was frustrated. They could both hear the sobs and whining voice but were too far away to understand what was being said.

"How about we see her room?" said Myers, and after a short pause for thought, Standing relented.

The noise of the sobbing subsided, and Myers followed Standing up the stairs. Jennifer's room was at the rear of the house.

"You have a strong family, Mr Standing. Jennifer will need that."

They reached the top of the stairs and Standing turned to see where Myers was going with the statement.

"I can't imagine what you're going through. I have a daughter about the same age as Jennifer and if the tables were turned, I have no idea how I'd handle it. Not as well as you are, that much I do know. Jennifer is fortunate to have parents like you. A stable home is what she needs now."

Myers reached the top of the stairs and met Standing eye to eye. Man to man. He was about to enter the man's teenage daughter's bedroom. He needed to be trusted.

"I don't know if this helps, Mr Standing, but keep doing what you're doing. Keep loving her and you'll get through this. She'll never get over it. But if you and your wife do as you're doing, she'll come to terms with it. In time."

Standing nodded and the two shared a moment, father to father. Myers looked away to give Standing time to wipe his eyes and take a few deep breaths.

"Is this her room here?"

Standing waved his hand for Myers to go in.

The room was like any other teenage girl's room. There were no posters on the walls; the family had too much style for that. But there was a shelf with stuffed toys, presumably from the girl's childhood. There were photos of her and her friends and her parents. The bed was unmade, but hadn't been slept in. Only a thin blanket lay on top which Myers imagined the girl had curled beneath the night before. It was a comfort thing that Harriet would have done too.

There was a small dressing table with a mirror and a few cosmetics. Not the full array that Myers imagined Harriet to have. Jennifer was still just fourteen. But if Mrs Standing was anything like Alison, Jennifer would be allowed a handful of products and a hairdryer. She was a girl, after all.

The room was decorated in white with accents of pink and the furniture was expensive. Myers knew all about expensive furniture, even in a child's bedroom. He could tell the difference between solid oak and flat-packed chests of drawers and handmade wardrobes over factory-built products. He could also tell the difference between expensive clothes and cheap counterfeits. The collection of shopping bags and boxes in the corner of the room was a token of Jennifer's pride in owning the items. People didn't do that kind of thing with knock-offs.

Then Myers' eyes fell on a familiar item. And just as Mr Standing had described that uneasy feeling of borderline paranoia when he had described Jennifer's initial absence, Myers felt the same.

"What is it?" asked Standing when he saw Myers staring too long.

"Nothing," said Myers. "I've seen enough."

"You saw something. I might not be a detective, Mr Myers, but I do know a liar when I see one."

"It's nothing, Mr Standing. Just that bag." He smiled a thin-lipped smile. "My daughter has the exact same one."

CHAPTER TWELVE

While Julios had walked anti-clockwise around the grounds, Harvey had taken a clockwise route.

He stepped through the orchard and stared down at the party below. The children had long since returned to their parents, and the relative silence gave him time to contemplate what Donny had said.

There had been a genuine desire for Donny to change and for the two of them to get on, as brothers should. But Donny had a long history of being weak. He had an affliction for drugs and lived a life so far removed from Harvey's that empathy had been impossible for most of their childhoods. Donny lived several lives. While he wasn't running businesses under the thumb of Sergio and the ever-present thumb of his father, he mixed in shadowy circles and ventured into the world of crime that even hardened criminals like his father refused to sink to.

To the right of the wooden archway, a stage had been built for the band. The guests had finished their meals and were still reeling from the speeches as they swarmed to the bar. The first poignant notes from the upright bass player sounded as he led the group into their first set. The guests hushed, craning their necks trying to put a title to the bass line. But it was one of the brass players who revealed the melody and drew the excitement from the crowd.

A few of the women, who were already fuelled by a few glasses of Dom Perignon, raised their arms and danced their way to the temporary dance floor while their partners clutched their pint glasses and leaned on the high tables to talk business.

Donny and Julia were in the distance, perched atop the crest of John's land following the photographer's instructions. It was the perfect place for the photos as the land fell away behind them and the clear sky framed the newlyweds in vivid blue.

But Harvey wasn't interested in his foster-brother or his new wife. He moved behind the fattest of trees that bordered the orchard, aware of the sound of feet moving through the long grass behind him.

But the footsteps stopped.

Harvey reached for his knife, but the suit that John had made him wear hadn't had any-where for him to keep it. It was still in his leather jacket.

He waited. His mind blocked the dull thrum of the party below and the melody of the swing band. He cast aside the rustle of leaves and branches in the gentle breeze and felt his pulse in his clenched fists.

There was a faint swish of grass. The snap of a tiny twig underfoot and the rustle of clothing.

Ten metres, thought Harvey, and waited for the next movement. He pictured who-ever it was as only a shape, tracking him as a leopard might stalk a deer. The fat tree be-hind Harvey shielded him from view, but whoever's footsteps he could hear would come from either direction. He stepped away from the tree and turned to surprise them.

But nobody came.

He moved right half a step.

Nothing.

He moved left half a step.

Again, there was nobody there.

Another half a step, his senses alive with adrenaline.

Nothing.

He took two steps, stopping with his feet planted, ready to defend himself, circling the fat oak, sure that he would see whoever was stalking him.

He moved back into the orchard, checking behind him as he went, and he stopped to listen.

Had he imagined the footsteps?

A bird fluttered in the treetops and the hum of wasps and bees feasting on the fallen fruit was louder than before. It was as if they had been disturbed.

Then movement, thirty meters away. A shape moved from tree to tree, moving away from Harvey back through the orchard.

But nobody knew that orchard as well as Harvey. It had been the playground for him and his sister. Their names were carved into the trunks of the fattest trees and the ground itself was rich with their blood, which had been spilt from countless grazed knees.

He flanked the dark shape through the thickest part of the orchard. He moved in silence but cursed the suit he wore. Each time he stopped, the shape moved further away. They were heading toward the far side of the property where the grass grew long, and the fruit-bearing trees gave way to fat oaks older than the house itself. John used to say that Henry VIII had planted one of them. It was one of John's favourite boasts that he announced to awestruck guests and he'd said it so often that Harvey felt there must be some truth in there.

He caught a glimpse of the shape as it moved out of the orchard. The strong breeze blew on the far side of the trees, giving Harvey a little lenience on the sounds he could make. He ran full pelt to the edge of the trees just twenty metres from the spot he'd seen the shape. Then, slowly, using all the stealth he could muster in the tight dress shoes, he moved towards the spot.

From one tree to another, he stepped, surveyed, and then planned his next move, until there were no more trees to conceal him, and he stepped out into the open and realised his foolishness.

He closed his eyes, cursing his shoes and himself, then turned as a voice he didn't recognise spoke to him with the clarity of education and the confidence of wealth and good breeding.

"You must be Donny's brother."

CHAPTER THIRTEEN

"She's telling the truth," said Fox. She pulled her seat belt on and checked her eye makeup in the mirror. "Poor girl. Nobody should have to go through what she did."

"Don't let emotions rule your head. Give me the facts," said Myers.

"The facts, sir, are that she was stripped naked and forced to watch Hussein..." She paused. "It was like you said, sir. He wanted her to watch him first."

"From the top, Fox. Just the facts. She was at home. Her parents were upstairs."

"Hussein tapped on the front door."

"So, he must have been familiar with the house," said Myers.

But Fox ignored him and ran through the headlines.

"She opened the door but there was nobody there. She stepped outside and he grabbed her. He covered her mouth with a rag. She said she remembered a bitter, chemical taste and that's all. She woke up in the woods."

"Rohypnol," said Myers. "Or some variation of it. We'll find out when we search Hussein's house. Then what? Was she tied up at this point? Give me the facts, Fox."

"Yes, she was tied up. She was stripped naked and couldn't move. She said she was aware of a camera flash but wasn't sure what it was until she opened her eyes."

"He wanted to capture the moment," said Myers, as Hussein's mind opened up a little. "He wanted to capture the very moment she woke up and realised what was happening. He wanted the fear. Keep going."

"He gagged her so she couldn't scream. Then he stripped."

Fox paused, not wanting to explain the details. But Myers needed the details. He had to see it in his mind. He said nothing, waiting for Fox to take a deep breath, compartmentalise, and recite.

"He made her watch him, sir. Just like you said."

Fox was stronger than Myers thought. She stared out of the passenger window. Unable to meet his stare, perhaps. Or maybe it was to hide the bitter hatred on her face?

"He dug the hole in front of her. He told her that the hole was for her. He told her he was going to choke her. Then he..."

She exhaled and cracked the window for some air then turned to him, red-eyed and angry.

"He licked the tears off her face, sir."

They were both silent.

Myers pulled the car into a lay-by and switched off the engine. They weren't too far from Harriet's school and as angry as Harriet had been and as confused as she was, Myers was grateful she wasn't going through the same ordeal. Stories such as Jennifer Standing's somehow made all other problems in life seem insignificant.

Perhaps that was why Alison had eventually had enough of him. He'd never reacted to her outbursts. He'd never shown her any kind of emotion, and maybe it was because the dramas in their own lives, the leaking pipes and the unkempt lawns, had been in the shadow of his work. While they fought over who did the most work in the house, there were people out there who'd had their lives altered forever. Murders, rapes, and even victims of robberies who were so traumatised they couldn't even return to their homes.

Myers pondered the thought while Fox gathered her senses. Time was often all people needed.

"You want me to carry on?" she asked.

"In your own time."

She cleared her throat and shifted in her seat.

"When Hussein had finished digging the hole, he turned his attention to Jennifer. She said his voice changed from being nasty and cruel to a soft, caring tone. He stroked her hair and hugged her. She said he hugged her for what seemed like forever."

"He liked the feel of skin on skin," said Myers, but kicked himself for interrupting Fox's flow.

She turned to him with raised eyebrows.

"Do you understand what I'm talking

about when I say there's a security that comes with the touch of skin on skin?" said Myers. "There's a warmth, a vulnerability, which strengthens the trust. It's what makes us close to our partners. You might love someone with all your heart, and they might reciprocate with similar feelings, but there's nothing like the touch of flesh on flesh. Naked and afraid."

"Is that a long-winded way of saying Hussein was just a sad creep who couldn't get a girlfriend?"

"Flippant, but yes."

"Afraid?" said Fox. "You said Hussein was afraid."

"Why wouldn't he be? There's case after case of men like him. Many of them can't perform sexually. Many of them regard themselves as inadequate. Do you remember the first time you were naked in front of a man?"

"He wasn't a man. He was more of a boy."

"But it's the same thing. The same experience. You were opening yourself up to him. You had to fight through the inadequacies. But over time, you feel more comfortable. You get to know each other's bodies."

"Of course," said Fox.

"So, imagine that you never had that experience. Imagine that you never had that closeness or that comfort or that trust. Imagine if you were so deeply ashamed of your body or your inadequacies that you had to force people to see it."

"And if you're weak like Hussein was," said Fox, falling in line with where Myers was heading, "you have to pick weaker people. Children and young girls."

"That's why he hugged her. That's why he was soft and gentle with her. He was experiencing what you and I and the rest of society experience with mutual concession."

"I get the feeling you empathise with him, sir."

"Of course I don't empathise with him, Fox. I don't even know if I'm right. All we have to go on is historical cases. But we have to understand him, or at least try to see his motive."

Fox was still. She looked across at Myers, trying to read his thoughts.

"She said he cried."

Myers said nothing.

"She said he held her, pressing himself against her, gripping her throat with one hand, and she felt his hot tears on her shoulder and his warm breath on her skin. She said they were cheek to cheek when he closed her throat completely. She felt him tense against her, but she could hear him crying. Even as she fought against her restraints and struggled for air, he held her as if he was helping her. She said it was like he was comforting her. She knew she was going to die, sir. Nobody should ever go through that. Nobody. She said that her blood felt cold. It was the only way she could describe it. She felt her legs go numb and the rope that held her to the tree took her weight. She said there was no pain. She was just frightened, and he kept whispering to her."

"Whispering what?"

"That's the strange thing, sir. He said..."

"Go on," said Myers. "In your own time."

"He said he didn't want to share her anymore."

Myers knew what was coming next. The girl they had just seen had been seconds from death.

Fox waited a moment and cleared her throat once more. Myers waited patiently. Cars passed them and people walked by, oblivious to the hideous conversation that was taking place.

"At first she thought he was an angel, sir," said Fox, and there was a hint of Fox's pride in the young girl and an admiration of her strength.

And she repeated the girl's words verbatim.

"An angel rose from the shadows. A black shape darker than the trees..."

She hesitated, as if recalling what Jennifer Standing had said and reliving her emotions.

"And the angel tore him from me."

"Our man," said Myers. "The silent man. She saw it happen. What did she say?"

Fox turned to stare through the side window and seemed to track an old man carrying a plastic bag ambling along the street with what appeared to be all the time in the world.

"She said one word," said Fox, then turned to stare at him as Myers imagined Jennifer had done. "Fury."

CHAPTER FOURTEEN

The voice was clear, smooth, and confident. The way the owner articulated her consonants then cut them off sharply as if every syllable was practiced and intentional somehow grabbed Harvey's attention.

He turned to see who it was that had managed to elude him and find a patch of sun in the long grass.

She was stretched out on the grass, resting on one elbow with her heels kicked off. Her long, brown hair almost touched the ground and her fingers rolled the stem of a champagne flute back and forth. Her slender legs stretched from beneath her short, tight dress, and her bare feet danced and writhed in the grass and stretched and flexed in the sun.

On the lawn before her was a bottle of Dom Perignon and an empty flute lay beside it.

"I've heard a lot about you," she said, and sipped at her champagne, her eyes never leaving Harvey's.

Harvey didn't reply.

"Donny told me you're the strong, silent type."

She smiled at Harvey's lack of response.

"He said you were all business and no play. Well, why don't you relax a little? Come join me."

Harvey glanced at the empty glass and felt the trap tighten.

"Come on. There's nobody around. It's your brother's wedding day. You can let go a little."

She set her glass down, balancing it against the grass, and filled the empty flute from the bottle. She held it out to him, and a naughty smile spread across her face revealing perfect, white teeth that bit her lower lip.

"Humour me," she said, and there was a touch of vulnerability in her voice that somehow managed to break through the confident facade.

Harvey stared at the glass then back at her.

"Don't leave me hanging here," she said. "Please."

He took the glass and she raised her own in the air.

"To Mr and Mrs Cartwright. May they have many babies," she said, then sipped at her drink. "It's good manners to sip after a toast, Harvey."

"I've never been one for manners that involve alcohol."

"But you took the drink from me."

"You begged."

"Do you often give in to people who beg?" she said, pleased to have led him into a corner.

"I should get back," said Harvey, and glanced down at the house through the trees. The view was mostly blocked, and the hum of the party was faint but audible.

"Oh, I remember now. Donny said you would be keeping us all safe."

It was as if she toyed with words, her lips and eyes playing games with each annunciation.

Harvey didn't reply.

"Do you think they'll miss you?" she asked. "Do you think they'll miss you if you keep *me* safe? Just for a while?"

"You don't look like you're in much danger."

"Oh, I'm in danger, alright," she said, raising herself up onto one arm to get closer. Her eyes darted from side to side, then rested back onto Harvey's, and she adopted a conspiratorial whisper. "I'm in danger of being lonely. Imagine it. A girl like me all alone in this beautiful place with just a bottle of champagne and the birds for company. What will a girl do?"

She lay back and stretched out.

"But wait," she said. "What if there was a man who could save me from such a fate? A strong man, handsome and fearless. What if he were to sit with me for a while to ward off the pangs of loneliness? A man like you, Harvey Stone. Won't you sit with me a while and keep me company?"

"I should really-"

"Get back, yes, you said," she said with a tone of utter disappointment. "I guess a man like you must have girls lay themselves before you all the time. I suppose, for a man like you, a girl like me comes along every day of your life."

"This man," said Harvey, reverting to the girl's drama, "what if he were to sit with you for a while? What if he disregarded his duties and sat with you?"

"He wouldn't regret it," she said, and teased her fingers along her slender thigh. "In fact, I'd do everything in my power to make sure he had an afternoon he'll never forget."

Her fingers raised the hem of her dress a little. Just enough to bare the tantalising flesh of her upper thigh and a hint of toned cheek.

Harvey gave his surroundings a scan and looked back at her.

"Are we safe?" she said, adopting the part of the frightened girl she had imitated before.

Harvey didn't reply, and the girl laughed then slid over, inviting him to sit beside her.

"Are you always so tense?" she asked when Harvey had crouched. "Sit properly. Relax. It's a beautiful day."

Harvey set his glass down with no intention of drinking it, then sat with his arms wrapped around his knees.

"Oh, come on, you can do better than

that," she said, and climbed to her knees. She moved behind him and began to pull his jacket from his shoulders. Harvey resisted at first, then relented when she slid her hands across his neck and found the tight bunches of muscle.

The first thing Harvey thought of was Julios' disappointment if he found Harvey frolicking in the grass with a woman while he was working. It wasn't that Julios was against such interactions. But Harvey had been asked to do a job and leaving Julios to look after the party alone was unprofessional. A single unprofessional act would cause Julios to doubt Harvey even more. And if there was doubt in his ability to stay in control, that doubt would spread like a cancer.

He had worked with Julios since he was a boy. Julios had mentored him and nurtured his mind into a permanent state of awareness and caution. He trusted nobody but Julios and John, and he trusted the former far more than the latter.

As a young boy, Harvey had taken to Julios' training well and he had progressed fast. For a teenager, Harvey's fitness levels had grown so quickly that his body had changed in a matter of months and hadn't altered much when he hit his twenties, save for the usual signs of maturity.

"So lean and hard," she said, as her fingers traced his spine, pushing any thoughts of Julios from Harvey's mind.

Her perfume was sweet yet subtle. He could feel the warmth of her face beside his own and she tugged at his tie, loosening it with one hand, and with what seemed like a practised movement, she slid it from his collar to begin working on his shirt buttons.

"I should..." Harvey began, and made to stand. But her grip was strong, and she pulled him back down.

"Shh. You should do nothing but let me take care of you," she whispered into his ear.

Her hands grazed the skin on his chest and traced the outline of the tight rows of muscles at his core. Her lips found his neck and she seemed to inhale his smell as she kissed her way along his shoulder.

"Lie down," she said, her voice soft but commanding, and she applied a little pressure to coerce him forward. He lay on the grass with the sun high in the sky behind the girl so that she was faceless in the silhouette and a halo of light framed her as she straddled him. She opened his shirt further and pulled it apart, seeming to revel in what she saw, and she explored him with inquisitive fingers, then lowered herself down onto him.

The girl knew what she was doing. She clamped her thighs around his to hold him there and to pull him closer, and with every touch of her tongue on Harvey's chest and neck, she ground herself into him.

Harvey's hands ran along her bare thighs, feeling the smooth skin and taut muscles. His fingers worked the hem of her dress up to reveal the flesh below. The further he explored, the more frantic her grinding became. She pulled away the straps of her dress and the material fell to her waist. Then she pulled Harvey's head up to bury his face in her chest.

She began working Harvey's buckle with her delicate touch, stopping only to squeeze at him through his trousers with feverish fingers, then returning to his belt with little care for delicacy.

The lace thong she wore was thin and tore with a signal tug from Harvey, a move that seemed to excite her even further as she worked him free and lowered herself onto him once more.

It was at that moment, at that point of no return, that their eyes met. She smiled while Harvey bucked and pulled her closer.

It was then that thoughts of anything but the electricity between them fell away and only her perfect body, energy, and lust filled Harvey's mind.

And it was at that moment of connection, when the two lovers' bodies met with the summer sun high above and the long grass rolling with the breeze, that in the distance, in some far-off time and world, a single gunshot rang out and echoed through John Cartwright's estate.

CHAPTER FIFTEEN

Beyond a mass of tangled weeds and perennial shrubs, a small patch of lawn grew wild and unkempt. The garden was a stain on the street. A thorn between roses.

The dead-end street was lower class but respectful. Myers was familiar with the types of people who would call it home. The neighbourhood wasn't full of sponging low-lives; he could see that by the cars and the tended gardens. The saloon cars and hatchbacks were mostly clean and there was an order, as if residents kept up with the Joneses and those that failed to maintain the look and feel of the street were the topic of bitter, over-the-fence discussions.

"I get the feeling the neighbours won't miss him," said Myers. He shook his head as a curtain twitched in a house across the street and he released his seat belt.

Fox was ready to go in. They had everything they needed: the warrant from Allenby and Hussein's keys from the evidence room. But before they went inside, Myers wanted to make sure Fox had recovered from her interview with Jennifer Standing.

In Myers' opinion, Fox was strong. She would go far. In a few short years, she had made detective sergeant, but for her to progress further, there were a number of firsts she would need to experience. It was those firsts that made or broke careers and her first interview with a victim of a sex attack had revealed far more of her capabilities than he had seen to date.

It was fortunate for all that Jennifer Standing was not interfered with, although she would carry the trauma for the rest of her life. The Jennifer Standing her parents had known and loved was gone. A new Jennifer Standing existed. It was fortunate that Standing hadn't been killed and that her abductor had. By Fox's account, she had been close to death. If things had taken a different turn, they might have been searching the woods for her body instead of sitting outside Hussein's house.

It was a blessing for Fox that she had been exposed to a survivor of such an attack. It was an experience that happened so rarely. What she did with that experience was down to her. Myers imagined that when she got home that evening, she might have a little cry. That would be okay. He'd cried a hundred times as the events of the day accumulated, and the walls of his home had removed the barriers for his emotions.

But there was anger in Fox that Myers was cautious of. Nobody enjoyed cases like the Standing case. Nobody enjoyed having to hear about the ordeal the victims went through. And nobody enjoyed trying to put themselves into the minds of the abductors or rapists.

But that was where Myers differed. That was where he shone. He was able to be that person, think like them, understand their behaviour, and find that motive.

And the motive unlocked doors to success.

Motives told Myers a hundred different things. Guilt alone does not solve a case. You have to see beyond the guilt.

"Shall we?" said Fox, her cool demeanour seeming to rise to the occasion.

Myers studied her for a second, then opened his door.

They entered through the front door with little fuss and stopped inside the hallway. Memories of Myers' childhood came flooding back to him, spurred by the flock wallpaper and patterned artex ceilings that had browned with time and nicotine. There were a few pairs of shoes with jackets hanging above them and a telephone table with a pile of un-opened post upon it. Myers pulled on a pair of latex gloves and flicked through the en-velopes, but there was nothing that his own hallway table didn't have. Gas bills, electricity bills, and a few other franked envelopes.

Beyond the hallway was a galley kitchen. Orange tiles ran across the walls. A free-standing oven was at one end and a small fridge-freezer at the other. It wasn't an immac-ulate kitchen, but it certainly wasn't a hovel. Hussein had taken care of himself more than many bachelors did. There were no crumbs or food on the sideboard and the sink was free of the countless days-old washing up that he'd seen so often in the abodes of social outcasts.

"Are you looking for anything in particular?" said Fox, as Myers peered into the fridge. "We know he was guilty, and we have his body."

"Something," said Myers. He turned to her and closed the fridge. "Something else. It'll be here somewhere. Why don't you take the lounge and I'll look upstairs?"

Fox sucked in a deep breath and nodded, clearly unsure of what he was looking for. But the truth was that Myers didn't know himself if he would find anything, or what he might find.

He ventured up the stairs, being careful not to touch the handrail. There were two bedrooms and a bathroom. The clean but tired appearance was continued in the bathroom, featuring an off-green suite. The toilet had a wooden seat and the bath had a makeshift shower curtain that had probably needed replacing five years ago.

There were the usual bathroom accessories: a shaver, a facecloth, and a bar of soap. Nothing fancy. Nothing to say that the guy took care of himself well but enough to say that Hussein did in fact keep himself clean.

The bath had a line of grime around the edge, but other than that, there was nothing blocking the plug. Myers moved to the master bedroom. The curtains were closed and there was a smell of dirty linen that reminded Myers of the first few months when he and Alison had split, when he had to do his own cleaning. That was before he'd found a routine and before he'd become self-sufficient.

There were dirty clothes on the floor and Myers picked through them to find they were all male clothing. They were the baggy, cotton pyjamas that Pakistani men wore. He'd heard them being called kurtas before. But there was nothing out of the ordinary. He pulled open the wardrobe and found a few items hanging, but not many. A chest of drawers was where Hussein had stored most of his clothes. Creased t-shirts and jeans and old socks and underwear. Myers sifted through them. Despite the cliché that detectives found clues in sock and underwear drawers, people still hid things there. It was something Myers had never understood, as if the suspect thought that nobody would be rude enough to search there. Myers always searched them and had struck gold enough times to carry on searching there.

He moved to the bedside table but disturbed the curtain as he passed. The narrow sliver of light that shone through lit a cloud of dust that seemed to hang in the air.

There were a few crude magazines in the bottom drawer. Nothing sinister or out of the ordinary. Myers had seen worse. He tossed them onto the bed and pulled the drawer out to search the spot that often contained the most gold. The space below the drawers.

But there was nothing save for a few coins of small denomination and a few old tissues that, even with gloves on, Myers didn't want to touch. He fanned the pages of the dirty magazines and dropped them back in the drawer, then kicked it closed and pulled open the top drawer. He found nothing of any significance. A few coins, an old, cheap watch, pens, and some loose batteries.

He shut the drawer just as Fox called from downstairs.

"Sir, how are you getting on?"

"Nothing earth shattering. How about you?"

Myers glanced under the bed, then stepped out onto the landing and looked down at her.

"Nothing any other young man wouldn't have in a rented house, sir."

"Okay, do me a favour and pick up that phone. Tell me if it's connected."

She did as he instructed. "It's working, sir."

"Good. Call Allenby. Tell her we're on our way to Hussein's parents' house to break the news. There's nothing here that says Hussein was anything other than a sex-starved loner. I'll check the spare room and be down in a second."

He opened the door to the spare room. It was smaller than the master with enough space for a single bed and a small wardrobe. But there was no bed. In its place was a desk with a comfy chair and a computer.

Myers stepped inside. There was something different about the room. The walls had the same yellowed and aged appearance. The ceiling was rippled with artex circles and the pattern of the carpet had faded long ago. The curtains were blackout curtains, thick and dark, and there was a mirror on the wall beside the light switch.

Myers flicked the light on.

It was the tidiest room in the house. There were none of the little keepsakes that people keep on their desks, or even a little monkey pen pot. There was no notepad, no books. Just a chair, a wardrobe, and a computer. He moved the mouse a little, then tapped a few keys on the keyboard, but nothing happened. He dropped to a crouch to see below the desk and found the computer's power button. The computer jumped into life with a noisy fan. Flashing lights on the rear illuminated the space below the desk enough to see that it was immaculate.

But his thoughts were interrupted by Fox calling up the stairs.

"Sir?"

Fox's voice was distant but still an interruption to Myers' thoughts. The scene began to fade away, his imagination letting the trails of possibilities go as if they slipped through his fingers.

The door opened behind him.

"Sir?"

"What?" he snapped, and he turned to see

Fox wide-eyed and staring at the room. "Fox? What is so urgent that you keep interrupting me?"

She looked at him, trying to read if he was genuinely angry or if it was a slight falter in his usually calm temperament.

"It's Allenby, sir. She wants to talk to you."

He sighed. He hated the interruptions. It took at least five to ten minutes for Myers to get into somebody's mind. Five to ten minutes of uninterrupted silence and mental freedom. What did the person do when they entered the house? Did they hang their keys up on a hook, or drop them in a pot? Or maybe they threw them on the kitchen work surface? Or simply put them back in their pocket? What was their routine? In fact, did they actually have a routine? Did they drop their clothes on the floor or fold them neatly and put them away? All of these things gave Myers an insight into their minds.

And the interruptions destroyed his empathy. Even more so when it was Allenby who was responsible for the interruptions.

"Ma'am?" he said, when he reached the phone.

"Detective Inspector Myers, Fox tells me you're in Hussein's house."

"That's right, ma'am."

"What are you looking for? I didn't ask you to go there. Did you listen to *anything* I said this morning?"

Three questions. None of which required an answer. Myers said nothing.

"You're still trying to find the link to Rashid Al Sheik, aren't you?"

"I'm just trying to find the killer, ma'am."

There was a pause and Myers pictured her sitting at her desk, toying with his career with a sickening delight.

"You're off the case."

"*What?*"

"I'm putting you on another case. I'll find another DI to take over. You can debrief them later."

"What are you afraid of, ma'am?"

"I'll remind you who you are speaking to, Detective Inspector Myers."

"We can't not investigate just in case Rashid Al Sheik makes a complaint."

"I cannot have this department tainted with allegations of racism and harassment, Myers. Not while I sit here."

"Ma'am-"

"Do you have your notebook?"

He sighed and fished his pad from his pocket and clicked open his pen.

"There's been a shooting. I want you and Fox to attend. Maybe a fresh case will give you some perspective, Detective Inspector Myers."

CHAPTER SIXTEEN

There was screaming. There was chaos. And there was the familiar tone of John's baritone voice at the centre of it all. Harvey broke free of the orchard and stood looking down at the party from the elevated viewpoint.

The band had stopped and were packing their kit away as fast as they could. The caterers had fled and were huddled behind one of their vans while the wedding organiser tried to calm them down. And cars were being started by husbands who called through open doors to their wives who were running across the lawn with their heels in their hands.

But there were two groups of people who were not running away.

The first were three of John's men. One had a man pinned to the ground. His knee was pressed into the back of the man's neck and he had twisted the man's arms up behind his back. The other two stood close by in case the man on the ground escaped.

The second group of people included Donny, who was being restrained by John while Sergio was on his knees beside a mass of white, blood-stained dress.

Julia.

He searched for Julios and found him standing at the gate checking the passengers in the cars in rapid departure. He waved them through one by one.

The gunman wasn't alone.

Harvey, with his bird's-eye view, watched one car join the queue to leave. It was a long, sleek, black Jaguar with dark windows that had been parked at the far end of the row of cars. Even during the chaos, Harvey had not seen anyone run to it.

The gunman's driver was waiting in the car.

There were more than twenty cars lined up on the driveway and the Jaguar was some-where in the middle.

Harvey ran. He called out to Julios but was too far away for him to hear Harvey over the crunch of tyres on the gravel and the rumble of engines.

He tore across the grass and reached the gravel, but there were people everywhere, too lost in their own fears and panic to get out of his way.

A man opened a car door for his wife and was ushering her inside when Harvey collided with him. He stumbled, but regained balance, scanning the cars for the shape of the black Jaguar.

He saw it. It was ten cars back from the gate. He signalled to Julios, but Julios was busy searching the cars.

Without a weapon, Harvey would have to rely on surprise and violence in the hope that Julios would see him. If there was more than one man and they were armed, Harvey would need to act fast. A plan formed in his head as he ran. He ducked behind another queueing car two cars from the Jaguar and slowed. He didn't want the driver to see him in his mirror. He moved to the next car, annoyed at himself once again for agreeing to wear the suit and not being armed.

A couple hurried past him. The woman was hysterical. She was being comforted by her husband as they moved, and Harvey saw the spatter of blood across her dress, her chest, and her face. The man's hands were also covered in blood, but the pair appeared to be unhurt.

Harvey glanced over to the small gathering that was huddled around Julia. John was shouting orders at his men who were crowded around the man on the ground, each of them venting their anger at him. Sergio was arguing with the wedding planner, coaxing him away from Julia's body. And between them, Donny was on his knees, cradling the head of his new wife on his lap.

The beautiful, white dress she had been wearing was soaked in dark, fresh blood and her skin had lost the colour of life.

Harvey steeled himself. He was crouched and holding onto the car beside him, trying to see how many passengers were in the Jaguar through the tinted rear window. But he saw nothing. Along the line of cars, Julios had seen him. He was more than one hundred meters away, but the big man recognised Harvey's expression and nodded.

Harvey made his move.

In four long steps, he made it to the car door and tore it open with his right hand, reaching in with his left.

But in that terrible moment as the door opened and daylight lit the interior, Harvey saw the old man at the wheel, he saw the look of horror on his wife's face, and he realised his mistake.

It was the wrong Jaguar.

"What the bloody hell!" said the old man, but Harvey slammed the door and straightened to see Julios a few meters from the gate walking toward him and pulling a weapon from inside his jacket.

It was wrong. It was all wrong.

Julios gave him a quizzical look and removed his hand from inside his jacket just as the driver of a sleek, black Jaguar beside him gunned the engine. The rear wheels sprayed gravel, the front end raised with the torque, and the Jaguar shot through the gates with its tyres squealing on the country lane.

The sudden burst of energy caught Julios by surprise. In a flash, he saw the Jaguar beside Harvey, saw the Jaguar speeding away, and knew Harvey's mistake.

He fired three shots after the car, but to little effect. By the time the car had disappeared from view, Harvey was beside him.

"Where have you been, Harvey?" said Julios, his voice low and bitter.

"No time. Give me the gun."

There was a second-long delay while Julios searched for something in Harvey's expression, and noted the unbuttoned shirt. Harvey revealed nothing. He held out his hand in urgency. Julios made the gun safe, then slapped it into his palm.

"I'm going after the Jaguar," said Harvey, and he ran towards his little cottage beside the gates.

He opened the garage door, tore the cover off his motorcycle, and started the engine, giving the oil time to heat while he pulled on his helmet. Then, before he climbed on, he ripped off his suit jacket and pulled on his old, leather biker jacket.

He revved once, hearing the growl of the engine in the confined space, found first gear, and shot from his garage and through the gates, leaving the chaos behind him. He reached the end of the narrow lane in a few seconds, where there was a T-junction. To his left, he saw the tail end of a black car disappear around the long, sweeping bend at least half a mile away. The main road connected Theydon Bois with a neighbouring village, Abridge. It was a three-mile stretch of wide and winding road, and Harvey was already nearly a mile behind.

He glanced right to find the road clear, revved the engine, and put the bike to work. The Jaguar, with its four-point-two litre V8 engine would have the power to outrun Harvey's BMW GS1200. But Harvey knew the roads. He knew every bend, bump, and pothole, and could take the road at close to full speed. If the Jaguar reached Abridge before Harvey, the driver could turn left or right, and Harvey would lose them for good.

Harvey worked through the gears, watching the rev counter, checking the road, and searching for a sign of the Jaguar. He worked the bike, pulling as much performance from each gear, making each gear change fluid and fast to maintain the momentum. Every second counted. Every drop in revs or drop in power during the gear changes mattered.

There was a long downhill straight before

Harvey passed beneath the M11 motorway, then the road snaked right and left in two long, sweeping bends. He emerged from the bend using all of the road and there, in the distance, was the Jaguar.

The driver was keeping below the speed limit, a sign that he was a professional. To be caught speeding after a shooting would risk being stopped by the police. In Harvey's experience, only a true professional had the nerve to keep calm and avoid suspicion.

The BMW was not the fastest motorcycle, especially with the panniers and the backbox Harvey had added. He had bought the bike for the on and off road capabilities as well as the freedom of being able to blend in. Superbikes were heavy to handle, awkward, and turned the heads of far too many people. But with a few tweaks of the engine and exhaust and an upgraded suspension, Harvey's bike was fast enough to catch most cars or, more importantly, evade the police.

He closed the distance to two hundred metres, but the driver must have seen him. The rear end of the Jaguar dropped as the driver kicked down and the powerful V8 roared into life. It was what Harvey wanted.

The Jaguar was fast on the long straights, but clumsy and unwieldy on the bends.

He maintained the distance, gauging the driver's ability, but as expected, he handled the power well. The long straight ended at Abridge with a small humpback bridge over the River Roding and a busy T-junction on the other side. But the driver seemed to either not know about the T-junction or was more skilled than Harvey gave him credit for.

Sensing a large collision, Harvey eased off. He couldn't take the bridge and the T-junction in excess of one hundred miles an hour. At the last minute, the driver braked. At the crest of the bridge, he tore the wheel left, forcing the long saloon into a slide. He powered on again as Harvey followed, now just twenty metres behind. The driver controlled the slide, playing the steering wheel to keep the Jaguar under control, and the rear wheels kicked in under a riot of blaring car horns and shouts from other cars that had swerved out of its way.

Harvey pulled his clutch in, found second, and dropped his left knee, taking the sharp turn as fast as he could and relying on the chaos the Jaguar had caused to leave him space. He was already climbing through third gear when he straightened, leaning forward to keep the front wheel on the ground. The Jaguar was just one hundred yards ahead and accelerating just as hard as Harvey. The landscape passed by in a blur of green trees, yellow rapeseed fields, and the winding River Roding that ran parallel with the road. To Harvey's right, the traffic in the other direction seemed to be moving in slow motion. The colours of the cars were the only discernible detail.

And then there was the flash of blue lights.

Harvey pushed down harder, crouching as low as he could behind the tiny windshield, trying to gain distance inch by inch. His side mirror vibrated with the speed so that any details were imperceptible, but he could see the blue lights at least half a mile behind him. The average police car would stand little chance of catching Harvey or the Jaguar at high speed, but they would call for back up and the road somewhere ahead would be closed.

He had to make the long straight to Stapleford count. It was less than a mile to the end of the road where a roundabout formed the junction. The Jaguar would need to slow from one hundred and forty miles per hour at least three hundred metres before the roundabout to hit it at a manageable speed.

Spying a gap in the traffic, Harvey moved into the opposite lane, anticipating the driver's next move, which would be to slam on his brakes so that the bike crashed into the rear of the car.

Harvey's bike crossed the dotted white lines just in time. Red brake lights flashed. The roundabout loomed ahead and the blue lights behind grew even closer.

Harvey shot past the Jaguar, braking hard, and fought as the bike snaked. He slid the rear wheel around and came to a stop at the entrance of the roundabout, giving Harvey just enough time to retrieve Julios' gun from his jacket, pull back the slide, and fire three times into the wide-eyed driver.

CHAPTER SEVENTEEN

"What did you find?" asked Myers, as he wound the car through the little maze of back streets, leaving Hussein's house behind for somebody else to pick up where he had left off.

There was unfinished business there, and he hoped to be back at some point.

"Nothing an ordinary young man in his first rented home wouldn't have. He was actually quite clean."

"You thought he'd live like a slob?" asked Myers.

"Yes. Yes, I did. It's a cliché, I know, but from what I found downstairs, he could have passed as a respectable guy. He took care of himself. Either that, or he didn't use the place from day to day and only went there to..."

"To what, Fox?" said Myers.

"To use the spare room."

"Nice idea, but I don't think so. He was unemployed. He didn't have much and from what I saw, there were enough personal effects there for him to call it a home."

Myers pulled onto the main road and flipped his notepad open to see the address that Allenby had mentioned over the phone. There wasn't a house number, only a road name.

"Look up Coopersale Lane in the A-to-Z," said Myers, and reached across her to pull down the glove compartment. "The thing you have to consider with men like Hussein, Fox, is that there's two of them."

Fox was flicking through the index of the little map book for the letter C but stopped when Myers' statement registered. He saw her look across at him in his peripheral and kept his eyes on the road, indicating to take the next right.

"One of them," he continued, "lives a normal life. Just an ordinary guy going about his business. He might have a hobby. He might have a few friends, but they know nothing of his alter ego."

"You think the change is that distinct?" asked Fox, as she flicked for the right page number. "So Hussein was an ordinary guy but had this kind of Jekyll and Hyde thing going on?"

"Not quite Jekyll and Hyde, Fox. But he would have urges. The normal Hussein might even have been ashamed of the other Hussein. But urges *are* urges."

He glanced across at her as she found the road and placed her finger on the page, then returned her attention to him.

"And when those urges come, Fox, it's like a drug. A powerful drug. I think he sat there alone but the urges grew stronger. But he hated himself. And then, one day, the desires grew so strong he had to do something. He had to reveal himself. He had to show the other Faisal Hussein."

Fox took a breath and exhaled long and slow through gritted teeth as Myers braked and joined a queue of traffic.

"There's something I don't understand, sir. If what Jennifer Standing said is true, and we have no reason to believe otherwise, then how did the suspect know that Hussein would be there? Unless, of course, he was with him when Hussein snatched her. But that theory doesn't sit well with me."

"Why?" said Myers, letting the car roll forward with the speed of the traffic. He opened the window fully and leaned out to see what the hold-up was, and saw the flashing blue lights, yellow jackets, and white-capped hats of traffic police.

"I don't know. He just didn't seem to be the type."

Myers raised his eyebrows and gave her a look as if to question if she'd listened to anything he'd said.

"I know," she said. "I know it takes all sorts. But I have a feeling. I can't explain it. Hussein's killer was-"

"An ordinary guy?" said Myers.

"No. No, not an ordinary guy. Far from it. But he just didn't have that look. He didn't look deprived. I think you were right before, sir. I think he's a vigilante. Some kind of psycho that goes after sex offenders. I think he followed him."

Myers smiled as Fox fell into his way of thinking, then braked to stop beside the traffic police. They had reached the front of the queue and saw ahead of them the twisted and smouldering remains of an expensive looking Jaguar on its roof. There was an ambulance at the scene and the fire brigade were wrapping up their hoses.

Myers flashed his ID.

"Anything we can do?" said Myers.

The traffic cop nodded a greeting and waved the car behind to go around them.

"Sir, do we have time for this? There's been a shooting," said Fox. Her concern, if Myers was correct, was based on what Allenby might have to say for their delay in arriving late at the shooting scene.

"Pull up over there, sir," said the traffic cop, and he pointed to a space on the grass verge.

Myers did as he was instructed but felt Fox's quizzical stare.

"We have a shooting three miles away," said Myers to Fox. "And I don't believe in coincidences." He opened the door. "What happened here?" asked Myers, as they walked from the car.

The cop held the traffic back so they could cross the road, then waved a more junior colleague over to take his place keeping the traffic moving.

"The car was involved in a high-speed pursuit," said the cop, and he pointed toward Abridge with a well-seasoned hand. "The car hit the roundabout side on and flipped."

"How many casualties?" asked Fox, as they made their way toward the wreckage.

"One. The driver. Thankfully, there were no passengers."

He shared a grim expression with Myers while Fox was looking at the scene.

If the officer had been younger and hadn't held such a command over the scene, Myers may have been tempted to guide him and offer his insights into the crash. But from what Myers could tell, the traffic policeman was experienced. He talked with authority and a calmness that only comes from seeing hundreds of incidents and fatalities.

They approached the scene as two paramedics were loading the ambulance with a gurney. There was a sheet covering the body and their movements were slow and careful out of respect for the dead, as opposed to the urgency they might have had if the man had still been breathing.

"Take a look around the car, Fox. I'll examine the driver," said Myers.

"Don't touch anything," said the officer. "I have a forensics unit on its way."

A fireman escorted Fox, a security measure to ensure she didn't get too close to the still-smoking wreck. The traffic cop followed Myers and stood beside the rear doors as he climbed in.

"The officer in pursuit managed to pull him out before the fire took hold," said the officer, as the paramedic pulled back the sheet to reveal the man's face.

The victim was Asian. Blood and splinters of glass in his face made his exact ethnicity unclear. But what was clear was the hole in the man's face.

"Why was he being pursued?" asked Myers, as he pulled the sheet back further and found two more holes in the man's bruised and battered chest. "Was the pursuing officer armed response?"

"The pursuing officer is one of mine, sir. Traffic police," said the officer. He flicked his head at the victim. "He was being pursued by a man on a motorcycle."

Myers looked down at him. He covered

the man's face with the sheet again, nodded a thanks to the paramedic, and stepped down from the ambulance.

"And where is this motorcycle now?"

"The rider left the scene before the pursuing unit arrived," said the officer. "They were travelling in excess of one hundred and twenty miles per hour. The pursuing unit was more than half a mile away when this happened."

"Sir?" said Fox. "I found something."

The two men approached her, and she dropped to a crouch in the grass twenty feet from the wreck.

Myers restrained his smile when he saw what Fox had found.

"We're on our way to a firearms incident a few miles away," said Myers to the officer. "I think you just found our suspect."

Fox pulled a pair of latex gloves from her pocket. She flipped the weapon over and, without picking it up, checked the safety was on. Myers was surprised at her familiarity with the gun and her approach to a crime scene. She barely touched the weapon but managed to release the magazine and hold it up with two fingers lightly gripping the very tip to avoid any fingerprints being disturbed. She bent and smelled the weapon in situ, then looked up at Myers.

"It's a full magazine, sir," she said. "This weapon hasn't been fired."

CHAPTER EIGHTEEN

Skirting around the edges of fields and meandering through small forests, Harvey found a series of paths and trails that led him off-road back toward Theydon Bois. He came to a ditch at the edge of a field and cruised along the path searching for two things.

The first he found beneath an overhanging tree. The drainage ditch connected with another via a nine-inch pipe. It was deep enough for Harvey to hide the weapon inside, after he'd wiped it clean. He pulled in a few handfuls of mud to cover it. It wasn't a permanent disposal, more of a precaution.

The second thing he was looking for was at the far edge of the field where two fields connected. The ditch had flattened out and there was a space for him to cross to reach the narrow country lane that led to the estate.

After a short stretch of tarmac, he rolled through the iron gates to a scene that was far removed from the grand wedding he'd seen earlier. It was hard to even know if it was the same estate.

Julios was on the gate. He nodded once to Harvey, who raised his visor and nodded back. It was all the information Julios would need to know that he had succeeded.

The last of the guests were being ushered from the grounds. And while Donny sat by Julia's side with his head in his hands, John was focusing his attention on a man who was pinned to the ground by four of his men.

Harvey rolled the bike into his garage and closed the door. He crossed the driveway and the lawn and stopped beside Donny. In the distance, approaching sirens sang through the village below; their tune was a far cry from the quartet's finesse.

"I'm sorry, Donny," said Harvey, and placed his hand on his foster-brother's shoulder. Donny dropped his hands to his lap, stared at Julia's body, then looked up at Harvey through bloodshot eyes.

"Harvey?" called John from the other side of the lawn.

But Harvey held Donny's stare.

There was loss in the stare. Nothing Harvey could say would ease the feeling.

"Harvey?" called John, for the second time.

Harvey nodded once to Donny and let his hand slip from his shoulder. All four of John's men turned their heads to watch Harvey walk across the grass. John issued no command, but they all stepped back as he arrived and glanced at each other. They were fearful and loyal men, some of John's best. But they knew their place.

The man lay flat on the ground. He tried to turn to see what had caused the men to let him go, but John's foot pressed his face into the grass.

"Anything I need to know?" asked John. He was referring to the man Harvey had gone after. As usual, he was covering himself and wanted to be sure that nobody got away.

"Not anymore," said Harvey, but kept his eyes on the man on the ground.

"He's the gunman. But he's not talking. I thought you might convince him to."

Harvey looked at each of the four men. The sirens were closing in and would be arriving any second.

"Take him to the barn," said Harvey, and walked ahead to avoid having to walk beside John and listen to him rant on about making somebody pay. It would be Harvey and Julios who would be set to work. That much was clear.

"Drop him there," said Harvey to the four men when they reached the barn.

He swung one of the large doors open and stared at John.

"I'll come and find you when he talks."

"I thought we'd stay, Harvey. I'd like to see him suffer, given what he's done today."

"I'll work alone," said Harvey, and flicked his head at the men, a gesture for them to leave.

John watched the men leave. From where they stood, the house and the gates could not be seen. The barn was situated at the foot of John's estate. Tall conifers and leylandii had been planted to shield the small outbuilding where John kept his prized possession: an original E-Type Jaguar in immaculate condition. The bright red classic was one of the first things John had bought when he'd found success and it was kept in the barn beneath layers of dust sheets to preserve it in all its glory.

It was the arriving ambulance and police cars that convinced John to leave. Though out of sight, the gravel drive beneath tyres was enough of a warning.

John nodded at Harvey.

"For Donny, Harvey."

Harvey didn't reply.

He watched the older man leave, circling around to the south side of the property so inquisitive policemen wouldn't wonder where he was walking from.

The man on the ground looked up at Harvey with unease. He'd already taken a beating from the men. His lip was burst and his nose bloodied, plus whatever body damage the men had been able to inflict with the heels of their shoes.

"Get up," said Harvey, and offered no assistance.

The man held his left arm close to his chest as he struggled to his feet and he breathed in short stabs. It was a sign that the man had broken a rib or two. Across his neck were two scars. The wounds would have been deep. The man saw Harvey looking and covered them with his hand, but the back of his hand and his forearm bore more scars than any Harvey had seen on one man.

They shared a moment, the man daring Harvey to ask how the scars occurred, and Harvey, in his silence, trying to understand who the man was.

"In," said Harvey, and checked the crest of the hill above them to make sure nobody had seen.

He closed the door behind them and slid a heavy bar into place to lock the doors. In addition to the two huge barn doors, there was a single door at the far end of the building. But that would be locked.

Harvey enjoyed the barn. There was a peace to the building. It was a wooden structure with rooftiles to match the house, despite their distance apart. Above him was a huge vaulted ceiling with oak beams spanning the distance. The walls were timber-framed, and the floor was poured concrete topped with screed for an immaculate, polished finish. The building had once been used by John to store anything he didn't want found. He'd had narrow rooms built into the walls accessible only by hidden panels in the timber.

It had always been a gamble for John to store anything on his own land, but he trusted very few people and very few people trusted him. The barn had been the best compromise he could find.

Over the years, the small, hidden rooms had stored bags of money from cash van robberies, bags of gold, diamonds and jewellery from safety deposit boxes, and people. People who had needed to disappear for one reason or another. Sometimes with their consent. Other times, John had been less gracious.

The building was Harvey's workshop. To the untrained eye, the barn was like any other. There was a bench along one side and tools hung from hooks on the wall. There were bags of cement, lime and plaster, sheets of plastic, hose pipes, and shovels. It was a beautiful building, and it contained items that any other man may have stored in his garage.

But the cement had never once been used to build a wall. The plastic had never once been used in decorating. The hose pipes had never once been used to water flowers. The shovels and spades had been used to dig holes, but never for gardening purposes.

The light was dim. Just how Harvey liked it. Tiny gaps in the vaulted roof allowed narrow slivers of light to illuminate the ever-present dust that hung in the air.

And the silence was perfect.

"What now?" asked the man. His accent was strong. He was Asian. But his English was good, perhaps second generation British.

Harvey didn't reply. He slipped into the darkness and moved with practised silence, allowing the weight of the atmosphere to start the process. And under that weight, amidst the dust and heavy timber beams, a battle began.

"I will never talk," said the man, searching the shadows with nervous, twitch-like movements.

Harvey didn't reply. He timed his movements with the man's voice, working his way through the shadows, collecting his tools.

"You saw my skin," the man continued, and spun at the sound of the aging, creaking timbers. "It is scarred with my strength. There is nothing you can do to me that I have not already endured."

He wore a beard in the European style and was dressed in the Pakistani kurta. But above his clothes and style, he had the passion and pride that was so strong among the race.

Race, gender, nationality, and origin had little effect on Harvey's judgement. He judged all men as equals. He'd seen the biggest, hardest, and toughest of men cry, and he'd seen them in all shapes, colours, and sizes release their bladders in fear.

"So, you see, my friend," said the man, his bravado betrayed by his ragged breaths, "you have no power over me. You hide in the shadows like a coward. Come out and face me."

Harvey didn't reply.

"No one can break me," called the man. "No man can hurt me."

And Harvey was behind him.

"*I* can," he whispered.

CHAPTER NINETEEN

The huge wrought iron gates to the house were at the top of the hill outside the village of Theydon Bois. A gravel driveway led from the gates, where an old gatekeeper's cottage stood, to a large house that was surrounded by manicured lawns, pruned hedges, and tall trees.

"Looks like we're interrupting a party," said Myers, as he manoeuvred the car to a stop beside a large man in a suit. He hit the button to lower the window.

The man said nothing.

"Detective Inspector Myers. This is Detective Sergeant Fox," said Myers, and nodded at an ambulance parked on the grass. "I hear you've had some trouble."

Still, the man said nothing. He seemed to be reading them both, judging, and making a decision. His nose had been flattened and his hair was shaved almost bald. His shoulders were as wide as both Myers and Fox together, and some more, and he stood so tall that even when he bent to see them, it wasn't low enough.

Two men looked up from where the ambulance was parked. The big man caught their attention and nodded at Myers. They returned the nod and muttered something between them. It was enough of a gesture for Myers to assume permission to enter. He rolled and stopped on the gravel driveway.

The lawn was littered with chairs and tables, some of which had toppled and spilt drinks, crockery, and cutlery onto the grass.

And for the second time that day, Myers and Fox watched as two paramedics loaded a gurney into the rear of an ambulance. The body had been covered with a sheet and the men moved unhurried.

Two uniformed officers approached.

"Detective Inspector Myers," said Myers,

as he flashed his ID. "This is DS Fox. What happened here?"

"Hard to say for sure, sir," said the first of the uniforms. He was tall with strong facial features and his voice was clear. He had confidence and a calmness about him that couldn't be taught. He was the type of officer that might do well one day. He spoke without turning or pointing and held Myers' stare. "It was a wedding party. The bride is in the ambulance. She was shot."

"Small arms?" asked Fox, and her question took the officer by surprise.

He studied her for a moment.

"If I had to guess, I'd say it was a handgun. Nine millimetre, judging by the size of the entry and exit points. Forensics have been and gone, sir."

"Been and gone? Already?"

"I don't think anybody was comfortable hanging around. They got photos of the scene and, as you can see, they closed it off for you. There's just a few of us left now."

"Have you spoken to anybody?" asked Myers. "Any guests?" He glanced past the officer toward the two men he had seen before. They eyed him with unease. But something was niggling at Myers. There was a familiarity he couldn't put his finger on.

"Nobody's talking, sir," said the officer.

"What do you mean nobody's talking? It was a wedding. Look at all the chairs. There must have been hundreds of people here."

"The guests have gone, sir," said the officer. Then he seemed hesitant to continue, as if he might offend Myers' intelligence. "They left before we even got here. You do know whose house this is, don't you, sir?"

Myers looked at Fox, who seemed just as ignorant as himself.

"Enlighten me."

"The house belongs to John Cartwright. This is the Cartwright family home. It was his son's wedding."

"John Cartwright?" said Myers, and in that moment, the case took a whole new turn, and he wished he was back on the Standing job.

Fox hadn't reacted. She wouldn't let on that she didn't know who Cartwright was to the two officers, so Myers nodded and took control.

"Good work, boys. What's your name, son?"

"Casey, sir," said the officer.

"Well, Casey, you seem like you know what you're doing. Get two men on the gate and get that big goon off. If he doesn't move, arrest him. Then see if you can find me a guest list. If this is John Cartwright's place, that guest list will be the who's who of organised crime."

"Yes, sir," said Casey, and he took the other uniform with him.

"Do you think you'll know who it was just from looking at the list, sir?" said Fox.

"No. But we'll have an idea of who it might have been from who isn't on the list. Come on. Let's go and meet our man Cartwright."

"Sir?" said Fox, and she waited for him to turn. "I feel like I should know who these people are."

"How long have you been in Essex, Fox?"

"Three months, sir."

"So how should you know them?" said Myers. "You need to learn fast. Do you get much organised crime in the sticks?"

It was the second time he'd used the phrase 'in the sticks'. He was hoping for a rise from her. Maybe he could see some emotion.

"A little," she said. "But it was mostly small-time in Bristol. The biggest problem we had was drugs coming in and out."

"Well, we get that here too, plus a hell of a lot more. The public-facing John Cartwright is squeaky clean. He owns nightclubs, bars, betting shops, and even launderettes."

"Cash businesses, sir?"

"That's right. You don't get many men like John Cartwright anymore. They're all either locked up or dead. Most of them don't survive or they make a mistake. Crime isn't what it used to be, Fox. It's not as easy. Technology catches them now. All the police have to do is rock up and nick them. Evidence is evidence."

"But not John Cartwright?" She stared past Myers, watching the old man in the expensive tuxedo in hushed conversation with another man who was smaller and slighter.

Myers sighed. The questions disrupted his analytical mind. He didn't need to be holding anybody's hand. He needed somebody to think like him.

"No. He's one of the old-school. Nobody knows how many men work for him. I bet he doesn't even know. He has a security firm on the doors of every club in South East London, even the ones he doesn't own, and underneath all that legitimacy is a web of crime and filth so murky, Fox, that once you're in it, you'll never get out."

"Surely a murder on his property is a chance to get him, sir?" said Fox, hopeful that they might make a big hit.

Myers stared at John Cartwright, watching his every move. The man spoke only to the smaller man, who, from his looks, appeared to be Eastern European and, from his expression and demeanour, to have intelligence.

"He'll be clean. There's no way John Cartwright would allow this to happen on his land. The last thing he wants is for *us* to be snooping around."

"Shall I contact Allenby, sir? To see if I can get a warrant?"

"Be my guest, Fox," said Myers, as John Cartwright and his sidekick began to walk over to them. "But by the time you get it, Cartwright will have cleaned this place from top to bottom."

"Have you got everything you need?"

called John Cartwright, as he approached right on cue. It was an invitation to leave.

"Not yet, Mr Cartwright. I wonder if you'd mind answering a few questions for me?"

"We answered all your questions earlier," said the thin man. "We'd like some time to grieve now, if you please."

"You didn't answer *my* questions, and *I* wasn't talking to you," said Myers.

"My name is Sergio. I represent Mr Cartwright in all legal matters. You can address me, and if Mr Cartwright feels he has anything further to offer, you'll know."

"What happened?" asked Myers. There would be no tripping them up with underhand questions. They were as experienced as he was at interview techniques and as well-versed in the legal system as any detective on the force.

"Someone shot my daughter-in-law," said Cartwright. "Her body is in the ambulance." He leaned in close so Myers could smell the alcohol and cigars on his breath. "With a big bleeding hole in her."

"Any ideas who?"

"No," said Sergio.

"Nobody saw anything?" said Myers. "There must have been two hundred people here, judging by the number of chairs. You're telling me nobody saw a thing?"

"No comment," said Sergio.

"Do you know of any reason why somebody might want her dead?" asked Myers.

"We all have enemies," said Cartwright, staring Myers in the eyes. "Don't we?"

"You're saying she had an enemy? Somebody who had a grudge maybe?" asked Fox.

"I'm saying that we all have enemies, sweetheart. Even you." Then he returned his stare to Myers. "But we don't go announcing them, do we now?"

There was a silence. It was a power play and they were standing on Cartwright's land. His legal adviser would know the law inside out and would know exactly what they could and couldn't say and do. It was time to work with them, or at least appear to.

"Listen, Mr Cartwright, I think we got off on the wrong foot. I'm not here to investigate you."

"Investigate me? What is there to investigate?"

"Like I said, I'm not here to investigate

you. There's been a murder. We have to investigate that. At the minute, there's half a dozen uniforms here, plus us. That's pretty light given the severity of the case. I can make a call and have this place swarming with uniforms. I'll close the road off. I'll have uniforms on the gates twenty-four-seven, and you won't be able to take a crap without asking an officer to pass you the toilet roll. That kind of police presence attracts the media, Mr Cartwright. You know the worst thing about a case like this is when the media are fed the wrong information. They'll print anything, you know. That kind of publicity can destroy a man. Years and years of hard work all gone in the blink of an eye. It's all about reputation, Mr Cartwright. You do understand, don't you?"

Sergio leaned in and whispered in Cartwright's ear, then straightened as Cartwright nodded his agreement to him, then turned to face Myers.

He said nothing.

"I'd like to have a look around, Mr Cartwright. If I may, of course. There may be some evidence. Do you think you can ask your men to leave the scene for us? Maybe they could wait in the house until we're ready to talk to them?"

"We'll co-operate where we can, Mr Myers," said Sergio. "You may search the grounds, but not the houses. For that, you'll need a warrant, I'm afraid. It's a sensitive time. I'm sure you understand."

"And the men?" asked Fox.

"I'll make sure nobody else leaves."

"Thank you, Sergio," said Myers. "Do you happen to have a guest list?"

He knew that Casey would be searching for one, but it would be interesting to see the difference in the two lists if there was any.

"Of course," said Sergio, with a smile. "I'll get you a fresh copy."

CHAPTER TWENTY

A single rope hung from the high beams in John Cartwright's barn. It emerged from the shadows and clung to the man's neck like the iron grip of something not of this world.

The man had done well. His bravado had not entirely been hot air and ego. He had endured far more than many men, and Harvey considered his scars to have been well-earned.

But there were few men who could resist the charms of Harvey's imagination. It was time to get serious.

"Who gave the order to kill Julia?" asked Harvey, his voice flat and emotionless, as if he was asking for the time.

The rope around the man's neck gave his

sneering laugh a hoarse rasp and he sucked in a shallow breath; it was all his broken ribs would allow.

Harvey stepped closer to him. The rope was taut and allowed only the man's tiptoes to steady his body and take some of his weight. It was the perfect balance of life and death.

"I will never talk," he rasped.

Harvey had hung him in the single shaft of sunlight that broke through the rooftiles. It was as if the man was in a spotlight, a move designed to impair the man's vision enough for the dark shadows to become as black as night.

The light glanced off Harvey's blade as he stood before the man, fascinated by the process of death. The blade cut through the man's shirt with ease and Harvey pulled open the two flaps of material to reveal a muscled torso, adorned with more scar tissue than flesh. Along the man's flank was the remains of a burn that spread onto his front with shiny, finger-like tendrils. The two scars on his neck continued across his front, and on his far side were fierce, raised lines that were criss-crossed, and, as Harvey moved around the man and ripped his shirt free, he saw the scars continue across his back.

Harvey touched the whip marks with morbid curiosity. He ran his finger along the length of one until it crossed paths with another. The scars were not fresh. Years had passed since they had been inflicted. Harvey could see that by the smooth flesh.

And the man's strength was apparent. His bravado was not the voice of fear summoning the numbing powers of adrenaline. It was memory, and it commanded respect, which Harvey honoured with memories and pain of his own.

Harvey moved around him until he stood before the man, and he stepped into the light, allowing him to see the empathy on his face.

"Who are you?" asked Harvey.

The man's nostrils flared as he exhaled. His teeth were gritted, and he fought the pain in his ribs with awesome tenacity.

"I am Asif," he said

"How did you get those scars, Asif?" asked Harvey.

Asif fought to keep his balance and choked as his toes danced to keep him upright.

"A man like you would never understand."

Harvey smiled, humoured to be likened to ordinary men. Asif would never talk while he held that belief. There was still work to do to convince him.

"Torturing a man is never pleasant," said Harvey.

And Asif laughed once before the movement inflicted pain and he choked as his feet sought the concrete beneath him.

"I often find that most of the work can be achieved by letting the victim know just how far you're willing to go, what lengths you're willing to reach to get what you want."

"Many men have tried," said Asif. "They have all failed."

Harvey stepped closer, close enough to smell the odour of spices through the man's skin. He held his gaze and let his smile soften.

"I am no ordinary man, Asif," said Harvey, and raised his knife to catch the sliver of light.

An ordinary man would have bucked and pulled away. He would have fought against his restraints with every ounce of energy he had. He would have cried out for help, for his mother, or for God.

But Asif was still. Few men had the courage to face death. Even fewer were strong enough to face inevitable agony.

"Who gave the order, Asif?" said Harvey. He spoke as an equal. Asif had earned that much through his tenacity and unwavering fortitude. "Tell me and I'll make it quick."

But Asif said nothing. The shine of his eyes was prominent against the shadows behind him. The sheen of his scars appeared moist in that narrow shaft of light and his ragged breath was that of a mortally wounded animal, wild and beautiful, with fight to carry him to the end.

And the end was close.

The tip of Harvey's knife touched Asif's brown skin. But the man did not flinch, cry, or call out.

The keen blade sliced the flesh from Asif's throat and worked its way down. The taut skin fell apart, leaving a deep, angry slice.

And blood found its way to the surface. It followed the cut like water in a canyon, as if it chased the very blade that carved the gorge.

Harvey stopped with the blade poised above the man's stomach.

"Asif?" said Harvey. "You know what comes next. Tell me who gave the order."

Despite the man's strength and tenacity, Asif was fighting an inner battle, restraining his pain and banishing it to the darkest parts of his body with a mental command that left Harvey awestruck.

But even the strongest soldier grows weary.

Asif grew unsteady on his toes, his face was contorted with the fight, and his short, sharp breaths spewed from between gritted teeth with spittle and the faintest of moans.

"There's no shame, Asif," said Harvey. He grabbed onto the man's sweaty, black hair and forced Asif to look at him, wanting him to see the respect in Harvey's eyes. "You've earned a fast death. You've earned the right not to suffer. I've never seen a man hold on for so long. I can leave you, and you'll bleed out. Death will be painful. Your body will shut down slowly. All you have to do is say the name and I can make it all go away."

Harvey searched for some kind emotion

in his eyes but found only signs of the battle inside.

"Or I can cut a little more," said Harvey, and teased the tip of the blade at the lowest reach of the wound where the swell of his stomach pulled at the flesh. The effect was electric, and Asif's body jolted back, causing him to choke and struggle and to cough and retch when he regained balance. Harvey leaned closer so that his mouth was beside the man's ear. "I'll cut out your organs, Asif. One. By. One."

And there it was. With Asif's lifeblood oozing from his chest and Harvey's blade teasing at the wound, Asif sprang into life with the dying fight of that wild animal Harvey admired. He kicked high and hard, but his final efforts lacked the strength of a balanced stance. Harvey caught his leg and trapped it against his shoulder. But before he could react, putting all his weight onto his neck, Asif kicked up with his other leg and began to squeeze.

The effort was gallant. Asif choked as the rope tightened around his throat. He squeezed his legs tight against Harvey's neck and, in the struggle, Harvey's hand, slippery with blood, dropped the knife to the floor.

Harvey held him there. The effort opened Asif's wound even further and as the man hung from his neck with blood pulsing from his chest, he seemed to push back, forcing the rope tighter.

With every second that passed, the hopes of Asif spilling a name slipped away. He tried to pull the man's legs free, but they were clamped on with an iron-like grip with his feet entwined behind Harvey's neck. Harvey tried to pull away to release the rope, but Asif saw it and held him tighter. He pulled Harvey closer, grunting and choking with the effort and seemed to roar as his core tightened. His wound stretched open and he raised his body up so that he was looking down on Harvey with the slackened rope trailing behind and all his weight on Harvey's shoulders.

Breathless and with eyes wilder than ever, Asif seemed to grin through his bloodied teeth, as if he relished the pain and welcomed the cold rush of death that would sweep through his body.

"I will never talk. I am Asif," he rasped.

Then his body tightened further as he

contracted his muscles and summoned every ounce of energy that remained.

Harvey saw it coming but was powerless to do anything. With the full weight of Asif on his shoulders, he tried to drop to his knees to reach the knife, but Asif was fast. Though his body was broken, his mind was true and keen.

"I am Asif," he said again.

With a speed as fast as when his legs had wrapped around Harvey, Asif once more sprung into life. He pushed back, hard, and slammed his neck down. The rope whipped and snapped taut with a deathly crack of spine, and his legs fell from Harvey's shoulders to hang limply and graze across the bloodied concrete floor.

CHAPTER TWENTY-ONE

"Do you mind if we ask you a few questions, sir?" said Myers. "I appreciate the timing is awful, but if we're to catch the killer, we'll have to act fast."

The man seemed lost. He was standing in the centre of the lawn on his own watching the ambulance drive away. His arms hung by his sides in that despondent pose borne only from the weight of loss.

"Were you close?" asked Myers, as he too tracked the ambulance as the driver manoeuvred through the array of chairs and onto the gravel with as much care as he could.

The man turned to stare at him. His face

seemed to twist in disbelief. His fingers flexed and he faced Myers with repulsion.

And only then did Myers see the boutonniere that was fastened to the man's lapel. His eyes were glazed and reddened by hot tears.

"I'm so sorry," said Myers. "I didn't realise you-"

"Get out," said the man, and he strode towards Myers filled with rage. "Get off our land."

He shoved Myers in the chest, forcing him to take a step back to maintain his balance, and Fox intervened in time to stop the man's assault, but for her efforts, she received the back of his hand across her face.

"Right," said Fox, and in a few quick moves, she locked his arms behind his back.

"Sir, I must warn you," said Myers, holding his hands up to both fend off another attack and to show he meant no harm. He reached for his ID wallet in his pocket and let it fall open. The man stopped fighting. "I'm Detective Inspector Myers and this is Detective Sergeant Fox. I'm sorry, I assumed-"

"What? You assumed what?" said the man.

His rage was easing, but his bitterness still held true.

Myers nodded for Fox to let him go and she dabbed at her mouth with a tissue. Behind her, at the top of the steps of the house, was Sergio, John Cartwright's legal adviser. He saw them and made a move.

"Are you the groom, sir?" asked Myers, hoping to make some progress before the interfering man reached them.

But he was too late.

"Donny?" called Sergio from nearly fifty metres away. "Donny, don't say a word."

"Sir? I asked you a question," said Myers.

And he nodded.

"Did you see what happened? It's Donny, is it? You must be Donald Cartwright. Is there anything you can tell me?"

Any son of John Cartwright would have been taught from an early age to say nothing to the police. It was their way. The *us* and *them* split was ingrained in the blood of men like Donald Cartwright. It was a wonder that resources were even spent on helping them. They would offer little help, if any, and would show even less gratitude if Myers actually found the culprit.

"They killed your wife, Donald. I'll find them. Just give me something to go on."

"Can I help, Detective?" said Sergio, as he approached. It was a question designed to re-instate his position as legal adviser for Myers' benefit and to inform Donny that Myers was a cop if he didn't already know.

"It's okay. I was just hoping to get a head start on finding the man who killed Mr Cartwright's wife," said Myers, and rolled his eyes as Fox opened her mouth. "We're here to do a job, but if you're only going to make it difficult, then perhaps we'll move on."

"I understand, Mr Myers."

"Detective Inspector Myers," Myers corrected.

"We've had a traumatic day, Detective," said Sergio. He placed a hand on Donny's shoulder and began to lead him away.

"I'm trying to help you," Myers called after them. "Mr Cartwright, if you know something that might help..."

Donald Cartwright stopped and turned. It was the response Myers had been looking for. It was emotion. Emotion never lies.

"Donny, don't-" said Sergio.

But Donald was re-incensed, and Myers

prepared for him to fly at them both again. He found himself stepping forward to protect Fox.

"All I know is that my wife was shot dead today."

"So help me find her killer."

"*You* won't find them," said Cartwright, and his eyes darted left. It was a subtle movement, involuntary at best, but in that tiny flick of nerves, he said more than he had with his bitter words. "The only thing you lot can find is the gate on your way out."

Myers nodded and let Donald re-join Sergio. He allowed him to walk a few steps further.

"Mr Cartwright?" he said. "Just one more thing."

Both men stopped.

"It'll only take a few moments. I promise."

Cartwright turned and Sergio followed a few seconds after, his face displaying all the impatience of a man with everything to hide.

"Something's bothering me," said Myers.

Cartwright's expression said all that was needed to say. He raised his eyebrows expectantly, as if giving permission for Myers to carry on with his muses.

"I'm sure you loved your wife, Mr Cartwright, and I hope you cherish those few short moments with her."

"You're treading on dangerous ground, Detective Myers," said Cartwright, but his advance was halted by Sergio, who placed his hand flat against Cartwright's chest.

"Make it quick, Detective," said Sergio. His voice had lost its mock-friendly and innocent tone.

"Well, it strikes me that if it were *my* wife that had been killed, I'd be in that ambulance with her. In fact, I wouldn't leave her side until I lowered her into the ground," said Myers. He lowered his voice and his tone deepened at the thought of Alison being carted away. "Even then, they'd have to drag me away."

The two stared at each other, Myers searching for some kind of guilt, and Cartwright with his eyes dancing from left to right and back to Myers, never resting in one place for long.

Cartwright's voice was filled with the phlegm of genuine grief and the fatigue that would haunt him for days and weeks to come.

"We all grieve in different ways, Detective," said Cartwright, then he turned, and it was he who led Sergio away towards the house.

"Cutting it a bit close, sir," said Fox under her breath. "He has a hundred reasons to make a complaint."

"Shut up, Fox."

Myers didn't face her. He watched Cartwright walk away. He studied him as the man fixed his jacket collar and smoothed his hair and adopted the confident stride of a man who had life handed to him on a plate.

"I only need one reason to nail him," said Myers, and he turned away from the house.

Fox walked beside him, matching his stride. She held herself well, and Myers was pleased she hadn't pushed for an assault charge, but he wished she'd hold her tongue until she'd learnt the ropes. This wasn't the sticks. This was London.

"How's your lip?" he asked, seeking distraction more than a response.

"I've had worse," she replied. "Are we heading someplace special?"

Myers laughed, but it wasn't a laugh of humour. It was more of a snort to avoid answering.

"Something funny?" she asked.

Myers stopped.

"Men like John Cartwright are, for the most part, untouchable, Fox. Do you know Frank Carver?"

"DI Carver, sir? Of course. *Everyone* knows Frank. He works in organised crime."

"Exactly. He's been onto John Cartwright for years. Carver probably dreams about the day he can walk these grounds. Men like Cartwright keep men like Carver at arm's length."

"Keep your friends close, sir?"

"Exactly, Fox, and keep your enemies closer," said Myers, and nodded at the roof of an outbuilding at the foot of the hill. It was surrounded by trees save for a gap where a small track led out and up the hill. "Let's take a look around, shall we?"

CHAPTER TWENTY-TWO

The barn door creaked open and filled a portion of the barn with bright light. An elongated shadow stretched across the concrete floor and then split into two.

From the confines of John's hidden room, Harvey watched through a narrow slit in the wood as two people moved into the barn. From the size and shapes of the shadows and the clicks of heels on the concrete, Harvey surmised it was a man and a woman.

"He did say we should stick to the estate, sir. The buildings are off-limits," said the woman.

Something passed in front of the slit and blocked Harvey's view. It stayed there, close enough to reach out and touch and close enough to hear him breathe.

"He said a lot of things," said the man. There was a familiarity to his voice. "They know more than they let on."

The man moved away from the slit and the heels of his shoes clicked a slow circle around John's car.

"The man in the car a few miles away hadn't fired a single shot. Therefore, there are two possibilities. The first is that he worked for John Cartwright and went after the man who killed Julia."

"And failed," added the woman, still out of Harvey's view.

"The second possibility is that the man in the Jaguar was with the killer. A driver maybe? But things went wrong. He had to get away."

"And Cartwright sent his men after him," said the woman.

"Something like that. Did you see the way Cartwright's eyes darted about? He couldn't look me in the eye. He's hiding something."

"His wife was killed, sir."

"Exactly. And why aren't there any guests here?" said the man from the far side of the barn, where the shadows were deep. "Did you see the chairs scattered on the ground? There must have been two hundred people here. Where are they now?"

"Scared? I'm not sure if I'd want to hang around after a shooting, sir."

"They were scared alright. Scared of what John Cartwright and his men might do if they opened their mouths and said the wrong thing. Two hundred people with two hundred versions of what happened. That's too much even for Cartwright to control. No. No, he got rid of them. Something happened and he made sure nobody was here to talk to us."

"You mean they killed the killer?"

"Imagine it. The wedding is going well. The bride and groom are in love. The guests are smiling. And the sun is out. The band is playing. And John Cartwright's ego is riding high."

He paused to let the image take shape. It was something Myers did when he had a point to make.

"Then someone kills the bride. A gunshot, loud and clear. People run. John's men tackle the killer, but the driver gets away. John calms the guests down. A man like John Cartwright could do that. He's very persuasive. But while he's calming the crowd down, telling them everything is under control, the groom lets his emotions get the better of him."

"The groom, sir? Donald Cartwright?" said the woman.

"He's an emotional, reckless mess. He's scared."

"Of what?"

The man ignored her question and continued with his hypothesis. He leaned back on the rear end of the covered classic car, a move that would infuriate even the calm and collected John.

"Donny does something stupid," said the man, and Harvey adjusted his position but still couldn't see the man's face. He saw the man fold his arms. He saw the man's fingers tapping as if he was playing a melody on his arm.

"Myers?" mouthed Harvey and stepped back to the wall behind him. There would be no explaining his presence on the grounds of a known villain just an hour after a murder had taken place.

"Things get out of control," continued Myers. "The guests are sent away.

Cartwright knows that we'll turn up, so he hides the body of the man who killed Julia..."

Myers paused, maybe due to a last-minute doubt as his theory voiced its unwanted opinion.

"In this room," he finished. He pushed himself off the car, pulled the sheets away, and, using a tissue from his pocket, carefully pushed the car's chrome boot release.

He stood back to admire his ingenuity and his face was framed perfectly in the slot from which Harvey spied them.

The look of disappointment on his face was priceless.

"Well, well, well."

It was John's voice. A huge shadow moved across the concrete floor in the doorway. Then, one by one, smaller shadows peeled off, accompanied by the clicks of heels. Expensive, heeled dress shoes.

Harvey closed his eyes and completed the picture with his imagination and hearing. John's heavy paces. The shuffle of Sergio's feet on the polished concrete as he moved out of harm's way. Donny's faster, less methodical steps following John. He mimicked his father's presence when he could but could never match him mentally.

And still, the giant shadow that belonged to Julios remained in the doorway. Julios would fill the space. There would be no escape.

"Sergio," said John, in that condescending tone of voice that Harvey hated so much. "Do I have cause to make a complaint?"

"You do, John," replied Sergio. "We gave strict instructions that Detective Myers and his friend were not to enter any building. There were four of us present and the instructions were quite clear."

"I see," said John. "Could that be deemed as harassment, Sergio?"

"Not yet, John. But if the detectives were asked to leave and they failed to do so, then I'm sure we could seek a harassment charge."

"Make all the complaints you want, Cartwright," said Myers. "A young girl died here today and you're hiding something. I know you and your type better than you think."

"Sergio?" said John.

"Unsupported allegations, defamation of character, and trespassing." Sergio pointed to the empty boot of the E-Type. "And clearly, you have no evidence."

"I think it's time you left, Detective Myers. Don't you?" said John.

Myers said nothing. He nodded to his partner and they edged to the door, where Julios' shadow seemed to sidestep to allow them through.

But Myers stopped at the threshold, his shadow tiny beside Julios', but clear enough for Harvey to see his stretched profile.

"A girl died here today, Mr Cartwright, and a man died a few miles from here. I believe the cases are linked and I'm just trying to find who did it," said Myers.

"Well I wish you all the best with that," replied John. "Sounds like you're far too busy to be hanging around here."

"If we find you taking the law into your own hands, there *will* be a price to pay, Mr Cartwright. Don't let me catch you interfering. The consequences of perverting the course of justice far outweigh that of an allegation that is, by all accounts, your word against mine."

"I won't," said John.

"You won't what, Mr Cartwright?"

John smiled and winked at Myers' partner. "I won't let you catch me," said John, then turned to Sergio. "See them out, Sergio, will you? Make sure they don't run into trouble on the way."

Myers' shadow shook its head, and he turned to leave again. Julios allowed Sergio through then returned to his space in the doorway and nodded to John when the detectives were out of view.

John looked about the space. His expression was mildly amused but confused.

Harvey stepped from the shadows and John offered him a proud smile.

"Right, it's just us four" said John. "And things are getting out of hand. What I need is honesty, Donny. Tell me truthfully. Do you know who they were?"

"No, Dad. Of course. I would have said."

John looked him in the eye, but Donny couldn't meet his stare. It wasn't unusual. Donny had never managed to look a man in the eye. It was one of the reasons nobody trusted him. That, and his history of deceit.

"Do you know of any reason why somebody would want to kill, Julia?" said John.

Donny's eyes teared up. They shone like beacons in the dim light.

"Don't start all that now, Donny. Now is not the time."

"No, Dad. No. Why would anyone want to kill her?"

"In that case, we can only assume they meant to get you," said John.

"The detective thought the same," said Harvey. "I heard him say before you arrived. He thinks Donny is involved somehow."

"What?" said Donny. "Why would I be involved in my own wife's murder? We were married an hour-"

"Donny, shut up, will you?" said John, tiring of Donny's emotional outbursts. "Do you or do you not know anything about what happened? It doesn't matter if you did. I'll stand by you. But I need to know the truth."

"I told you the truth. Why would I lie? They killed my wife."

John nodded and turned to Julios.

"Julios, Donny, pack a bag each. Make it fast. You're going away for a while."

"What?" said Donny. "Where are we going?"

"You're going to a safe house and you're

going to stay there until all this is over. Sergio will give you the details. Nobody, not even me, will know where you are."

The message was far from subtle. John was mad at Donny but was holding his temper back. He took a deep breath, leaving Donny to deal with his emotions by kicking a bucket across the barn.

"Harvey, how did you get on with the driver?" said John.

"He couldn't talk," said Harvey.

"And the other one?" said John, searching around the room. "Where is he?"

"I told you *I* wanted him," said Donny. "I *told* you not to give him to Harvey. He messes everything up for me. What did you do with him? Did you let him go?"

"Shut up, Donny," said John.

"They killed my wife, you idiot," said Donny, ignoring his father. He closed the distance between himself and Harvey but stayed closer to John.

"Donny, watch your mouth," said John.

"Oh, that's right. Stick up for Harvey. Nothing changes, does it? Even when his sister was alive, it was the same."

Harvey drew his knife.

"Donny," said John, drawing his name out long and slow in a warning but keeping his eyes on Harvey's and raising his hands to keep everyone cool.

But Donny continued his rant.

"The one time I need him to help me and he lets me down. Of all the people that should know grief, it's him. I remember how he cried when Hannah died. I remember how Julios helped him get his revenge."

Harvey walked toward Donny, his knife in his hand ready to strike.

"Harvey, no," said John.

"Yeah, what?" said Donny, in a rare act of bravado that could only be fuelled by his emotions. "You're going to kill me as well, are you? You're a nut job, Harvey. You always have been. I'm glad Hannah died. At least you know how it feels. It wouldn't surprise me if you were in on it. In fact, where were you when Julia was killed? You were supposed to be security. It's a bit of a coincidence, isn't it?"

In a flash, Harvey whipped his knife across the front of Donny's face. The blade passed just fractions of an inch from Donny's eyes. It was so fast that Donny barely had time to register the move. He silenced and stood with his mouth ajar and eyes wide.

Without looking, Harvey jammed his knife into the upright beam beside him and sliced the rope. There was the sound of whipping rope tearing through the pulley and Asif's plastic-wrapped body fell to the concrete floor with a sickening thump.

"There's your man," said Harvey, and yanked the knife from the beam. He held the blade up to Donny's face, staring into his eyes.

"Harvey," warned John.

But Harvey stayed there, long enough for Donny to heed the warning. Then he turned the knife in his hand and offered the handle to Donny.

"See if you can make him talk," said Harvey.

But Donny was in shock. He stood motionless and his face dropped from a bitter sneer to that of the weak man he was.

"Go on," said Harvey, and jabbed Donny with the handle of the knife. "See if you make him talk. You make it all sound so easy, Donny."

He jabbed again, but Donny just stood there.

"You want revenge, Donny?" said Harvey. "Do you want to make someone suffer? Do you want to know how it feels?"

Harvey grabbed his hand and placed the knife into it, closing Donny's fist around the carved, wooden handle. He raised Donny's limp arm to his own throat and held the blade against his skin.

"There, Donny. There. All you have to do is cut. Go on. Cut *me*, Donny. See how it feels."

A trickle of blood both warmed and whetted Harvey's neck, but Donny's arm was limp and weak.

"Cut me, Donny."

"Enough," said John, and his voice boomed around the vaulted roof, amplified by the empty space.

Feeling his own hand shaking and the trickle of blood drip onto his chest, Harvey held Donny for a moment longer, until John spoke again.

"I said that's enough," said John, his voice quieter but authoritative.

Harvey pulled the knife from Donny's hand and shoved his arm away. There was so much he wanted to tell Donny about grief and revenge. But his words would be wasted. Donny had neither the strength nor the will to go through with revenge of any description.

"Right," said John. "This is a bloody mess and we aren't going to get through it by fighting each other. Do I make myself clear?"

Neither man answered.

"I said, do I make myself clear?"

"Yes, Dad," said Donny, and found a patch of shadow to avert his gaze.

"Harvey?" said John, and he waited for Harvey to look him in the eye. "Have I made myself clear?"

Harvey didn't reply. He nodded once and stared back at him. It was all John was going to get and he knew it.

Sergio re-entered the barn and took in the scene. A man like Sergio, as despicable as he was, could tell what was happening and was wise enough to stay silent.

"Pack your bags, Donny. Julios, I want you gone in under an hour," said John. Then he turned to Sergio and growled, "Sergio, I told you I wanted that guest list checked and checked again."

"But, John, I-"

"Get Julios the address to the safe house

and get out of my sight. I'll come and find you when I'm ready. I mean it, Sergio. I don't want you back here until I say."

Sergio, embarrassed to be berated in front of everyone, led Donny from the barn.

John turned his attention to Harvey.

"Harvey," said John, and Harvey waited for the command, "I don't want to know what happened. I don't want to know your thoughts about Donny. I want answers and I want somebody to pay. If you want to carry on with this family, you need to become part of it, not stand on the side lines."

Harvey didn't reply.

"I can't begin to tell you how disappointed I am right now, and you dare to stand there saying nothing. You're one step away from losing everything so buck your ideas up. Find whoever gave the order to kill Julia..."

He paused, lowered his voice even further, and leaned in to speak into Harvey's ear.

"And make them pay, Harvey, or God help you."

PART II

CHAPTER TWENTY-THREE

The first-floor office at Romford Police Station was open plan, dated, and loud. The walls were painted a hideous light blue and the row of offices where Allenby was situated were nothing more than cheap, timber-framed cubicles.

But the office was a palace compared to the gents' washroom. A tiny amount of the budget had been spent on keeping it tidy, but layering paint on flaky paint had only worsened the look, and years of grime ran along the edges of the linoleum floor.

Once again, Myers found his reflection in the mirror. He ran the cold tap and let the basin fill, then splashed the water over his face and used a paper towel to dry himself.

Behind him, one of the lavatories flushed. A man coughed and spat into the bowl before snapping the latch and easing himself from the stall.

"Myers," said Carver, as Myers dried his face. "Having a bad day, are we?" The strength of his Scottish accent fluctuated. The more condescending he was being, the stronger the accent was.

"Nothing I can't handle, Carver."

"Good to hear it," said Carver, and rinsed his hands. He let the water run and banged the soap dispenser harder than necessary, then pulled a handful of towels from a small pile on the sink. He dried his hands and tossed the towels into an overflowing wastepaper bin, even the dry ones that hadn't touched his hands. It was when Myers noticed little moments of inconsideration or imperfections in people that he knew he was wound up. He couldn't care less about a bunch of hand towels or how hard somebody hit the soap dispenser. But he knew himself well enough to know that the little twitches would lead to something much larger.

"Myers?" said Carver, and he realised he was staring at Carver's hands. He had no idea how long he'd been staring. "Maybe it's time you took some time off?"

"I'm fine," said Myers, knowing that Carver was trying to make something out of nothing.

"You look fine," said Carver, without even an attempt to hide the sarcasm. "How's young Fox settling in?"

"Fox is good. She's got a good head on her shoulders. She just needs to adjust to the way things are done here."

"I'm sure she's in capable hands."

Everything he said was worded to be complimentary, or at the least, pleasant. But underneath the shroud, there was an undertone of spite. It was all an attempt to get in Myers' head. He left Myers no plausible reason to complain. Carver had just told Myers that Fox was in capable hands, he'd shown compassion, and even displayed concern for Myers' wellbeing.

But it had all been part of an attack. A series of tiny flicks of a blade could do just as much damage as a single stab to the heart.

And on top of the underhand blows,

Carver's confidence bore down on him like a weight. It was an unmovable rock. It was a cloud that darkened with every laugh he raised and case he solved.

It was suppressive for a man like Myers, who lacked the people skills to meet him head on.

"You look like you have the weight of the world on your shoulders, Myers. Do you want me to have a word with Allenby? See if she can ease off a little?"

Another little flick of the blade. Carver's relationship with Allenby was flawless. It was based on case after case of Carver's relationships with criminals. The ability to see through the muddy waters of organised crime with the help of the criminals themselves. Carver appeared to be in control, and, in return, the criminals had an easy time. Maybe a few charges dropped here and there. Or a favour or two in the bank.

But that was the organised crime world. A world where Myers rarely ventured. It was a world where the players rarely changed and the shift in power was the only real change. Myers' world was so very different. Homicide.

Murder. A different case every time, and every case was a blank sheet.

Carver shook his head, and Myers realised he was staring again. He pushed past Myers with a quiet laugh to himself.

"You need to wake up and smell the roses, Myers," he said. "Or at least wake up."

"How do you do it?" said Myers, as Carver opened the door.

"Do what?" said Carver, holding the door open. The noise of the office along the corridor grew louder and Myers tried to find the right words to say. Words that wouldn't make him appear weak. But there was no other way of saying it.

"How do you manage to appear so magnanimous despite being a lying, cheating, and despicable criminal?"

Carver smiled.

"It's a skill."

Myers despised him.

"I need something," said Myers, still leaning on the basin. "I need a favour."

"A favour?" said Carver, and his tone changed from the condescending and patronising sneer he usually used to one of opportunistic interest.

He let go of the door and it banged shut.

"You have my attention, Myers. But be quick. The governor has a case for me."

And there it was. As clear as day. Myers straightened. He checked his reflection, smoothed his hair, and cleared his throat.

Matthew Myers was back.

"What do you know about Donald Cartwright?"

Carver shrugged off the comment as if the name meant nothing to him.

"And why would I do you a favour, Myers?" he said. "Even if I did know him."

It was the question Myers had been waiting for.

"Because Donald Cartwright was married today."

"Well? What do you want me to do? Send a bottle of champagne?"

"And your name was on the guest list."

CHAPTER TWENTY-FOUR

The office where Donny worked was inside a dull 1970s office block. It was a grey building that offered little motivation or inspiration. It was the type of building Harvey assumed to be full of administrators and back office clerks. It was a place of watched clocks. It was also a place for John Cartwright to house his more legitimate dealings and keep an eye on his less-than-trustworthy son at zero cost.

The building belonged to John, the security worked for John, and all the business owners who occupied the commercial spaces inside owed John a favour in one way or another.

The building was set back from the main

road in Chigwell, a few miles from John's house. There was a car park at the front and to one side, but few cars parked there on Saturdays.

Harvey parked his motorbike far from the entrance, stowed his helmet in the back box, and walked. The car park appeared normal. There were no unmarked vans parked up and none of the cars had occupants.

The security efforts matched the building's drab look. The door opened without a lock, key, or card reader and closed behind him with a lazy sigh. The sound of the road was cut off and all that remained was the dull hum of an air conditioning unit regurgitating the stale air. There was a small security desk to one side of the reception room. The desk was unmanned but there was a jacket hanging over the seat and an old rucksack on the floor. There were several small CCTV monitors on the desk showing black and white representations of various parts of the building, two for the elevators and four more that showed areas of the car park, the entrance, and the public spaces in sequence. He watched them for a minute, allowing for a full cycle. None of the monitors showed the fire escape, so that was the route Harvey took.

He opened the door and listened for movement above him. The stone-coloured painted walls were duller than white yet brighter than the heavy blues that had been used in the reception. Sounds echoed off the hard surfaces. The steps, which were concrete tipped with an aluminium grip, offered little chance of stealth unless the individual stepped over the metal strips, which felt un-natural, but Harvey did it anyway. He didn't like to announce his arrival, but was sure that, should someone pursue him, they wouldn't have the patience to do so. The sound of somebody climbing the stairs would be heard all the way up on the top floor.

There were only five floors, each with six or more office spaces partitioned off. Harvey stopped on each landing and peered through the small window in the fire escape door. As the car park conveyed, there were few people working on a Saturday afternoon.

Donny's office was on the fifth floor. Harvey had been there once before and had been far from impressed. He turned right out of the fire escape and walked to the far end of the corridor, glancing through the mesh-lined windows of the other spaces as he passed, until he reached the very end of the building, and the corner office.

The door to Donny's office was as insecure as the others in the building. Applying a little pressure at the top and bottom offered enough of a space for Harvey to wedge the back of his knife in the gap. He eased the wood back, pulling the lock from the door jamb, and with some gentle persuasion from his knee, he popped the door open without leaving any sign of a break in.

Using a spare key from the filing cabinet, he twisted the lock and closed the door. If anything, Donny would think he had just forgotten to lock it when he returned.

It was a large space for such a small and feeble man. Dual aspect windows offered plenty of natural light and the vertical blinds had been opened to reveal a view over the rooftops of the picturesque town of Chigwell.

But Harvey wasn't there for the view.

Harvey was there because Donny had been lying and his office was the only place that would offer an insight into his wretched foster-brother's world.

Beside the windows were three armchairs, which the interior designers had clearly chosen for style over comfort, considering how sleek and futuristic they looked. They were arranged in a half-circle with a coffee table in the centre. There was another door behind the chairs which Harvey opened to find a large storage space full of stationery, boxes of files, and the junk Donny had collected over the years. He switched on the light and saw the dust that had been disturbed by the door opening hang in the air. The space was rarely used.

He moved to Donny's desk. It was as Harvey had imagined, littered with papers. The man lacked discipline. Harvey had never owned a desk, nor had he ever felt the need for one. But if he did have one, he was sure it would be kept in order. There seemed to be two piles of paper. Forms of some kind. They were spread out as if Donny had been looking for one in particular.

Harvey studied the topmost form. It bore the company name on the top left-hand corner and had boxes for the relevant information. They were import documents and the pile on the left had been stamped with the words *DUTY PAID* in red ink along with the seal of the UK Customs and Excise. To a man more familiar with paperwork, the forms may have meant something. But to Harvey, they were just import papers for the alcohol that was served in John's establishments. He tossed them to one side and opened the top drawer. Inside the drawer, he found nothing of use. Some papers, pens, and takeaway menus. He tried the second drawer and found an envelope full of photos. They showed Donny at a party with friends. It appeared to be a red carpet event. The men wore tuxedos and the ladies wore ball gowns. Harvey recognised some of their faces from the wedding. Donny's friends. Others, he had never seen before. But the last photo caught Harvey's attention. It showed Donny and a friend posing for the photo against a sponsored backdrop that was adorned with the names of high-profile brands. Harvey imagined the highest bidding brand would have the company name in the most prominent spot. But in this particular photo, the most prominent spot was obscured by a woman.

She was elegant, long-legged, and her hair rested on her shoulders. Her dress appeared expensive. It concealed enough to remain tasteful yet revealed sufficient skin to stir the memory in Harvey's mind.

It was the girl. Harvey hadn't caught her name. He hadn't even thought of her since he'd heard the gunshot ring out. He'd left her lying in the long grass and she hadn't crossed his mind once since.

She was staring at Donny and his friend with the type of smile a person adopts on occasions such as high-profile events. It was the always-happy expression, the carefree, fun-loving gaze that hid all those things that Harvey had read in her eyes a few hours before. She had appeared lonely behind a mask of confidence. Seductive and powerful yet fragile and tender. He gave her some thought, then dropped the images into the envelope and tossed them back into the drawer. He closed it and was about to open the third drawer when a dull and muted ping announced the arrival of the elevator along the corridor. He glanced around the room looking for a place to hide. His eyes settled on the stationery cupboard just as he heard the grumble of a man's voice outside.

CHAPTER TWENTY-FIVE

"I'm not sure that Mr Cartwright would appreciate you in his office without him being here," said the guard.

He had a northern accent that Myers placed on the outskirts of Manchester. He wore a pair of plain, black trousers, unpolished shoes, and, judging by the state of his shirt, he was due a laundry day.

"I'm not sure that Mr Cartwright would appreciate a visitor having to spend ten minutes looking for the security guard," said Myers. "So, what do you want to do? Let us in or make a call to see what he says?"

The guard stared between Myers and Fox. His expression wrote cheques that his size and physique couldn't cash. There was a weakness in his eyes that gave him the appearance of being sly and underhanded.

"Five minutes," he said, and he pulled a big bunch of keys from his pocket. Each of the keys were marked with various colour tabs which Myers presumed to relate to each floor. A number was also inscribed on each key and he found the correct one. He inserted the key and tried to turn it, but it was already unlocked. He glanced back at Myers then tried the door handle. "He must have left it unlocked."

"Perhaps I didn't need to disturb you from your extended toilet break after all," said Myers, and he moved past the man into the space.

"It's nicer than I thought it would be," said Fox, as she followed Myers and began studying the shelves of files.

She raised her hand to pull a folder from the shelf.

"Don't touch anything, Fox."

She paused and glanced at him.

"Nothing is to be moved," he said. "We don't want your grubby prints on anything we may need later."

The guard was leaning on the door frame, watching with interest as they made their way through the office.

"I suppose you'll want to be getting back to whatever it was you were doing?" said Myers without looking at him.

The man said nothing, then raised his eyebrows when Myers eventually looked his way.

"You must be busy?" said Myers, inviting him to leave them to it.

"Not really," the man said, and shook his head. He checked his watch and slid his hand back into his pocket. "No, nothing to do for an hour or so."

He wasn't going to leave.

"What is it you're looking for?" asked the man.

"I'll know when I see it," said Myers, as he flicked through the papers on the desk.

"You said Mr Cartwright owns several drinking establishments, sir?" said Fox. She had followed Myers to the desk and was eyeing the papers that were sprawled out.

"He doesn't own them, his father does. Donald just runs them," said Myers. She was irritating him. The office was large, and they didn't need two people to look at the same desk. He moved across to one of the large windows that looked out over Chigwell.

"So that's what all these import certificates are for. There are a lot of them. How many establishments does he run?" asked Fox.

"I don't know how many exactly he runs, but his father has bars and clubs all over East London."

"But why does he *import* the alcohol?"

She was a distraction and he let her know it with a heavy sigh.

"I guess he saves money by importing it, Fox. Is this relevant to..."

He stopped himself from saying too much in front of the guard. Fox looked up from the papers and seemed to understand.

"Why don't you tell us what you know about Donald Cartwright?" said Myers, and the guard lost his carefree demeanour. He pushed off the door frame and jingled his keys in his pocket.

"Me?"

"Yes, you."

"I don't know anything about him."

"You know who he is?"

"He's the boss' son."

"So, you work for John Cartwright?"

"Yeah. But listen, I don't know anything about anything. I'm not getting involved."

"What's your name, son?" said Myers.

And the man silenced. Myers waited a moment. He would talk. It was just a matter of time.

"Charlie," said the guard.

"Okay then, Charlie," said Myers, knowing full well that Charlie was the first name he had thought of. "Just relax. You're not in any trouble. I just want to know a little bit more about Mr Cartwright."

"Which one?" said Charlie, and Myers knew he would talk.

"The younger one."

"Donny? He's a nice guy. Doesn't say much to me."

"Have you ever tried to talk to him?"

"Well, once, yeah. But he didn't seem to be in the talking mood."

"Do you work the desk every day?" said Fox. She was still at the desk studying the papers. Her interruption irritated Myers but he let it go. It was a good question and he could see where she was going.

"Well, no. We do shifts. Me and others. It rotates."

"So some weeks you do mornings and then other weeks you work the afternoons?" said Fox.

"Yeah, and the evenings. I do the mornings every three weeks."

"So you see Mr Cartwright coming in and out of the building?" said Myers.

"Yeah. Every three weeks."

"Do you say good morning, Charlie?" said Fox.

"Eh?"

"Good morning. Do you tell him good morning when you do see him? He is your boss, after all."

"Oh, no, he's not my boss. His dad's my boss."

"So you don't say good morning to him?" said Fox.

"Well, no. Not really," said Charlie, and he checked over his shoulder. "He's not very friendly. A few of the other guys have had run ins with him."

"Have you?" said Myers, standing with his back to the large window.

"No, not me. I prefer to keep my nose clean."

"How long did you get?" said Fox, and the question caught Myers off-guard.

"Eh?" said Charlie.

"How long did you get?" repeated Fox. "In prison. The tattoo on your neck. It's a prison tat."

Charlie pulled his collar up to hide the tattoo.

"Two years. But that was a long time ago, mind. I don't do any of that stuff anymore."

"What stuff?" asked Myers. The man named Charlie who Myers was sure was not named Charlie had become interesting. What started out as an innocent probe to get an insight into Donald Cartwright had developed into something more.

Charlie squirmed.

"Ah, look, I should get back to my desk."

"You'll stay right there, or I'll get John Cartwright on the phone right now and I'll tell him that his security guard opened the door to his son's office without even looking at our IDs."

Charlie sighed and realised his mistake.

"What was your crime?" asked Myers.

"Armed robbery," said Charlie, and Myers

smiled at having broken such a man with relative ease.

"Guilty?" said Fox.

He nodded.

"Two years for armed robbery. Did it pay well?"

Charlie said nothing.

"I thought the going rate for armed robbery these days was seven years. Is that right, sir?"

"Unless the prisoner decides to relay a little more information than what he gave in court," continued Myers.

"Hey, I'm not a grass," said Charlie. "I just..."

"Go on," said Myers. "You just what?"

"I did what I had to do. I never grassed on anyone that didn't deserve it."

"I see," said Fox, and she smiled at Myers. Myers didn't smile back.

"Seems funny to me that a convicted armed robber would be working as a security guard," said Myers.

"Mr Cartwright is alright. He's a hard bastard sometimes. But he's fair. He sees me alright and I'll not say anything against him."

"You're referring to the older of the two Mr Cartwrights?" said Fox.

"Eh? Yeah. Of course. John Cartwright. He's okay in my books. Gave me a second chance, he did."

"But you don't have the same affection for his son?"

Charlie shook his head.

"Charlie, tell me something. Does Donald Cartwright have many visitors here?" said Fox, and again, Myers was pleasantly surprised at her line of questioning.

"Yeah. Sometimes."

"Do you know them? Are there any records?" asked Fox.

"Well, they're supposed to fill in the form. It's for health and safety and all, but..."

"But what, Charlie?"

"I don't like to ask him. He's the boss' son and all."

"So he has guests here but you don't register them?"

"What am I supposed to do? He could fire me like *that*." Charlie snapped his fingers as if to accentuate his point.

"Do you remember any of them?" asked

Myers, and he moved to sit on the back of a stylish looking armchair.

"Maybe. But I don't know their names."

"A description will do."

"It's girls, usually."

"Girls?" said Fox. "You mean women? Businesswomen?"

"No, girls," said Charlie, and he laughed. "You could call them businesswomen, but I doubt they'd take a credit card, if you know what I mean." His smile faded.

"Anybody else?" asked Myers, keen to move on from Donald Cartwright's lewd goings on. He stood from the chair with a sudden awareness of how tainted everything must be in the room.

"Some men. I can't remember them. It was weeks ago."

"Businessmen?" said Myers.

"Yeah. There was some men. Asian fellas. They had a woman with them."

"A businesswoman?" asked Fox.

"Yeah, she wasn't a call girl. She had eyes that would tear you apart just by looking at her. Posh tart, she was. But that's all I remember. They got in the lift and that's all I saw."

"You didn't see them come back down?" asked Fox.

The lead was going nowhere. Some men that he didn't remember visited Donald Cartwright a few weeks ago. Myers shuffled across the room to a doorway. He hadn't noticed it before.

"My shift was over by the time they were done. One of the other guys must have seen them leave. It was probably Joey. You should talk to Joey."

Myers opened the door and stirred the dust. He peered into the darkness and fumbled for a light switch.

"Sir?" said Fox, and Myers peered out of the cupboard with his eyebrows raised. "I've got something."

Myers closed the door and Fox met him halfway across the room. For the first time, he noticed the scent she was wearing. It was nice. It was sweet and smelled of innocence.

She unfurled a balled piece of paper and flattened it out.

"This was in the bin, sir."

"In the bin? So?"

"It's been stamped, sir. Why would he throw away a consignment and keep the rest?

Surely he'd need this for accounting purposes."

"Maybe it's a duplicate?"

"No, the duplicates are yellow and blue. I dealt with these all the time, sir. In Bristol, sir."

"In the sticks?"

She ignored his comment. "This is the original. The yellow is kept by the port and the blue is kept by Customs and Excise. There's a number scrawled on the top of this one, sir."

"A number?" said Myers, and he took the form from her to study the number himself.

"That's a container number. I'm sure of it. I recognise the format. Three letters followed by three numbers, then nine more."

"So?" said Myers. "They import alcohol. We already established that."

"But this one has the number handwritten on it."

"So? He could have just jotted it down while he was on the phone."

Fox deflated before his eyes. It was clear she was trying to make a good impression.

"Okay, sorry, sir. I just thought it could have been something."

She reached to take the form from Myers, but as she did, something occurred to him.

"Hang on," he said, and pulled the form away. "You might be onto something."

"Sir?" she said, and she moved closer to get a better look. He inhaled again and enjoyed the scent. It was calming, even if she was irritating.

"What does he usually import?"

Fox reached for the stack of papers and sifted through them.

"Looks like cases of beer, wine, champagne, some spirits. It's just alcohol, sir."

"Some spirits?" he said. "What spirits?"

She gave the first few forms a quick analysis and Myers watched her analytical mind ticking away.

"Vodka mainly, plus a few cases of gin. Then it looks to me like small amounts of scotch, brandy, Jagermeister-"

"And they are all similar?" he asked.

She looked again and nodded.

"And the quantities are always the same?"

She nodded.

"It looks that way."

"I think you found something, Fox. Find

out everything you can about that container number."

Myers headed for the door, pleased that Fox had found a purpose. The research would keep her busy for a while.

"I don't understand, sir."

He sighed and closed the door on the guard.

"Picture Cartwright's bars. These aren't your average working man's clubs, Fox, where men order brown ale and women sip at Cinzano and lemonade. The clientele will drink wine, bottles of beer maybe. They'll start the evening with a gin and tonic, then as the night draws on, they'll order vodka. The barman will line shots up on the bar and they'll down them one by one."

She was coming round to his idea. Those country cogs of hers were ticking.

"So why did he order forty-eight cases of middle-grade scotch on a separate consignment, write the container number on the form, and then throw it away?" she asked.

"Exactly, Fox. There's more scotch there than he's ordered in the past six months. Find me that container."

CHAPTER TWENTY-SIX

On the far side of Theydon Bois, beyond the pubs and shops and the village green, tucked away on the edge of Epping Forest, was a small two-storey block of apartments. The finish was pleasant. It was modern brickwork appointed with wooden features that were sympathetic to days gone by. Tall, lush trees lined the small driveway and the entrance to the below-ground car park. Harvey parked his bike in one of the few guest spots and waited. Before long, a taxi arrived, and a young couple emerged from the building. They were laughing about something Harvey hadn't heard and the man even held the door for Harvey as he climbed the steps.

He watched the taxi pull away and hit the button for the elevator. There would be no need for stealth for what Harvey was about to do.

The doors opened to the second floor and Harvey turned right. The carpeted corridor smelled of pine and the bright hallway lights with the light oak finishing offered a clean environment, tainted with the aroma of various foods that were being cooked in the apartments. There was no tantalising smell coming from the last apartment along the corridor, only muted and muffled shrieks of joy.

Harvey opened the unlocked door and closed it behind him. He gazed around the living space. The light oak had been continued throughout with tasteful artwork on the walls. It looked as if it had been designed by a top interior designer, with tall potted ferns beside the balcony and polished work surfaces that ran from a breakfast bar into the kitchen, leading the eye toward the stunning treetops of the forest.

The bedroom door was open, and Harvey could hear the groans of passion coming from inside. There was talk of how bad he had been, and the man begged for punishment. Harvey stepped inside the bedroom to find Sergio lying in a star shape on the bed. He wore a blindfold and each of his limbs were tied to the bed posts with shiny, black, leather straps. The girl Sergio had been talking to at the wedding was standing with her back to the door wearing only stockings and heels. Her arm was raised ready to strike his naked flesh with a horse-riding crop.

"That's it. I've been such a bad boy," he teased in his Eastern European accent.

"You want more?" she asked.

"Yes. Yes, please. I deserve more."

And she spanked him with the crop hard across his bare foot. She toyed with the loose, leather strap on the end of the crop, running it up his leg. Sergio's excitement was evident, and he twitched in anticipation.

She raised the crop once more and Sergio inhaled a long, jittery breath.

Gently, Harvey took her wrist from behind and signed with a finger to his lips that she should be quiet. She released the crop into Harvey's hand, and he moved her toward the door. She smiled at the game, not even trying to cover herself, and watched from the doorway with delight as Harvey delivered the first blow across Sergio's genitals.

Sergio bucked and writhed on the bed, pulling at his restraints. His twisted face eased from excruciating pain into delight the way violent white-water froths at the foot of a waterfall then trickles downstream in search of the sea. He straightened, panting with delight, and licked his lips.

"More," he said.

Harvey whipped the crop down onto his bare chest leaving a red mark on his skin, and Sergio laughed with pleasure through his gritted teeth, growling with the sensation.

"Again."

Harvey struck his stomach with the crop, harder than before, and Sergio bucked. He tried to double over but the tight leather straps held him down.

"Oh yes," he cried.

And Harvey hit out again across the hard arrogance that was the result of his twisted mind.

The effect was immediate. The pain was fierce, and Sergio's voice rose in pitch between his ragged breath.

"Not so hard," he said.

But Harvey was not one to take orders. He struck out three times in rapid succession leaving Sergio no time to recover. He growled with the agony and writhed on the silk sheets. Harvey glanced back at the girl, whose wandering hands had stopped exploring her own body and now covered herself. The excited expression on her face had faded to a wide-eyed and horrified stare.

And Harvey struck out three more times while holding her in his stare.

"Softer, Alina. Not so hard, please."

He waited for Sergio to settle and he admired the angry welts across the man's chest.

The girl, convinced that this was no longer a sordid game, collected her clothes from the floor, using them to cover herself, and she ran to the next room.

"Alina?" Sergio called.

"She's gone," said Harvey.

There was a moment of pause as Sergio's mind deciphered what was happening. He no longer stood proud and cavalier. His body softened and the blood that only moments before had hardened his sexuality now pooled in his cheeks.

"Harvey?" he said, as if he dared not utter his name.

The front door slammed as the girl left the apartment.

"Alina? What's going on?"

"I'll tell you what's going on, Sergio," said Harvey, and he struck Sergio's stomach hard across an already furious looking welt.

"No, Harvey, stop. Please."

"You know something."

"What, Harvey? About what?"

"Who killed Julia?"

"I don't know. How could I know? Harvey, stop. Untie me."

He ran the crop along the length of Sergio's leg, stopping at his foot.

"Harvey? What are you doing? This is crazy."

Harvey struck the sole of Sergio's foot as hard as he could and watched as Sergio struggled against the straps, bearing the pain through gritted teeth.

"There was a container delivered. You wrote the number at the top of a form."

"What? A container? I don't know anything about a container."

Harvey gave the same treatment to Sergio's other foot and waited for Sergio to recover.

"You wrote the number at the top of the form. What was in the container?"

"What, Harvey?" said Sergio. "We have containers all the time. It's alcohol. We import it. You know that."

It was Sergio's small toe that bore the brunt of the next lashing. The pain was enough to instigate the tears Harvey had been sure would come at some point.

"There was something special about a particular container. I need to know what it is, Sergio. A girl died today, which means that either you or Donny upset somebody."

"I haven't upset anybody," said Sergio. "I just do my job. Talk to Donny. He does it all. He makes the orders. It's him that receives the shipments. All I do is make sure everything is done properly and report to John. Please, Harvey. Let me go."

"Where do I find Donny? Where did Julios take him?"

Harvey rested the crop on Sergio's already swollen toe.

"No, please, Harvey. I can't tell you. You heard what John said. I can't tell you that."

His foot trembled with the anticipation. His body tensed, and his genitals, which only minutes before had been swollen with joy and lewd excitement, were shrivelled and flaccid.

The second blow across Sergio's toe was sharper than the first. Harvey felt the perfect connection between leather and flesh and heard the snap of the crop as Sergio entered into a state of total panic and fear. His body jumped across the bed as far as his restraints would allow and twisted to protect his exposed groin. It took five more lashes across the soft and tender parts of Sergio's legs to calm him down.

"You're sick, Sergio. You know that?"

"*I'm* sick?" he gasped. "You're the one whipping me."

"Your best friend's wife has just been killed and you brought one of the hostesses home for some sordid sex games."

"He told me to go. John did. You heard him, Harvey. He said he didn't want to see me. Stay out of sight. That's what he said."

"Where do I find Donny and Julios?"

"Harvey, please. I can't tell you. I can't take any more of this." He must have sensed that Harvey had raised the whip because the moment Harvey's body tensed to deliver another strike, Sergio crumbled. "Okay, okay. Stop. Enough, Harvey. I'll tell you."

Harvey let the crop rest on Sergio's shrivelled manhood and saw the man's chest rise and fall in quick succession.

He relayed the address with reluctance and a tear ran from beneath the fluffy eye mask.

Harvey lay the crop across Sergio's chest.

"If you're lying, I'll be back."

"What? Harvey, untie me. You can't leave me like this," said Sergio, his voice even more panicked than before.

Harvey listened to Sergio calling after him, his voice growing quieter as he reached the elevator and pushed the button to go down.

CHAPTER TWENTY-SEVEN

Myers pushed through the double doors that led from the staff car park. Fox followed behind, and as he placed his wallet against the card reader to open the next set of doors, he found her right beside him.

He sighed and she looked bemused at his annoyance.

"Find out whatever you can about that container number. I want to know where it came from, what was in it, who signed for it, and where it was delivered. Anything else is a bonus."

"I'm on it, sir," she said, and seemed to glow with the opportunity. Myers was close to telling her thanks. But he thought better of it.

He'd see what she came up with. He'd given her an opportunity to demonstrate what all that training can do. He stopped and let her walk on, partly to give him room to think and partly because he was tired of her incessant desire to be his shadow.

It was then that the door to his right buzzed. It was the door to the evidence room and the electro-magnetic lock clicked to release. Carver pushed the door open, but he didn't seem to acknowledge Myers' presence at all. He appeared vacant and lost in his own thoughts.

"Looking glum, Carver," said Myers. "What's the matter? Did you miss the party?"

"Not now, Myers," Carver replied.

"Oh, come on. That's not like you. Where's the banter?"

Carver turned, his face was angry and his eyes red.

"I said, not now."

"Okay, okay," said Myers, holding his hands up in defence. "I was just kidding around. I actually wanted to come and find you anyway."

"You're out of favours, Myers."

"I just wanted to say thanks."

Carver raised an eyebrow.

"Genuinely," said Myers. "The tip you gave me about Cartwright. We might have a decent lead. So, thanks."

Carver huffed. It wasn't like him to miss an opportunity to gloat. He cast his eyes away.

"What's got to you, Frank?" said Myers.

"Ah, just leave it, Myers."

"No, seriously." Myers pulled him from the doorway to let a couple of uniformed officers through. Then he led him out to the car park. "Talk to me."

Carver pulled some cigarettes from his pocket and lit one. He let his head fall back and released the smoke through his nostrils.

"I didn't mean to push the wrong buttons, Frank. You know how it is. The best form of defence is attack."

Carver nodded and leaned against the wall.

"Is Allenby on your case?" asked Myers.

"No."

A single word response and Carver slipped back into his own mind.

Myers gave him a minute to think but stayed close by, knowing he'd open up eventually.

"How do you do it?" asked Carver. He cleared his throat and spat.

"Do what?"

"How do you deal with it? The innocence."

Myers said nothing.

"I see death on a weekly basis, Myers. I see death everywhere I go. But it's mostly thugs. They deserve it, and if they don't, then they'd probably wind up doing something that does make them deserve it. It's part of the life. Organised crime. It's more like organised death, Myers. They all deserve it one way or another. But you'll never find out who pulled the trigger and part of you doesn't care who did pull the trigger. They deserved it."

The emotion had drawn out Carver's Scottish accent. He was a hard man and to see him cut up was humbling.

"But a young girl. A young girl far too young to have done anything so bad that she deserved..."

He paused and his eyes watered. He took a long drag on his cigarette.

"They don't train you for this, Myers. Well, maybe now they do, but..."

He stopped again and Myers knew what

he was feeling. His mind was showing him the image he was trying to block. Some images never leave. Over time, with enough death, those images merge into one.

"Did you get her name?" asked Myers.

Carver shook his head.

"They're identifying her now. What's left of her." He shook his head in disbelief and took another long pull on his cigarette. "So savage, Myers. So savage."

"Any leads?"

"Nothing." He shook his head again and flicked his cigarette, watching it spin away and land on the tarmac. "Not a thing. We have her belongings, but there's no ID. She's too young for a driving license and her bag was just full of..." He paused again and stared up at Myers. "Kids stuff, Myers. The type of stuff kids carry in their bags. Cheap makeup, chewing gum, and a sodding personal CD player that won't turn on."

"Sorry, Frank," said Myers. "Was she..."

It was Myers' turn to pause. He didn't need to say anymore.

"Not that we know of. Her clothes were intact. If she was, they'll find out."

There was a silence between them that said more than any of their words had.

"If you want to talk about it," said Myers.

Carver laughed a single shot of defiance.

"We have shrinks for that type of thing, don't we?" he said.

"Shrinks aren't out there seeing what we see, Frank."

"Why are you being nice, Myers?" said Carver, and he rubbed his face with both hands and straightened his jacket. He stared at Myers. "What's with the politeness?"

"Banter is one thing, Frank. Some things go beyond that, don't they?"

"I guess." He pushed himself off the wall. "I better make a start."

"I mean it, Frank. I know I'm a dick to you and, well, you're a dick to me. But if you need to..."

Carver nodded. "I'll bear it in mind, Myers. I'll bear it in mind."

Carver turned away and pushed through the door then stopped. He looked over his shoulder at Myers, tightened his lips in a half-smile, and nodded once, then let the door close. Myers waited for the buzz of the doors and then leaned on the wall where Carver had stood. There wasn't much that got to Myers. Back-stabbing and banter were all part of the fight. They were there to harden those who wanted to climb the ladder and to highlight those who just didn't have the resilience to handle it. But somewhere beyond all of that, something intangible that ran parallel with the to-and-fro of police life, was an emotional level that people rarely spoke of. Myers could see it in the eyes of nearly all of the officers he'd worked with over the years. Other signs of the disturbance included greying hair or balding, and the bags beneath their eyes. Some men even developed a tremble which they passed off with bravado as having had too much caffeine. But Myers knew. And that was what it was, a disturbance. A tremble in that parallel world could ripple through the real world that people saw. It could change things, alter outcomes, and the host could make a wrong decision. He understood that. He understood what Carver was going through. No doubt, Carver would be in the first-floor office now, wearing a shield to fend off the banter and backstabbing, and retaliating with comebacks of his own.

But Myers knew now. He understood that

whatever tremble in that parallel world had opened Carver up had rippled through into Myers' world. There was a shift in power. He considered what Carver had said. A young girl had been killed. It was London. It happened too often. No ID and no clues as to why she had been killed. He thought of Jennifer Standing and how close she had come to the same fate.

Perhaps there had been a tremble in some other dimension? Perhaps that's why the killer showed up when he did? Perhaps in another world he hadn't showed up? Perhaps then Carver's girl would be alive?

"Perhaps," he whispered.

He leaned through the exterior doors and fished his wallet from his pocket to open the security doors. But then he stopped. There were two small meshed windows inset into the doors to his right, and through them, he could see the duty officer maintaining the records in the evidence room. He stood as a shopkeeper might, leaning on the counter waiting to offer his wares.

Myers held his wallet up once more and the doors buzzed then clicked open.

"Afternoon," said the officer behind the

counter, and he stood up straight, waiting for an instruction.

"DI Carver just submitted a girl's belongings," said Myers.

The man nodded. "Yes, sir. About ten minutes ago."

"Was there a lot there? Can I see?"

"I'll need a ticket, sir, if you want to take-"

"I just want to look. Right here will be fine," said Myers.

The officer nodded again, glanced up at the doors, and then disappeared behind a corner.

Myers knew what it would be. Perhaps there had been a tremble in that other world. Perhaps the two worlds had shifted course somehow. By an unexplainable intuition, Myers knew what the officer would produce.

But he still felt a stab in his heart when the officer returned with a plastic tray and a Louis Vuitton bag sealed in a plastic evidence bag.

CHAPTER TWENTY-EIGHT

There were several houses across East London that were, in one way or another, owned by John Cartwright. The portfolio changed as months went by. The houses were used for a variety of purposes. On occasion, John would offer a released felon a place to find their feet in return for favours. Other times, the houses would be used to store items that needed to be kept away from prying eyes; robbery hauls and high-value items. Occasionally, the houses would be used as safe houses. They were a place for somebody to stay until the heat had died down and new faces adorned the walls of police stations' most wanted boards.

Harvey knew many of the houses, but as the portfolio changed and only John and Sergio knew what they owned and under what fictitious business' name, there was no way anybody but the two of them could compromise their plans. It was a security protocol that wasn't based on trust. Just principles and best practise.

The Horns Road house that Sergio had divulged was such a property. Harvey knew the road well. It stretched from the A12 in Newbury Park to Barkingside. It was a busy road with heavy traffic and suited John's purposes well. Busy residential areas so close to London were often full of transients. Nobody would pay a blind bit of notice to a few strangers entering a house.

Harvey parked his bike in a side street named Hamilton Avenue. He left his helmet in the back box, locked it, and walked to Horns Road. A quick glance at two of the houses told him which way the houses were numbered. He turned left and made his way to the safe house. Checking with discretion the insides of the parked cars was a habit he'd formed from Julios. A safe house should be kept safe and what he was about to do would break all the rules. The cars that passed were mainly single occupants. None seemed to even see him. The area was heavily populated with Asians. Their community was strong and there was even a local mosque to facilitate their religious needs. The community had done well in London. Each of the bay-windowed Victorian houses were worth well over one million pounds and the cars that were parked along the roadside were anything but old scrappers. None of the parked cars were occupied and none stood out as being suspicious.

Breaking protocol was one thing. But drawing attention to a safe house by entering from the rear would have been ludicrous. People knocked on doors all the time. So, Harvey knocked.

But doors to safe houses were usually closed and locked. They didn't usually push open with the slightest touch. He checked behind him and glanced up the street as casually as he could.

There was nobody about. A car passed but the woman driving paid him no attention. He entered and closed the door behind him without making a sound, and then he waited for a full minute, listening to the sounds of the building, listening for movement anywhere.

But there was none.

There were rules to using a safe house, rules designed to avoid the safe house becoming conspicuous. Curtains should be opened and closed in the morning and evening but under no circumstances must the occupants dwell on either the ground floor or at the front of the house. This limited the usable space to the rear bedrooms, which was one of the reasons John preferred the old Victorian houses. There were usually two rear bedrooms. Lights should be used as if the house was being lived in normally. But under no circumstances should the lights be used in the room where the occupants were dwelling. This limited the occupants' usage of the house even further. The rule wasn't a major concern in the summer but staying in one of John's safe houses during wintertime was akin to a prison sentence.

Nobody without strict instructions from John was to visit a safe house that was in use for whatever purpose.

They were John's rules, and nobody ever broke them.

Until now.

Harvey knew the downstairs rooms would be empty, but he peered inside the living room. It was furnished to look as if it was lived in. But the photos on the walls were all cheap prints and the framed wedding photos on the mantelpiece had been ripped from magazines.

The kitchen space had been used. Harvey felt the kettle and found it to be warm. Not hot. Just warm. There were tea and coffee jars on the work surface and a small spillage. That would be Donny. Harvey knew Julios well enough to know that he would have cleared up a spill. Through the kitchen was a back door. It was wide open, and Harvey could see a narrow garden path leading to a rear gate.

The gate was also open.

He felt his pulse flutter then ease. Something was wrong. Even if Julios and Donny were only just unloading the car, they wouldn't have left all the doors open. Julios wouldn't have. Harvey knew that much. But Donny was a wild card. When you were the only legitimate son of a millionaire criminal, rules were of little significance.

He was tempted to bolt up the stairs, but he crept. He winced when the fourth stair creaked, and he shifted his weight to the edges of each step. The stairs led from front to back, which meant the first bedroom on Harvey's left was the first of the rear bedrooms. The door was ajar, but Harvey heard no movement from inside. He checked the other doors. They were all open, but he could see little of the insides from where he was standing.

He tugged his knife from inside his jacket with his right hand and pushed the door to bedroom one with his left. The hinges announced his arrival, but still he stood back until he could see inside.

It was empty, save for a single bed, and the curtains were closed. Harvey moved inside. He lowered the knife and peered through a gap in the curtains. Julios' car was parked in the alleyway. He would have unloaded the bags through the rear entrance. There was an ancient sports holdall on the bed. Harvey recognised it as Julios'. It was leather with the name of an old sporting brand printed on the side. Julios had little requirements for a new, expensive bag. He was a frugal man.

Donny, on the other hand, would have

brought as much as Julios would allow. There was no way Donny would survive a spell in a safe house without some kind of entertainment.

Harvey stepped outside. Nothing had changed. The doors were all as they had been. There was still the same smell of dust in the air. Harvey moved to the second bedroom, the only other room at the rear of the house. He peered around the door. A large double bed occupied most of one end, upon which were two suitcases. They were unopened as if Donny had just put them down. What was more likely was that Julios had carried them up the stairs to stop Donny whining about how heavy they were.

There was nothing out of place. He stepped into the room, unzipped one of the cases, and flipped the lid open. Just to make sure they were in fact Donny's. Among two neat piles of clothes was a selection of DVDs and a games console.

They were Donny's.

He pulled the lid closed, zipped it up, then strode into the front bedroom only to be greeted by a cricket bat to his gut. The force of the blow knocked the wind out of him, and he doubled over with barely enough instinct remaining to roll out of the way.

The bat landed beside him and he rolled once and sprang to his feet, sucking in air and feeling his way to the window, his eyesight blurred, his eyes streaming tears. There was just time for him to see a white blur move from the room through the doorway.

Harvey ran at the shape and hit the wall. He clutched at his gut as he stepped onto the landing and his eyes refocused. The man was on the stairs moving fast. Harvey hurled himself at him. He felt his legs collide with the wooden banister rail and heard the splinter of wood. He hit the man with full force and grabbed for his neck. They both rolled down the stairs in a bundle of clawing fingers and grappling hands.

It was the other man that hit the floor first. He landed face first with Harvey's arm around his neck.

"Where's my brother?" said Harvey, and he increased the pressure.

With the man's legs on the stairs and Harvey's weight on top of him, the man had little room for manoeuvre.

But still, he said nothing.

Harvey added some weight to the man's spine, and he screamed out in agony. He was less than half the man Asif had been. Harvey needed him to speak.

"Where have you taken him?"

Harvey leaned forward to stare him in the face, keeping his knee in the small of the man's back.

The man spat in his face and Harvey pulled back on his neck, twisting his head and finding that place where the nerves end and brittle bone is all that stands between life and death.

The man sensed his predicament. He breathed a cry and a whimper. He moaned a prayer.

And still, he said nothing.

His eyes closed and the corners of his mouth tweaked to bare his teeth. And as Harvey pushed the limits of the man's spine and a prayer sang out in a hoarse and foreign whisper, his chances of finding Donny and Julios grew slimmer.

The body fell limp in Harvey's hands. The man's skull thudded on the floor as the last of his breaths escaped, and his foot gave a final, involuntary twitch. Harvey lashed out at the wall in anger.

He held his head in his hands and dropped to a frustrated crouch as the odds stacked against him weighed heavy on his mind. The sight of Julia in her blood-soaked dress. The dead driver who Harvey had shot. Asif, the brave man who had outwitted Harvey even in the midst of torture.

And now a useless, crumpled piece of meat that lay at the foot of the stairs in one of John's safe houses.

But, amidst the fog of self-hate and loathsome thoughts, hope showed itself. The swing of the bat. The roll down the stairs. Even during the chaos of the fight, Harvey had heard something.

The noise hadn't registered at the time. But somehow, his subconscious had noted it.

He searched the man's pockets which, in the kurta, were deep and wide. But he found what he was looking for and hope became a reality.

He left through the back door and found a black BMW parked behind Julios' old Subaru. He hit the key fob. The lights flashed once, and the locks popped up.

He checked both ways and then opened the car door. The door pockets were full of takeaway food wrappers. He pulled them out and dropped them on the carpet, then emptied the contents of the glove box.

Harvey sat back and let his head rest on the back of the seat.

Hope was a futile mistress.

He climbed out and was about to close the door when he caught sight of something. He sifted through the pile of trash and found something that wasn't rubbish.

And she smiled at him the way only hope can.

CHAPTER TWENTY-NINE

The rumble of chatter in the first-floor office ceased in unison when Myers burst in through the doors. The pause would have been worthy of a well-rehearsed orchestra. He grabbed the first available phone, dialled the number from memory, and waited. Thirty pairs of eyes stared at him while the line connected and the unhurried ringing began.

"Pick up, pick up," he mumbled.

But nobody answered.

He stared around the room looking for someone who knew and liked him well enough to carry on with the calls. He found nobody. One by one, they returned to their tasks and the rumble of chatter resumed like the sections of the orchestra supporting the lead violin.

He slammed the phone down.

"Sir?" said Fox, more out of duty than anything else. "Is everything okay?"

He found her in the mass of staring eyes, but the words failed him. It was just a whim. Just a terrible, terrible thought. He was wrong. He had to be wrong.

He said nothing.

Allenby must have sensed the change in atmosphere. She appeared at her office door and followed the stares.

Myers backed away. He had no allies in there. He nearly stumbled on the fire escape stairs from trembling legs and, for that reason, isolating his car key on a bunch of five keys was impossible to do while he ran. It was at this moment that his wallet decided to catch on his pocket lining, and he fought with it beside the security doors before tugging it free. He ran to his car, tossed his wallet inside, and fumbled once more with the ignition barrel. He had already put the car into first gear when the engine fired, and the car lurched into life. A few moments later, he slammed on his brakes as people walked across the entrance to the police station car park. Ordinary people in their own unhurried, ordinary lives.

He honked his horn and waved for them to get out of the way. But the only responses he received were a look of confusion from an older man and a dirty look from a young mother pushing her pram.

The exit cleared as he edged forward, and it was then that Myers wished he had a faster car. He'd seen the movies. Cops drove V8s and slid their cars around corners. It was all Myers could do to get his old motor up to fifty miles per hour, then he had to slow for a roundabout. He manoeuvred his car through the traffic to an ensemble of car horns and he floored the accelerator onto the main road out of Romford.

He checked the clock on the dashboard, which was an hour slow. He'd never got around to changing it since winter. It was 5 p.m. She should be at home. She would have walked or taken a bus. Myers considered the route. He thought about every conceivable way the bag could be hers.

But his panic only served to raise his already racing pulse and lift his blood pressure. He stopped at a set of lights that crossed the

A12 dual carriageway. He gave serious consideration to pulling into the oncoming traffic and working his way across the busy road. But it would be a lethal game of frogger. The cars were doing in excess of fifty miles per hour and his old motor was too large and cumbersome for such a move.

His fingers danced on the wheel. He checked the rear-view mirror every few seconds, but for what, he didn't know.

People had mobile phones in their cars. Some even carried them, large, brick-shaped devices that must cost a fortune to run.

But Myers did not.

The lights changed, and in a heartbeat, Myers resumed his impatient driving style. Two lanes of traffic crossed the dual carriageway, and if there was a gap, he moved into it, then hung on the bumper of the car in front, pushing for the next gap.

"Come on," he shouted, and slapped his hands on the wheel while he hovered in second gear waiting for the traffic to speed up.

He moved back to the outside lane, cutting off a beat-up, old work van. The driver honked his horn and leaned out of the window, hurling abuse. His curses fell on deaf ears. Myers was in a world of his own. The driver moved his van closer so that it filled Myers' rear-view mirror. The road changed to a single lane and the drivers ahead were patiently performing a zip formation. Myers stayed as close as he could to the car in front, but the car to his left saw the move and closed him off. He braked and the van nudged him, rocking the old car on its floaty suspension. There was no time to stop and look for damage. His car was a wreck and the van had seen better days. Instead, he checked his driver-side mirror, glanced ahead once, and pulled out into the oncoming traffic.

He knew there would be chaos. He knew he'd anger people. Cars swerved and pulled to one side. One car screeched to a halt, narrowly missing the car in front. Myers eased himself through the gap, saw the turning ahead, and floored it.

Only mildly aware of the chaos he'd left behind, Myers navigated the back streets he knew so well with ease. He knew where all the potholes were. He knew the places where he had to stand his ground. The old engine was smelling hot. The smell of hot oil was emanating from the vents.

But he was close.

His sweaty fingers slipped on the steering wheel, but he pushed on, working the old gears as hard as he could. Then, finally, he screeched to a halt in the first space he saw.

He wasn't aware if he closed the car door or not. He didn't give it a second thought. He just ran to the front door and jammed his finger on the doorbell.

Then came the wait.

The road was quiet. Only a single car passed. He stepped over the shrubs and peered through the front window. There was movement out in the back, in the garden, but he couldn't make it out. He knocked on the glass but caught nobody's attention and stepped back to the front door. He rattled the letterbox and slammed his hand on the little window as hard as he dared without breaking it. It was when he bent to look through the letter box that the door opened and Alison stood there, her face a dark cloud of thunder.

"What the bloody hell-"

"Where is she?"

Myers looked past her to the kitchen and saw a few people huddled around the back door. There was a gentle murmur of voices and a woman laughed.

"Matthew, what are you doing here? You can't just turn up."

"Is she home?"

"Yes. I think so-"

"Get her."

"Matthew-"

"Alison, just go get her."

"No, this is ridiculous. You can't just turn up, Matthew. We have guests. You know what today is, don't you?"

"I need to see her," said Myers, and then called up the stairs. "Harriet?"

One of the men peered through from the garden.

"Matthew, go home."

The man's curiosity got the better of him. He moved into the kitchen, sensing something was wrong.

"Alison? Is everything okay?"

She turned to answer him, and Myers saw his opportunity. He pushed past her and ran up the stairs, ignoring Alison's objections. He heard her following, but he had reached the top of the stairs and saw Harriet's bedroom door was closed.

He knocked once and waited. He closed his eyes and did the closest thing to praying he had done since he was a child.

There was no response.

Alison reached the top of the stairs behind him.

"This is enough," she scalded, her voice hushed but seething. "You have absolutely no right-"

He pushed the door open.

"Matthew?"

The tension in his body that had built since he first saw the bag in the evidence room fell from him and his knees buckled with the relief. He held onto the door and sighed.

Harriet looked up from her bed. She was propped up with her pillows, a magazine resting on her knees. She saw him, screwed her face up in confusion, then removed her earphones.

"What are you doing here?" she said.

"Honey, I tried to stop him."

Myers could say nothing. He wanted to go to her and hold her like he did when she was just a young, sweet child. But those days were gone.

"You can't just come in here. Mum, tell him."

"I tried, sweetheart. He barged in."

"Is everything okay?" said the man's voice, who had followed Alison up the stairs.

"Yes, Matthew is just leaving," said Alison. "He just wanted to ruin my birthday, that's all."

Her birthday.

He sighed again.

"Dad? What's going on?"

He clung to the door frame and let the voices around him, the questions and the tempers, flare and fade.

"I'm sorry," he said. "I'm so sorry. I thought..."

He paused and gave consideration to what he was about to say. Then decided against it.

"The bag, Harriet. Where's the bag?"

"What bag?"

"Matthew, you need to start talking."

"The bag you had this morning. The Louis Vuitton bag."

"What Louis Vuitton bag? She doesn't have a Louis Vuitton bag," said Alison, but her voice was distant. A distraction.

"The bag, Harriet," said Myers.

Harriet glanced at her mother then succumbed to the fact that she wasn't going to be able to deny it. She had never been a dishonest girl. A fighter, yes. Bad tempered, definitely. But a liar, no. Not his Harriet.

She reached for it from the floor and placed it on the bed.

"Harriet, where did you get that?" Again, Alison's questions were superfluous to the moment.

Myers stepped forward and opened it.

"No, Dad, you can't."

He tipped the contents onto the bed. Some chewing gum, a small bag of makeup, a little packet of travel tissues, and a book.

"Matthew, if you don't explain yourself, I'm going to have to call the police."

"Where did you get the bag, Harriet?"

"I told you, I got it from-"

"Honestly, Harriet, this is serious."

Her expression changed when she saw the grave look on his face.

"A friend of mine gave them to us. They're not real and I don't think they're stolen, Dad."

"Where did the bags come from?"

"I don't know. She just had them."

In the corner of the room, wedged between the wall and the wardrobe, was a large shopping bag full of smaller bags. It was typical of teenage girls to keep the bags from shopping trips. Something to do with having people know they bought from a particular shop.

"Did it come in a bag?"

Harriet nodded. She threw the magazine down and pushed herself off the bed, then rifled through the larger bag and began pulling smaller ones out.

"This one, I think," she said, and offered it to him. "Honest, Dad, I don't think they're stolen."

Myers held the bag. It was A3 size and good quality. It had strong, rope handles that were knotted inside and on the side of the bag was printed the name of the distributor.

And a ripple of change took place as he recognised the name.

CHAPTER THIRTY

The business card stated Regency Bags Limited as the company the man had worked for. The card design was stylish and, if anything, appeared a little too gaudy.

The address on the sign for Old Ford Industrial Park in Bow, East London, was anything but gaudy. It was much like any other unit on any other industrial estate. A forklift rattled around ferrying pallets and boxes, driven by an Asian man, and there were two more Asian men working close to the doorway.

The panniers and back box on the motorcycle gave the impression Harvey was a courier looking for an address. It was a good cover to make use of. Harvey rolled past the unit then an old, dented van that bore no sign-writing. It was parked behind some pallets forty yards from the unit. He parked his bike two hundred metres away and walked back to the van. A few scraps of paperwork on the messy dashboard bore the same company logos as the business card: a pair of snakes wrapped around a quill.

He knocked once on the side of the van and waited for a response. But there was no reply. He checked the men hadn't seen or heard him and he tried the side door on the off-chance. If the door was unlocked, the chances of the van being full were slim. It was not the sort of area a man with any sense would leave a van unlocked.

It clicked open.

Watching through the side window of the van, Harvey slid the door open, letting the sunlight fill the dark space.

It had been a long shot and was worth trying but, as expected, the van was virtually empty. There was a pile of flattened card-board boxes with the Regency Bags Limited logo printed on the side. He was about to close the door when, beyond the cardboard, something caught his eye. Tied to the rear pillar was a length of old rope that to any other man would appear harmless and normal. Most van drivers carried rope to tie down cargo.

But most van drivers wouldn't have a length of rope with two wrist loops set twelve inches apart inside, and the body work of other vans were rarely dented from the inside out.

Harvey studied the rope from afar and a sequence of events began to form in his imagination. The loops were too small for Julios' hands to pass through, but Donny's would have fit just fine. He considered the thought. There was no way any sane man would untie Julios for any reason other than to set him free, which meant that they had untied Donny, knowing he was too weak and pathetic to give them any trouble, and they had kept Julios tied up because they feared him. The thought also supported Harvey's theory on the number of men he was up against. If there were any more than four of five men, they would have kept both prisoners tied up.

He considered Julios in that space liked a caged animal and he ran his finger along the dents in the van's bodywork. Julios' large boots kicking out at everything and anything.

He watched the men for a while, and over the course of five to ten minutes, he was able to ascertain a clear hierarchy within the Regency Bags Limited workforce. The man on the forklift was the eldest of the three men, but the man in charge was the eldest of the two in the doorway. He barked orders in what Harvey imagined to be Punjabi but could just as easily have been Urdu or some other variation. Language wasn't Harvey's strong point, but he had a keen eye and sharp reactions, which made up for any flaws in his communication skills.

All three of the men wore a loose form of kurta, a long-sleeve shirt that hung below the waist with loose matching bottoms. On their feet, they wore sandals. It was the type of workplace where health and safety officers would run their pens dry with red crosses and reports, but the Old Ford Industrial Park in Bow was not the type of place a health and safety executive would venture alone.

Within that same square mile, Harvey could name half a dozen yardies who would crush an old junker with no questions asked and without even looking in the boot. The old warehouses that ran alongside the canal were rarely used for anything above board. It was just one of those places that uniforms turned a blind eye to. It was safe to say that the Old Ford Industrial Park was a great place for Regency Bags Limited to get away with whatever it tried to do.

It was also safe to say that there were more than three men in the unit. The flash Mercedes saloon and the brand-new Toyota were pricey toys more suited to executives than men who ran workshop floors and drove forklifts.

Harvey peered across the forecourt, which was littered with boxes and pallets, and into the sliding shutter doors. It was dark inside and he could see little except for rows and rows of boxes stacked as high as the ceiling. A mezzanine floor ran around the edge of the inside and Harvey heard footsteps walk across it. A door opened and a man's shape appeared in the light, then disappeared when the door closed.

Even from a distance, Harvey could see the man was not a manual worker. His hair was slicked to one side with grease and he wore a kurta like an ankle-length shirt.

It was a safe gamble that the man wearing the kurta drove the Mercedes, leaving the manual workers to drive the Toyota and the van.

Harvey reached through the van to the front passenger door and unlocked it. Then, keeping his eyes on the three workers, he opened the passenger door, leaned in, and released the handbrake. It took a little persuasion to start the van rolling, but it rolled and gained momentum on the shallow incline.

Harvey waited behind the pallets.

Three, two, one.

"Ruko, ruko," one of the men called, then the other two joined in. Their sandals slapped on the concrete and they passed Harvey together with all the grace of three lead donkeys in the Grand National. They pushed and shoved and shouted for the van to stop and didn't look back.

Harvey strolled into the unit. He pulled the sliding shutter closed and locked it, fished his knife from inside his jacket, then stood in silence. If the man in the mezzanine office had heard the others, he would be out in less than a minute.

He wasn't. Harvey moved on. There were rows and rows of boxes piled high in what seemed like no order at all. Among the dirty smell of old dust, Harvey could smell the leather bags. It reminded him of John's office. All it needed was a crystal decanter full of brandy and a tumbler set on a silver tray and he could have been at home.

He glanced up at the office and all around. There was no way even five men could have manhandled Julios up the stairs, conscious or unconscious. There was only one other door downstairs. It was in the far corner of the space and there was a pathway of worn floor paint indicating it was used with some regularity.

Harvey had timed it well. He pushed open the door just as the men outside began to bang on the shutter doors. There was shouting in the main room behind him. In a few moments, they would burst through the door. Harvey had a few seconds to search for Julios and Donny.

The thing with warehouses is that, large

as they are, there are usually very few places to hide. Businesses need large open spaces.

The back room was small, and the breeze block walls were lined with shelves.

There was no exit and there was no sign of Donny or Julios.

He listened at the door. The space beyond was silent. There were no footsteps or men's voices. He placed the flat of his hand against the wood and pressed his ear to the door.

There was nothing.

Then there was everything.

The door came crashing inward, forcing Harvey back. He fell against the shelves and as he picked himself up, the youngest two men rushed inside while the man in charge shouted orders that Harvey did not understand.

They cornered Harvey, edging closer with arms ready to grip and lash out, and the youngest, a lean and tall man who seemed yet to grow into his body, edged closer. Harvey pulled a small box from the shelf and threw it at him, then another. The man in charge rushed in and he and Harvey fell to the floor in a grappling mass of arms and legs. He was strong for his size and he pinned Harvey down, forcing his face onto the hard concrete with the palm of his sweaty hand.

Harvey reached up, flailing for something to hit him with, but found nothing. He gripped the metal shelves to haul himself up and felt them topple then settle.

The man on top of him shouted something to his younger friend, who kneeled and rummaged through Harvey's pockets.

Then the shouting began. Through the man's fingers, Harvey saw the youngest holding the business card he had found in the BMW. They shouted at him, but Harvey didn't understand. The man on top released his hand and bent, so that his face was inches from Harvey's. The smell of spiced food and foul breath turned Harvey's stomach.

The man growled an unfathomable, spite-filled curse with his lip curled like the hood of a cobra, and Harvey pulled. He pulled with everything he had on the upright of the steel shelves. They swayed, and the youngest man shouted. Harvey pulled harder, rocking the tall shelves, and the man on top hit him with everything he had.

But it wasn't enough.

The shelves toppled and seemed to hang on the very edge of their balance. The man on top forced Harvey's face back to the floor, but the move only strengthened Harvey's resolve. He pulled one last time, using the man's weight against him.

And there was a silence.

The man's eyes widened in disbelief. Boxes fell from the very top, crashing onto the floor around them. The youngest of the men tried to run but the shelves had already gained momentum. They crashed into his skull with a sickening thud and he was out cold before the weight of the shelves crushed him.

Boxes fell all around, glass smashed, and the men called out in fear.

The man on top of Harvey was ripped from where he knelt, and his body lay twisted beneath the mass of steel. He groaned as the chaos settled, his fingers outstretched, reaching for the business card that lay on the floor.

Harvey was balled in the void of the first shelf. If he had been lying just a few inches to his right, the shelves would have crushed his skull.

He lay there in silence, his eyes closed,

and he felt the space around him, taking the moment to consider his options and to think of Julios and Donny. The thought was enough to spur him on.

He pulled himself up and stepped out of the mess and debris, leaving the two men pinned by the weight of the shelves.

At the door, he looked back at them and wondered when and where they saw Julios and Donny last. He wondered what secrets they held. But they spoke no English. Any attempts to force them to talk would be futile. He was about to leave when he gave the room a final look.

He remembered the sound of broken glass when the shelves fell. A pool of amber liquid had collected on the screed floor and was making its way toward a small, circular drain.

Harvey kicked a box and broken glass rattled. He tore it open and emptied the ruined contents on the floor. Glass fell and liquid dripped, but as the sodden box crumpled in Harvey's hands, a slip of blue, dot-matrix paper fell to his feet.

CHAPTER THIRTY-ONE

There were fewer stares when Myers returned to the office, but more smirks and hushed laughter. It was reassuring to see that, for once, Carver wasn't leading the cruel jokes. Myers wouldn't rise to it.

Nothing mattered.

He threw his light jacket over the back of his chair and plopped down with a sigh. He let his head fall back and tried to focus on something useful.

But nothing seemed important.

There was nothing more important than Harriet. It was plain and simple. The wife of a villain had been shot and, as Carver had said, that was the life they led. Even if they didn't deserve it, sooner or later, they would end up doing something to deserve it.

Jennifer Standing was alive. Faisal Hussein was dead. Who cared who killed him? He deserved it too.

The girl whose death had upset Carver, well, that wasn't his case. It was sad, but there was a separation there. It wasn't his responsibility to close the case. Not anymore. He glanced across the office at Carver, who seemed to take long bouts of staring between writing a report and making notes, or whatever he was doing.

And the hidden laughter and snide comments from the rest of the team?

They can go to hell.

Most importantly of all, Harriet was alive. It hadn't been her bag in the evidence room, and she was safe at home with Alison and a bunch of other people.

It was just a ripple.

But there was one stare he felt. It was almost laughable. He closed his eyes, gave a quiet sigh, and spoke.

"What is it, Fox?"

She hesitated, and in that tiny space of

time, he guessed there were two sentences on her lips. The first of which would be to ask him if he was okay. But it was both surprising and relieving that she chose the second.

"I traced the shipping container. I was right."

She could have the little moment of glory. It wasn't like she was a bitch. She didn't have a mean streak. In fact, if anything, she was too far the other way.

"Well done," he said.

A little motivation would go a long way. He slipped down in his chair and opened his eyes to stare at the Styrofoam ceiling tiles. The pattern was generic, much like any office space might have. But the deeper he stared, the more hypnotic it became. There seemed to be a pattern within a pattern. It was like time and space had been printed on a ceiling tile. A swirl of heavy and light dots swirled and met with another. But it was the spaces in-between that were of interest. He'd heard it said that music was less about the notes and more about the spaces between them. It was the same for art. The beauty was in the empty space.

"Sir?"

Sadly, reality was more about the facts.

"Do you enjoy the research, Fox?"

"I enjoy challenges, sir. I always have."

"Good career choice. If you're looking for a challenge, or fifty, you're in the right place."

"It's why I'm here."

"Well," he said, as he heaved himself up in his chair and pulled the chair closer to the desk. "Don't let the challenges become about anything other than the case. That's my advice. Take it as you will."

"Sir, do you mind me asking you something?"

What would it be? Would she ask the question that she chose not to a while ago? Would she ask about his life? Why he chose a career that would kill him before he retired? He could answer the latter. The former, well, he'd need the shrink to help him with that.

He looked up at her, and for the first time, he saw something in her. There was a resilience in those brown eyes. He hadn't been friendly with her. He hadn't been rude, but he certainly hadn't made an effort to make her feel welcome. Not like he probably should have. Perhaps she had grown hardened to people ignoring her or pushing her away as a result of her incessant desire to stand too close, to talk too much, and to be a part of something.

Maybe that was it? Myers had forged a career on the back of his ability to put himself in other people's shoes. But those other people were usually either victims or suspects. He never empathised with his colleagues. Not once had he ever considered what they were going through, how they felt, or what was driving them. It was only a chance meeting with Carver that had given him food for thought, an insight into the man's mind.

Just a ripple.

She was new in town, a country girl at heart, although she referred to Bristol as being her home city. Myers would bet all the money in his wallet that she was a country girl who maybe went to college in Bristol. It would have been the first time she had strayed away from home. He saw flashes of bright adolescent girls making her life a misery. She would have been singled out. Eating alone during breaks. Girls would turn their backs on her as she passed them. But she would have been the first to submit her coursework, or papers, or whatever they were called in college.

He considered her face. She was pretty. Her figure was great, and she would look great in a little dress. She had a chest, but not too much, and beneath the immaculate blouses she wore, her waist would be firm and lithe.

"Sir?" It was the former of the questions. "Are you okay, sir?"

He raised an eyebrow in question, still imagining her body. There was a good chance she was still a virgin. College boys would have tried and, since then, young men would have failed to impress the hardened, isolated mind enough for her to let their hands get anywhere near her.

"You seem distracted."

He sighed.

"I'm thinking, Fox. It's what we do here. Think. You can't solve a crime by just talking about it."

Her silence was enough for Myers to regret his tone just sufficiently enough to pull him away from his mental image of her taut, little waist. It was probably for the best. She was probably less than ten years older than Harriet.

"If you enjoy challenges, missy, see if you can find me the details of a..." He flipped open his little notepad. "Regency Leather Goods Limited. They sell bags."

She noted the name of the company down, enthused by the fresh challenge and not in the slightest discouraged by Myers' tone. A tough girl like her might do well in the force if she could learn to distance herself.

She finished writing and collected a bunch of papers off her desk.

"Now..." she began, and adopted the look of a know-it-all secretary telling her boss what appointments he had that day.

Myers' opinion of her, which had been swelling the more he empathised, sank a little.

She had a lot to learn about being personable.

"About that container, sir."

"Go on then. Thrill me with your intellect, Fox." He rested his elbow on his desk, preparing to engage with her, but his face slipped into his hands and stared at the blank desk space between his fingers.

"It was delivered to a car garage in Canning Town. Looks like some kind of repair shop."

"Superb," said Myers, unable to conceal the sarcasm in his tone.

"Using John Cartwright's import license."

"Again, that is truly outstanding."

"You don't find that interesting?"

"What? That a shipping container was delivered to a car garage? No, Fox. Unless you can tell me that particular shipping container was full of something interesting."

"I checked the records. I went back nearly three years."

His flippancy raised its head, but Myers withheld it. She was a distraction, at least. "Go on."

"Donald Cartwright imports anywhere between fifteen and twenty-two containers per year, all to serve his father's businesses."

"Seems fair, considering the amount of bars and clubs he owns. If he can save a few thousand by importing the booze, that makes good business sense."

"This particular delivery is the only one that hasn't been countersigned by Sergio and it's the only one that was delivered to a different address. Couple that with the hand-written container number, the larger volume of whiskey, and the balled-up shipping note we found in the bin…"

"*You* found, Fox," said Myers, offering her a little taste of success. "You found the shipping note."

"I think all that makes for an interesting find, sir."

He thought about the facts and whether she was reading too much into it. But, as usual, she had more to say.

"I have a theory."

"A theory? Already?"

"Donald Cartwright's wife was killed. But it was a mistake. It was supposed to be him that died."

"Plausible," said Myers. "Go on."

"He used his father's import license to do his own business. You saw him. He was cagey. He was defensive. He was using his father's license to undercut him."

"Or he was using his father's license to import something other than alcohol."

"I think he's made enemies, sir. I think whatever was in that container fell into the wrong hands."

Myers had to admit, it was the best idea they'd had.

"Or maybe whatever was in that container didn't fall into the right hands?" said Myers, turning her theory on its head in the most agreeable manner he was in the mood for.

"I think Donald Cartwright is in serious danger, sir."

CHAPTER THIRTY-TWO

The upstairs warehouse office was empty. The Mercedes was gone. Whoever was running the show was a coward.

For the second time that day, Harvey closed a door with little concern for the men he left behind or the destruction his presence had caused. The Old Ford Industrial Park was one of those parts of East London that people were blind to. Loose lips did more than just sink ships. Loose lips broke bones and destroyed lives. Nobody tolerated a grass and, as a result, nobody would be seen talking to the police.

So when Harvey walked past the neighbouring unit to his bike, despite there being a man outside talking to a delivery driver and despite there being several people in the distance scratching their heads over the van that had rolled into a few parked cars, nobody saw him.

He rode away with his helmet visor down and accelerated out of the park to re-join the A12 dual carriageway toward Canning Town. He maintained the speed limit, aware of his bloodied knuckles and swollen lip. A stop by the police could be catastrophic and, in Julios' words, it would be the mistake of a lesser man.

The trick to being invisible was to blend into the surroundings. To ride fast would turn heads. To change lanes without warning would flare tempers. And to break the rules of the road would be like placing himself under a spotlight. But when an old Toyota overtook him and swerved into his path, Harvey had little opportunity to do anything but shine that spotlight.

The car came from his right and forced Harvey into the next lane where he had to brake to avoid hitting the back of a large articulated lorry. He moved across one more lane and onto the shoulder, and tiny stones seemed to jump up from beneath his front wheel and gouge his legs. He shot past the lorry and moved in front just one lane away from the Toyota. The lorry driver sounded his horn as the driver of the car peered at him through the passenger window and veered his way. The front wing caught Harvey's leg and sent him into a wobble, from which he recovered just in time to swerve around another slow truck.

The lorry slowed, leaving just Harvey and the car. They were neck and neck. The road ahead was clear save for a few other cars faster than themselves, and the traffic behind them had seen what was happening and had all slowed.

Harvey chanced a glance at the driver. It was the man in charge. The man who had pinned Harvey down. His lip was curled in the cobra-like grimace of hatred and he pulled at the Toyota's steering wheel to close the gap.

Tired of being on the defending side, Harvey swerved across the lanes until he was just a metre away. He accelerated when the man swerved his way and he braked to retake his place beside him, toying with the car's lack of agility and coaxing the man into a rage. Harvey knew the roads like he knew the or-chard on John's estate. He was familiar with the bends and knew the sweeping curve of the next junction.

He also knew that a motorcycle stood little chance against a car. The only advantage he had was speed. He took the junction, teasing the driver to follow and staying just far enough in front to be out of reach. He slowed to take a slip road and the car followed with its front bumper grazing Harvey's rear wheel. The move off-balanced Harvey and he fought to stay upright, then accelerated away. He leaned through a bend and joined the road for the Royal Docks with a screech of tyres not far behind.

The road was empty, and the Toyota's engine roared behind him. The dockside was paved and retained the tall cranes that had once loaded ships destined for lands far away. Small, immature trees had been planted in two long lines with a clear run between them of empty pedestrianised space. The Toyota bounced onto the pavement and the driver floored the accelerator. Harvey's bike was fast, but the Toyota wasn't far behind.

He increased the speed, knowing that the dockside would end. He allowed the driver to pull alongside and he glanced down at the speedometer.

Seventy-five miles per hour.

He accelerated again and the driver did the same, matching him move for move.

Eighty-five miles per hour.

The window rolled down, and just as Harvey glanced across, he saw the dull, black muzzle of a handgun rise into view.

A single shot glanced off the petrol tank between his legs. He increased the speed a little more, but the long stretch of pavement was running out.

The second shot passed beneath his arms. The driver was grinning as he took aim for the third, which tore through Harvey's jacket seconds later, missing his chest by inches.

Harvey slammed on the brakes and the rear end fish-tailed out from beneath him. He rolled to one side, brought his arms into his body, and the friction of the concrete caught him. He rolled too many times to tell, then slid on his side, letting his thick, leather jacket take the brunt of the grinding concrete.

He came to a stop forty feet from his bike, just in time to see the Toyota crash through the waterside barrier. He heard the futile rev of the engine and saw the brake lights flash on with little effect. Then the car splashed down into the water below.

Harvey lay still. He let his heart settle and moved his limbs and digits. Nothing was broken. His hip was grazed, and his jacket was hot from the friction.

Somewhere in the distance, Harvey heard the sound of the first sirens, but he needed a minute. He lay there and thought of Donny and why the men would want him. What had he done? It had something to do with the contents of the container. It had something to do with the boxes of alcohol. And it had something to do with the owner of a car garage whose address was on the delivery note, which was just a few streets away.

The time for trying to understand it was over. He'd faced a mad man in the safe house, a bunch of men in the warehouse, and a lunatic in the Toyota. He needed to stop it. He needed to find Donny and Julios.

He got to his feet and limped the first few steps until his body adapted to the sores and scrapes. He heaved his motorcycle upright and turned the key. With a little throttle, it started on the second try.

The sirens were edging closer, and on the far side of the water, Harvey saw the flashing blues racing along the road that ran parallel to the docks.

He waited for a full minute and no man surfaced in the water. The car had filled through the open window, upturned, and disappeared into the dark water leaving only a ripple on the surface in its wake.

The ride out of the docks was calmer and shorter. The garage was just a few streets away and he navigated the back streets, adopting his role of a courier looking for a delivery.

But beneath the leather jacket were bloodied scrapes. Beneath his cargo pants, his skin was red raw. And beneath his darkened visor, his face was resolute.

He stopped the bike at a T-junction just as three police cars raced past from right to left. He glanced right and saw the name of the garage printed in large, yellow letters on a flaking, wooden signboard.

And he saw a familiar man open a car door and peer into the premises.

CHAPTER THIRTY-THREE

The back streets of Canning Town where Myers had parked his car were the wild west of London. To his left was a row of shady garages built into the elevated section of road that crossed the docks. There was a boxing gym and a pub that had appeared to be closed as long as Myers could remember. Its boarded-up windows and graffitied walls offered little in the way of a nice, quiet drink.

But Myers knew it to be a resource. Deals were struck in the corner booths, allies and enemies were made with equal regularity, and all behind the closed doors of a seedy, little pub that nobody knew about.

The other businesses around it basked in

the shade of the same crooked arm. Back in the eighties, the garages would have been cutting and shutting stolen and damaged cars into the early hours of the morning, and car identification numbers would have been ground away in a shower of sparks. Dodgy vans would have been loaded with the scrap parts and they would have been delivered to a no-questions-asked scrap merchant a few blocks away.

Men thrived in back streets like the one Myers was parked in. Men who were born and raised there could walk the streets and bathe in that shadow carefree. Even men like Donald Cartwright who thrived under the wing of his villainous father could walk carefree in the name of Cartwright. His father was a face, and lesser men would bend over backwards for a face.

But men like Myers were sniffed out in a heartbeat. Men like Myers were the black sheep. Men like Myers were outcasts.

Three police cars raced past with their sirens blaring and lights flashing. The noise faded and Myers climbed from his car. He looked up at the signboard. It was faded and the paint was flaking. There was a small forecourt outside the old garage with enough space to fit four or five cars. Parked in the corner were two old wrecks that looked as if they hadn't moved since the eighties. The tyres were flat and brittle. The windows were smashed, and the paintwork was all but rusted away, leaving just very faint reminders that the car on the right had been a Blue Ford and the car on the left had been a red BMW.

He glanced back at his car and checked his pocket for the keys then ventured further. It was unlocked, but nobody would steal an old wreck like that. Besides, without a warrant, he'd just be a few minutes.

Three large, round industrial bins were in the opposite corner filled to their brims with folded cardboard and balls of plastic wrapping that Myers thought might have been wrapped around a pallet to keep the contents from falling off.

There was a single door to the right and a large concertina door to the left. Myers presumed that the larger of the doors was to allow vehicles in for repairs and the smaller door was for human access.

Both doors were shut, but the security shutter on the smaller door was raised. Even a local man wouldn't leave his premises vulnerable to break-ins. Myers tried the door and found it unlocked. There was a small office on the right, or at least the remains of one. The desk had been upturned and there was paperwork scattered across the floor.

From where he was standing, the forms appeared to be motor test certificates. The drawers of the desk had been pulled out and the contents had been tipped on top of the paperwork: old cigarette packets, disposable lighters, pens, and a whole host of random objects that Myers himself might find in his own drawer at home.

The door was open but intact, meaning that whoever had made the mess hadn't needed to break in and there was no empty space that looked like it may have, at some point, housed a safe. Myers himself knew that the blank motor certificate pads were worth a large amount of money to a small-time villain, but they hadn't been taken, which meant that either the culprit hadn't known the value, or they were looking for something else. Something bigger. Something with a pulse, maybe?

He moved along the hallway to a final door that opened out into the workshop.

There was no sunlight, but the florescent lights were on. A yellow hydraulic car ramp was in the centre of the space, the far wall was racked out with what looked like hundreds of car tyres of all descriptions, and behind the wall to his right was a small lavatory. The door to the lavatory was missing and Myers screwed his face up at the sight of the mess inside. The place didn't need cleaning. It needed burning. There were a few random, oil-stained chairs dotted about and a collection of torn car magazines. It was the poorest attempt at a customer waiting area Myers had ever seen.

Along the back wall, however, was a large workbench and two tall tool chests. They were red with silver handles and covered in stickers. On the wall above the bench, which was covered in spare parts, drinks cans, and oily rags, were several calendars which fell into the category of cliché garage topless pictures.

To the right of the workbench was a fire escape door with a long, silver push-handle and Myers thought that even hovels like the garage needed to have some form of emergency exit. He wondered what he'd find out there, then shuddered at the thought.

He stepped into the space and felt a strange guilty pang of combined intrusion and fear. There were no cars in the garage, but the air retained a thick, oily smell borne of years of spilt oil and vapour seeping into the pores of every surface in there. He pulled his jacket in tight around him. It seemed as if every surface was coated in a thick layer of grease.

But there was something else in that smell. Something that had combined with the oil to form a sickly aroma. He knew the smell, but it had been tainted by the oil and he couldn't put his finger on it.

There was something not quite right about the place. It was the first time he actually wished Fox had been there with him. Another pair of eyes would be useful, and despite her annoying traits, she was actually turning out to be a smart thinker. It was she who had seen the slight variation in the forms. It was she who had known the format of the numbers reflected a container number. And it was she who had theorised that Donald Cartwright could be in trouble.

The fact that Donald Cartwright was not

in the garage did not mean he wasn't in trouble. In fact, it only gave weight to the theory. Something had happened in the garage. And Myers was sure the two were connected.

Donald Cartwright's shipment had been delivered to the garage, the only delivery for years that hadn't been delivered to his father's warehouse. The form was different and the adviser, Sergio, hadn't countersigned it. The office space looked as if it had been turned upside down and the place was empty. And now Myers was in the workshop, he looked at the space. Nearly every inch of floor was covered in something. There were car parts and more crumpled paperwork, tools, and overalls. To his left was a huge chest of small drawers and each of them had been pulled out and had their contents tipped onto the floor. Shiny nuts of all sizes, screws of various lengths and thicknesses, and pop rivets were scattered everywhere, and the empty drawers had been tossed on top of the mess.

He ventured further into the space, but the feeling of intrusion and fear gripped his stomach. He knew the type of men who owned places like the garage, and he knew that catching them by surprise might not be pleasant.

The nuts and screws on the floor crunched underfoot but there was no way to walk around them. He took another step and leaned forward to peer around the corner. He caught sight of a large tarpaulin. It was oil-soaked with grease spots dotted about like the skin of a teenage boy. Myers checked behind him and glanced back at the little, single door before he committed and ventured around the corner. If somebody returned now, there would be no arguing that he was looking for somebody. He was intruding without a warrant.

Something crunched under his foot. It wasn't nuts or screws. He knew the gravelly sound. Stuck to the sole of his shoes were tiny shards of broken glass and, when he raised it, tiny droplets of liquid fell. He was standing in a puddle. A huge puddle that, only then did he realise, stretched across the entire width of the workshop.

The pungent smell grew stronger and clung to the back of his throat, and he raised the corner of the tarp. There was no doubt what the smell was. It was sickly and he'd smelled it before a hundred times, just never mixed with the smell of grease and oil.

Beneath the corner of the tarp, he caught his first sight of a broken box. As he peeled it back, the smell greeted him like when a coroner unzips the body bag and the aroma seems to attack the senses.

There comes a point when a detective transitions from following up on a lead to being nosey. Myers was past that point. But when he pulled back the tarp and dragged it off the mess below, he moved from just being nosey into a full-on unwarranted investigation.

The stench found his nostrils like a swarm of angry wasps. Hundreds of broken bottles lay at his feet and the whiskey-and-oil-sodden tarp slipped from his fingers. The cardboard boxes that had once contained the bottles was mostly mulch or in the final stages of turning to mulch. A few of the bottles remained in-tact, but not many.

Myers picked one up. It certainly wasn't a single malt. And almost definitely wasn't the highest quality. The writing on the label was foreign but the brand name was in English.

Grasshopper Whiskey.

"Never heard of it," said Myers.

He was about to collect a second bottle from the mass of broken glass when the fire escape door squeaked open and a slice of light lit the cluttered floor in the far corner of the workshop.

He stopped.

A man was whistling the melody to an old tune Myers' mother used to listen to. He stepped into the garage, oblivious to Myers, and he put a bucket down on the cluttered workbench.

Myers moved his foot and the man froze at the sound of the broken glass. His head raised but he didn't turn.

"Detective Inspector Myers," said Myers. "Mind if I ask you a few questions?"

The man's head turned a fraction as if he was gauging the distance to the fire escape.

And he bolted.

CHAPTER THIRTY-FOUR

Only a fool would leave his car unlocked in the back streets of Canning Town. Harvey parked his motorcycle in the side street and was inside the policeman's old car in a heartbeat. Even if he hadn't seen the man's face, he would have known it was him by the way he walked with a curious disposition and drummed his fingers on his leg. The man's head seemed to have been at an angle when he read the garage sign and then again when he peered into the forecourt. The man was a nervous wreck.

But Harvey had seen his face from behind his own helmet visor. He had spent close to twenty-four hours in the same interview room, sometimes with the man's face inches from his own. He had smelled his breath, he had studied every crevice in his skin, and he had seen the misery in his eyes.

And Harvey remembered his name.

To find Detective Inspector Myers at the garage was not a coincidence. It meant that either Harvey was on the right track or both he and Myers were wrong. To see the man leave his car unlocked was a gift.

The glove compartment held a box of tissues and a fat, leather wallet stuffed full of the car's maintenance details and its warranty.

The pocket in the driver's door was of little interest too. There was a small rag and a bag of Murray Mints. Harvey recognised the smell from the man's breath. Some of the empty wrappers had been tossed into the pocket.

The back seat was clear save for an old tie. Harvey imagined him pulling it off after a bad day and tossing it into the back while he was driving.

He was about to get out of the car when a flash of blue caught his eye. Tucked down the side of the passenger seat was an A4 cardboard folder, the type that slotted neatly into a filing cabinet. Harvey checked the garage and listened. Nobody was coming.

The first page of the file was loose. It had been pulled from a notepad and kept in the folder, presumably as the man considered it to be important. The writing was messy, it had been rushed, and the collections of words were in patches across the page as if they were not connected. They were just thoughts. He studied the writing and made sense of them.

Louis Vuitton bags.

Regency Leather Goods Company.

Container number.

Miles Stein Auto Repairs.

He turned the page and found the yellow form with Sergio's handwriting at the top. The next page was blank, but after that, the folder became interesting.

The first page was a hit sheet on Faisal Hussein. It listed every one of his arrests and convictions and even detailed his release date. At the top right of the page, a mugshot was held in place with a paperclip.

He turned another page to find details of the crime scene, how he had died, and what evidence the police had. A suspect was mentioned but no name was given. The report said that the suspect had been released and it gave the date and time.

It was the next page that caught Harvey off-guard. Amir Farooqi. Found dead in his home. The report said that he had been tortured but the killer had left no prints. Every surface had been cleaned.

The next seven pages were reports of unsolved murders. Every one of the men had been made to suffer and then killed. Every one of them had a similar modus operandi.

And Harvey knew every single name in the folder. All except the last name. Rashid al Sheikh. There was a photo of an Asian man in a suit. But the report was brief. He had no convictions and held a good position in a public facing role. In place of the man's criminal record were the policeman's notes. He had linked Faisal Khan to Amir Farooqi somehow. And Farooqi had been linked to each of the others. There were arrows linking all of the names to Farooqi and one more linking Farooqi to Rashid Al Sheikh.

Harvey had limited means to identify the men he killed. The newspapers offered release dates with details of their previous crimes, and often when a new offender was caught, the local media would go wild. But the detective had means. He had all the power of the police behind him. Maybe they thought Harvey would go for Rashid Al Sheikh? Maybe they would lay a trap?

"He's building a case. He's tracking me."

The printout of Rashid al Sheikh's details were three pages long. According to the document, the man was a local businessman with his fingers in many pies. He reminded Harvey of John.

There was a short list of known activities. He had funded a local mosque and chaired meetings. He was a councillor for a local political party with links to names that even Harvey, who rarely read the national newspapers, had heard of. They were serious men. Powerful people.

Another police car rushed past and Harvey checked the garage gates and listened for Myers' footsteps.

He heard nothing, and he read on.

The total number of businesses that Sheikh was involved with was unknown. He was a silent party in many, and Harvey imagined that he leveraged his position and political connections to aid the success of his investments.

Sheikh was very much like John, except John would use the threat of brute force to aid his success in lieu of Sheikh's political connections.

Sheikh held the majority share of several known organisations, including a fabric company, an abattoir, and a transport company. The file listed other shareholders, each of whom had a strike beside their names. Sheikh's name was the only one to be circled over and over again.

Harvey imagined Myers circling his name at his desk. It was the type of thing a man does absentmindedly. A subconscious demonstration of hatred or obsession.

A few loose photos fell from the back of the file. They showed Rashid al Sheikh with a few other Asian men and one with a senior government official that Harvey recognised as the man behind the recent opening of the Millennium Dome.

He slammed the folder closed, then used the rag in the door pocket to wipe the surfaces down. Back at his bike, he put the folder in the back box and locked it. Then he pulled his helmet on. He sat on the bike considering what he'd just seen. Harvey had killed dozens of men. Most of them had been for John, but a good number had been of his own accord and the last six were all detailed in that folder.

But what did that have to do with Miles Stein?

It was often that an answer presented itself to Harvey. Usually, he had to work for his results. But the moment he was just about to turn the key in the ignition, he heard footsteps approaching. They were loud and fast. From around the corner in the direction of Miles Stein's garage, a man burst into view. He was running flat out, his face a picture of panic. He shot past Harvey without a glance and seconds later, Detective Inspector Myers followed. The detective eyed Harvey as he ran past. But the helmet visor was tinted. There was no way he could see through.

The two men disappeared around another corner into the warren of alleyways that connected the back streets and offered access to the rear of people's properties. Harvey had to admit, Myers was faster than he looked. He was giving the man a run for his money.

Harvey started the bike. He glanced once

in his mirror and pulled out onto the road. He glanced into Miles Stein's Auto Repairs but saw nothing and continued. He turned right into the next alleyway and gave a quick blast of acceleration then slowed.

It was seconds before the first man came around the corner and Harvey matched his speed. The man refused to look at him. He was breathless and fearful.

Harvey raised his visor and the man glanced across at him, a questioning look on his face.

"Get on," said Harvey.

CHAPTER THIRTY-FIVE

Myers kicked a garage door and the boom thundered along the alleyway and returned with a taunting echo. He doubled over to catch his breath and then straightened to see the bike disappear from view.

The garage door deserved another kick before he walked back to his car.

The journey home was a blur. He kept the stereo off and ran through the facts over and over. Donald Cartwright's new wife had been killed. A shipment of alcohol was imported but delivered to a random address. Clearly it wasn't intended for his father's pubs and clubs. Which meant that Donald

Cartwright had done a deal outside of the family business.

But why?

The alcohol had been delivered to a small garage in Canning Town and had been smashed up. He'd found a man at the scene, but he had run.

Why?

And who was the man on the motorbike?

He slammed the door to his apartment and tossed his keys onto the little table beside the door. They slid the length of the once polished surface and then dropped to the floor. Myers considered picking them up, then thought better of it.

It was usual for Myers at this point to open the fridge door, look at the fresh vegetables and cold meats he'd bought, then ignore them and opt for a microwave ready meal from the freezer.

But he did neither of those things. Instead, he poured himself a large scotch. He added a couple of ice cubes and leaned against the kitchen door frame staring at his small living room and pondering the broken shipment of whiskey.

The upturned office.

The demolished workshop.

Somebody was looking for something.

The TV was switched off, but he found himself staring at it anyway. The blank screen offered him a place of little distraction. Who would want to kill Donald Cartwright?

The first cold, hard truth of the matter was that John Cartwright hadn't got to where he was without upsetting a few people along the way.

The second cold, hard truth that struck Myers was something Carver had said.

"They all deserve it one way or another. But you'll never find out who pulled the trigger. Part of you doesn't care who pulled the trigger. They deserved it."

He exhaled, long and slow, through pursed lips and sank the remains of his drink, questioning why he was putting so much effort into a crime he would never solve. Nobody wanted him to solve it. The Cartwrights had made it clear they would deal with it themselves. The only reason he was on the case was...He stopped mid-thought and laughed. Just one sharp exhale that nobody heard but him.

"Allenby," he said, as he poured himself another drink. "You clever bitch."

He drank. He poured. And he drank one more.

"Well, if you wanted to keep me distracted, you should have just said."

Being off the case he'd been working on for months had been a welcome distraction, he had to admit. But nothing, not even the endless cycle of meaningless clues on a murder case, could stop the daydreams. Surely, she had known that. And it was Carver's voice again that rang true.

"How do you deal with it? The innocence."

Myers smiled to himself.

"You don't, Frank. You can never deal with it."

It was true. The faces of the young victims who hadn't deserved to die never left the minds of those who were unfortunate enough to see them. They weren't the faces of hardened men who, in Carver's own words, deserved to die. They were young girls, and boys too, who had fallen prey to the savage brutality of the sick and twisted.

He found himself sitting on the edge of

his bed. It hadn't been a conscious decision to leave the kitchen. It was an autopilot move made by his body while his mind contemplated the Standing case and the half a dozen more that preceded it.

Half a dozen girls who hadn't deserved a single thing but kindness and protection.

Allenby had said he was too close to the case. Maybe she was right? Maybe the men he'd seen had all deserved to die? Maybe he should take a leaf out of Carver's book and let whoever was killing them continue.

"It would be a damn sight easier," he said, and he finished the last of his drink.

He placed the glass down on the bedside table when the shrill bell in the old telephone began its song.

It would be Alison. He knew it would be. She would have waited until the evening when he got home so she could call up and berate him for turning up unannounced, for upsetting Harriet, and, more importantly, ruining her birthday.

He let the phone ring off but counted the rings.

Eight.

If she called again, she would wait longer.

It was exactly what she used to do when they were together. The first ring was a test call to see if he would dare to pick up. She would have more patience for the next call. But she would also have that annoying superior tone. The third call, if he answered, would be her venting her wrath. It would begin with, 'How dare you?' and it would end with a threat, 'If you ever want to see Harriet again...', and there would be many verbal missiles thrown his way in between, 'Do you know how you made me feel?' or, 'Do you understand the implications of your actions?'. That was always a good one. It always made him smile. Of course he understood the implications of his actions. He always understood the implications of his actions. Whether or not he gave a hoot about the implications or considered them of less value than the consequences of not doing the action in the first place was another question.

The phone rang a second time.

"Eight to beat, Alison."

He could picture her strutting around her brand-new kitchen with the cordless phone. She would, of course, insist on adding in audible effects to the berating. The subtle banging of saucepans on the stove was enough, in her opinion, to let him know that she was still a mother and had to look after their child.

Six rings.

But, hell, could she cook. It was one of things he'd loved about her in the first place. The way she could take a simple dish and turn it into something extraordinary. She would know which of the spices to use from the little pots inside the top-left kitchen cupboard. She would know which herbs to cut from her little herb garden that would bring out the flavours in the meat.

Seven rings.

She would even warm the plates, a simple thing many people overlooked in Myers' opinion. 'Hot food should be served on hot plates'. That's what she used to say. She would smile back then. She would smile and hum to herself as she danced from cooker to counter, working her magic.

But right then, with the phone wedged between her cheek and her shoulder, there would be no humming. Her rage would be building.

Eight rings.

He considered picking up the handset but thought better of it. The day had been hard enough.

Nine rings.

Maybe he should start by wishing her a happy birthday? Kill her with kindness, as they say.

There was no tenth ring.

Another day maybe?

He exhaled again, long and deep. He'd caught himself doing it more and more of late. It was something he'd seen people do as they sat opposite him in the interview room. It was something they did when they were tired of the questions, tired of his persistence. They just wanted to be left alone.

He knew how they felt. He wondered if he saw a suspect doing the same thing again in an interview room if he would empathise.

"Let's take five minutes, eh?"

Sadly, life didn't work like that. A five-minute break was five minutes they would have to conjure up another lie. He would be five minutes further from breaking them. Unless it was the silent man, the man who had not uttered a single word in an entire twenty-four-hour period. The man who had not even raised an eyebrow, altered his expression, or fidgeted in an entire day.

Myers hated the fact that the man had won. He hated the fact that he had helped Allenby push him further from the case. Yet, somehow, somewhere inside Myers, there was admiration for him. He had a resilience that, in the eyes of the law, held him innocent. Yet deep down, there was something much more there.

The phone rang for the third time.

One ring.

"Sod it."

He picked up the receiver.

"Alison, you have to stop this. You can't keep calling just to vent your frustrations at me."

"Sir?"

"Fox?"

With two women controlling every aspect of his life, Myers had little room for a third. Especially an annoying little know-it-all fresh from the countryside.

"You didn't come back to the station, sir."

"I, erm, had a late one at the garage."

"Miles Stein's, sir?"

"Yes. I haven't been back long." Myers

heard himself mumbling and doubted Fox understood a word of what he had said.

"Did you find anything? You didn't call in."

"No, I, erm...there wasn't much to see. I'll tell you about it in the morning. Good night, Fox."

"Wait, sir."

He heard her suck in a lungful of air in anticipation of his voice. He imagined her clinging to hopes that he'd show a little interest. He wished he could show interest. Maybe that was it? Maybe he just wasn't interested in the case. Carver's words had helped him resign himself to the fact that it was an unsolvable case and not worth the effort.

"What is it, Fox?"

"You asked for a name, sir. The man who runs Regency Leather Goods Limited."

He sighed, not wanting to even hear the name. He knew he would have to follow it up. She would have added it to the report already.

"Go on."

"Rashid Al Sheik, sir. He's a councillor for the Labour party in East London."

"Rashid Al Sheik? Are you sure?"

"Positive, sir. He's a silent partner of Regency. I requested his details from Companies House. Do you need his address?"

"No," said Myers, and he rallied with the name in his mind. "No, I know where he lives. Thank you, Fox."

CHAPTER THIRTY-SIX

The River Lea began in the calm and serene Chiltern Hills and wound its way across country into East London where it spilt its tainted and polluted burden into the River Thames. Harvey knew it to be tainted and polluted. He knew the names of at least three men whose rotting bodies poisoned the water.

And he knew the places on the riverside that were accessible and hidden.

Hackney Marshes was such a place.

He drew his motorcycle up beside a cluster of trees that wasn't thick enough to be a forest yet were numerous enough that only those on the river itself could see what he was about to do, and there wasn't a boat in sight.

"Off," he said, and he held his bike steady for the man to climb off.

"Oh God, thanks, fella," said the man, straightening out the stiffness of the ride from his back. He grinned. "They nearly had me then."

Harvey kicked down the bike stand and removed his helmet. He hung it from the handlebar and removed his gloves while the man spoke.

"What are we doing here?" he said. "You could have dropped me at the pub. I would have bought you a pint to say thanks."

Harvey punched the man square in the face and felt his nose break beneath his knuckles. The man doubled over and let the blood fill his hands. He stepped away from Harvey toward the riverside.

"What the bloody hell are you doing?"

Harvey hit him again and knocked him off balance. He stumbled backward and fell to the ground. Then, seeing Harvey's advance, he crawled away toward the water.

"Who are you?" he said, his voice rising in pitch. "What do you want? I haven't got anything. I haven't done anything."

Harvey dragged him to his feet and held his face close to his own.

"Donny Cartwright," he said. "Where is he?"

The man looked confused.

"Eh? Donny? How the bloody hell should I know?"

Harvey launched him backwards further and the man crawled to the water's edge.

"It's his wedding day," said the man. "I haven't seen him. I wasn't invited. Honest, you can check."

Harvey leaned over him and the man crawled back another metre until his hands found the shallow river edge.

"How do you know him?" asked Harvey.

But the man just stammered. Harvey took a single step into the shallow water and then dragged the man into the river. He tried to scramble to his feet, but in his panic, he fell again, and Harvey caught him by his throat. He pushed the man's face beneath the water and held him there. The man's arms and legs thrashed, and he fought against Harvey's hold until Harvey lifted him free and held his head up by his hair.

The man coughed up a mouthful of water

and mud streamed across his face. He fought
to regain his breath and then opened his eyes.

"How do you know, Donny?" said
Harvey.

The man lingered for a second too long
and Harvey plunged him back under. The
thrashing resumed, and then Harvey felt the
man tap him on the arms, as a wrestler might
tap out of a hold.

Harvey raised him up.

Once more, the man spat and coughed.
His eyes were red from fright and he clung to
Harvey's hands, squeezing them hard.

"Please," he said. "No more."

"Donny?"

"I work with him," said the man, and
coughed again. He took deep breaths and
seemed to calm down with each word he
spoke.

"You work for John Cartwright?"

"No. No, I don't," he said. "Me and
Donny, we're partners."

"Partners in what? Donny doesn't own a
garage."

"No, the garage is mine."

"You're Miles Stein?"

"Yes," said the man, nodding. "Donny and I went into business together."

"Doing what?"

The man paused and Harvey held him under for a few moments just to remind him that talking was a far better choice.

"Booze," he coughed when Harvey pulled him back up. He heaved and a sickly combination of mud and river water ran from his mouth and dribbled down his chin. "We import booze."

"Who for?"

Harvey prepared to dunk him again.

"No. No, I'll talk," he said.

Harvey waited.

"We only just started it. Donny met someone who said they needed alcohol on demand."

"On demand?"

"Yeah. To order. You know?"

"Not really."

"Unlicensed parties and that sort of thing. Private stuff. Wealthy blokes."

"So, Donny gets the booze. Where do you come in?"

"He needed somewhere to keep it."

"Why couldn't he keep it at the Cartwright warehouse?"

The man agonised over the answer. His mouth hung open ready to talk but his brain wouldn't allow the words to be spoken.

Until Harvey dunked him again.

"Drugs," he said when Harvey pulled him free of the murky water. "It wasn't just booze."

"Donny imported drugs?"

"Yeah. It was hidden in the cases. Donny said he knew a bloke on border force that could help us get it through."

"What drugs?"

"Cocaine. But listen, I just stored it. That's all I did. I didn't have anything to do with it."

"You said you were partners."

"Well, yeah, but..."

Harvey dunked him once then pulled him out before the thrashing began.

"I need the truth, Miles. Where are the drugs now?"

"I don't know. We had a break in."

Harvey dragged him up from the water and stared at the man eye to eye.

"Donny's wife was killed today. Now tell

me where the drugs are and who they were for. Nobody knows we're here, Miles."

It was Harvey's final words that tipped Miles over the edge. His face twisted as he fought back the tears and his bottom lip began to shudder. If it weren't for the river water, Harvey would have guessed he was wetting himself anyway.

"The drugs, Miles."

"We got rid of them," he said, and the honesty broke him. The relief of betraying Donny shattered any strength the man had left, and he flopped in Harvey's arms.

"Where?"

"Julia said something to Donny. I don't know what she said. But after that, Donny wanted to pull out of the deal. Honest, that's all I know. They broke into my garage and smashed everything, but Donny had already sold them to someone else. He said he didn't want to do business with them anymore." He clung to Harvey's hands. "Please, you have to believe me."

"Miles, Donny is gone. Someone has got him."

It was like time had been paused. Miles stared into space, his mouth ajar.

"I need to know who the drugs were meant for. I need names, Miles. I need them now."

"Sam," said Miles, as Harvey shook him to his senses. "I don't know the last name. Donny used to go there. That's where the deals were struck. Honest, I never went there."

"Where, Miles? I need answers."

"The Docklands. It's an apartment in the Docklands. One of those swanky ones that overlooks the river. I know the address."

CHAPTER THIRTY-SEVEN

Myers could smell the alcohol on his own breath, even with both the driver and passenger windows open. Fox hadn't had to give him the address of Rashid Al Sheikh; it was an address Myers had been to many times, but he had never once been invited inside.

Three times, Myers had submitted an application for a warrant, and three times, Allenby had denied the request, forcing Myers to work harder to get the proof he needed that Sheikh was involved somehow in the murder of those girls.

There had been six men killed over the course of a few months and all six of them had been on the sex offenders list and five of them had served time at Her Majesty's pleasure. But the connection didn't stop there. Every one of those men were connected to the untouchable Rashid Al Sheik.

Well, he wouldn't be untouchable for long.

He pulled his car into Vicarage Lane in Chigwell and slowed to a crawl. The house he was looking for was a gated property and had at least six or seven bedrooms. The lower half of the house was neat brickwork and the upper section was black, timber beams infilled with white painted render. It had class, of that Myers was sure. There were two black Range Rovers on the driveway and a smaller BMW that Myers knew belonged to Sheikh's wife. It was the dying hours of the daylight and a few of the lights were switched on inside.

Myers stopped the car beneath a tree and turned off the engine. He'd knocked before on many occasions, and each time, he had been sent away. To knock again would be pointless. But to catch Sheikh leaving or returning might give Myers the opportunity to rile the ostentatious prick enough for him to say something he'd regret.

The opportunity came sooner than Myers imagined.

"The rubbish is collected on Mondays, detective," said a voice. A familiar voice. "I wouldn't park there too long, or they might mistake your car for my recycling. Perhaps you should move along?"

Rashid Al Sheikh stepped into view wearing a trendy looking tracksuit and gleaming white trainers. He held an MP3 player and pulled the headphones from his ears, then wrapped the cord around the player while waiting for Myers to say something.

"Regency Leather Goods Limited," said Myers. "Do you know it?"

"I should do. I own it," he said. Then added, "Mostly."

"We found two of your bags, Mr Sheikh. Louis Vuitton rips offs."

"Good for you. Keep them. Maybe your daughter would like one for Christmas?"

He nearly told the man that she already had one, but that would only feed his ego.

"Is that what you came here to tell me, Detective Myers?" He laughed and made to walk back to his house.

"One of them was fourteen," said Myers. "Fourteen years old."

Sheikh opened his mouth to talk, but Myers had more to say.

"She was raped multiple times, Mr Sheikh, by multiple men."

"Raped?" He looked surprised. "How do you know she was raped? These white girls want more than children's dolls, Detective Myers. Perhaps she knew how to party."

"Charlene Briggs," said Myers. "Does the name ring any bells?"

He shook his head and offered his lower lip in denial.

"She was found dead a few weeks ago."

"Detective Myers, I don't know where you're going with this-"

"She didn't deserve that, Sheikh."

"Perhaps she made some bad decisions? You know these kids as well as I do. They think they know what's good for them." He stepped closer to the car and leaned on the door. "But they don't. They don't know any-thing, do they?"

"Amir Farooqi," said Myers, and stared dead ahead along the empty road of millionaires. He turned to stare up at Sheikh. "Does *that* name ring any bells?"

Sheikh was silent, his face expressionless.

"We found him in his home. His face had been burned off with a blow torch. In fact, the only way we knew it was him was because of the semen of his we found on his clothes," said Myers. "And on Charlene Briggs' body."

Sheikh met him eye to eye.

"It means nothing."

"What does? The semen or the name?"

"He was my cousin."

"We know."

"That doesn't mean he raped her."

"A fourteen-year-old?" said Myers. "A fourteen-year-old isn't old enough to have consensual sex. That can only mean one thing."

"Is that all you have to say?" said Sheikh, and once more, he made to head toward his house.

"Faisal Kahn," called Myers, enjoying the balance being in his own favour for once. "We found *him* pinned to a tree."

"The name isn't familiar."

"Oh, really? That's strange. Because he

worked for you. You gave him a job when he got out of prison, and his father, Mohamed Khan, is one of your best friends. I have some photos of you together. Would you like to see?" Myers fumbled blindly for his file, but Sheikh relented.

"So, I know his father," said Sheikh, and screwed his face up in dismissal. "That doesn't mean anything. Is this all you have, Detective Myers? Does this amount to anything?"

"I know you're involved."

"In what? If you can tell me what I'm involved in and you're right, I'm an honest man. I'll hold my hands up. But if you can't, Detective, then I suggest you leave and expect your pretty, little, white boss to tickle your pretty, little, white balls in the morning, because I'll make a complaint to people so high you'll be back walking the streets before Monday morning."

He wanted to say it. He wanted to blurt out that Sheikh was at the centre of it all. That it was his fault that the men had died. His fault that the girls had died, and that Jennifer Standing was scarred for life. That he'd pay. One way or another, Myers would make him pay.

But he had nothing. Nothing but a gut feeling that he'd been told a thousand times wasn't enough.

"I didn't think so," said Sheikh. "Now get out of my sight."

CHAPTER THIRTY-EIGHT

Three tall, glass towers dominated the London Docklands area. They were visual landmarks, icons of London, and the surrounding apartments housed the wealthy, and provided them with the shiny, glitzy lifestyle they sought.

The apartments were clean spaces with smooth, bright walls and crisp, shiny surfaces, and the surrounding waters reflected the image across its surface. Harvey had been to a few of them working for John and for all their lavish style, the apartments had felt like well-appointed, cold prison cells. They lacked the freedom of the outdoors, the green fields and forests, and the ability to step outside and breath the air.

The apartment building Miles Stein had divulged was on Westferry Road on the west side of the Isle of Dogs. There were three identical apartment blocks in a row. On one side of them was the road and the residential population of the island, and on the other was the River Thames.

Harvey passed the entrance to an underground car park and parked his bike between two cars outside the next apartment block. He stowed his helmet and removed his gloves, then made his way to Clover Court. The building was seven storeys of brickwork designed to be sympathetic to the old warehouse and dock building that had once been there. Only the south end of the building had two more levels and they were of glass and steel. It was a culmination of old and new.

Like Sergio's apartment building, the apartments were accessed via a card reader that all residents were provided. When activated, the card reader would release an electro-magnet at the top of the door and the door would open.

It wasn't the first time Harvey had encountered such a door system. He would often wait for somebody to enter or exit and to hold the door for him. However, his cargo pants and boots were still damp, and he could smell the river on himself. People would remember that smell should they be asked, should the situation develop into an event worthy of memories being recalled.

He ventured into the underground car park.

All security systems had flaws. The flaws were, Harvey found, typically design features such as enabling access in an emergency. An electro-magnet relied on a consistent electric current to maintain the connection. A card reader allowed a brief breaking of the current to disengage the lock long enough for somebody to enter or exit. Therefore, the key to accessing a building that relied on card reader access was to kill the electricity to the door.

Harvey found the electricity panel with other services including the dry-riser inlet and the fire alarms system on the wall two parking bays down from the underground doors to the basement. There were no markings to identify which of the fifty or so switches would isolate the doors, so Harvey flipped the master switch.

The lights went out, the hum of an extractor fan waned then silenced, and the electro-magnet above the door clicked off.

Harvey entered the building, pulled a fire extinguisher from the wall to hold the door, then returned to flip the switches back on. He returned the fire extinguisher and, save for a brief moment of darkness on basement one, nobody would be any wiser. The buildings had security cameras in place, but it was a well-known fact that men did not stare at monitors for twenty-four hours a day. The cameras were used, if ever, in retrospect of a crime.

Harvey could handle being seen in retrospect. It was a small price to pay. He chose to use the stairs to apartment 701. The apartment listings fixed to the wall in raised lettering displayed only two seventh-floor apartments. The ping of an arriving elevator would alert somebody.

On the seventh-floor landing, he stared through the fire escape window into the hallway. There were two doors, both of matching light oak and polished to a sheen that reflected the bright walls and artwork.

According to more raised lettering on the walls outside the apartment, 702 was to his right, and if he stood with his back to the wall and peered through at an angle, he could just make out half of the front door.

He looked through the window to the left, his hand poised on the handle. It was clear. He heard no voices and saw no movement, so he opened the door just as the elevator's digital ping sounded.

Harvey released the handle and pulled himself into the corner out of sight. A shadow passed by the window. Harvey waited for another, but none followed. He heard the faint ring of a doorbell and he peered right. The acute angle limited his view to the arm of a tall man who was waiting for a door to be opened.

He heard the click of the door and a woman's voice. It was stern and authoritative and spoke above the man when he tried to speak. But the distance and the heavy door muffled the conversation. Harvey pressed his face against the glass for a better view. The man was wearing a grey kurta and his slick, black hair and the intonation of his voice suggested he was of foreign origin.

The conversation became heated. He raised his voice, but Harvey could only make out a few words. He waved his arms, gesturing as he spoke, and Harvey caught a brief view of the woman. She wore expensive looking heels and a conservative, blue dress that was cut just above the knee. Her hips were narrow, and the cut of the dress concealed her ample chest. Long, brown hair hung across her shoulders, but Harvey could see no more. She turned and he watched her stride back into the apartment. The visitor held the door open and he cocked his head with interest as her hips swayed from side to side like the pendulum of a clock. He moved to one side and stepped into Harvey's view as she returned. And when she returned, she was joined by another woman.

The second woman's dress was cut far less conservatively. It was short enough to reveal her patterned stocking tops and a slice of bare, white flesh above. The top half revealed most of her small bust and her long, blonde hair reached her naval. But, once again, Harvey couldn't see her face. She stood with much

less confidence than her host. Her feet shuffled the way a schoolgirl's might in a display
of her insecurity. She folded her hands together in front of her and held her stylish bag
tightly.

The man and the host exchanged another
short burst of bitterness and then the three of
them walked to the lift and the door to 702
closed of its own accord.

Harvey didn't see the woman who had
answered the door. Nor did he catch a
glimpse of the man's face. His attention was
elsewhere. He was struck dumb by what
he saw.

The woman in the revealing dress with
the slice of white flesh topping tasteful yet
tantalising stocking tops wasn't a woman. It
was a young girl. Harvey's blood ran cold.

CHAPTER THIRTY-NINE

Getting into the office out of hours was a habit that Myers had broken only days after he had been made detective. It was only when he couldn't sleep or was well into a case that he spent any additional time there.

He wasn't into this case. He couldn't care less who had killed the newlywed Mrs Cartwright, and Carver's words had stripped any meaningful resolution from the killer he had spent months hunting. And he cared less about Donald Cartwright being in danger than he did about what films were showing at the weekend.

They all deserved it one way or another.

In fact, the only thing he really cared

about at that moment in time was seeing Rashid Al Sheikh behind bars. Not for the purposes of solving a crime, although the recognition would help his case with Allenby. But his reasons were far more personal. To stand in court and watch the smile fall from his smug face would be a highlight of Myers' career.

But for that to happen, Myers needed more on him. And to get more on him, Myers needed to be in the office while nobody was there.

He filled the coffee machine and hit the power button. The coffee would do him good and should he be found there, somehow the act of making coffee would add weight to the lies he would need to tell.

The police force was, in terms of security, on top of their game. Myers had sat in on briefings and lectures about how the digital data on suspects was gathered and stored. Although Myers didn't fully understand the ins and outs of what had been said, he understood the concepts. Cables connected the various police stations and the data was all stored in a data centre. The access to files was limited by rank, which meant that Allenby could access more data than Myers and Myers could access more data than Fox.

But as advanced as the security systems were, the transition to being fully paperless was a slow one, and that worked in Myers' favour. There were too many old dogs like him who preferred to use paper files that were then scanned and stored in digital format. Those digital files had to be stored somewhere, and as long as the individual knew where they were kept, the stripes on their shoulder played no part. The risk was the same for anyone in breach of the security policy.

The file store was located in a locker that was outside Allenby's office. Once per week, a contractor came and collected the files, and Myers had seen a hundred times Allenby fetching the key from her office and unlocking it for them. Then, when they were done, she would lock the locker and return the key to her office.

All Myers had to do was find where she hid the key. He made fresh coffee and let it percolate. Then he wandered over to the window to check the car park. There were a handful of cars all with the light bars and identification numbers on top. There was a riot van that was mainly used at weekends when drunken idiots needed a ride and a sticky, blue mattress to sleep on.

Myers' car was parked beside the duty officer's, who he knew to be in the evidence room, as the man had called out something about the late hour when Myers had entered.

He moved fast.

He opened Allenby's door and glanced around, half-expecting to see her waiting behind her desk with her feet up and her fingers linked like a Bond villain.

But the office was empty.

He tried the little monkey pot she kept on her desk but found only a handful of paperclips embedded into a ball of blue tack, some broken pencils, and used ballpoint pens. He glanced around the door. All clear.

He moved behind her desk and sat in her seat. In a childish whim, he had the urge to break wind in her chair, and somewhere inside, he smiled at the thought.

He tried her top drawer. It was stacked full of paperwork, but nothing of any significance. The forms and papers related to the office management more than any crimes or suspects, so he checked beneath the pile then closed the drawer.

The second drawer was locked.

He pulled hard on it, feeling for how sensitive the lock was, but nothing budged. In the end, it was an old trick he had learnt as a child that was the answer. The desks weren't designed for the police force. They were just standard desks that any office might have, only older and duller, in Myers' opinion. He opened the top drawer, and, with a little force, he was able to remove it, leaving the top of the locked drawer below exposed. And there, hanging on a small hook, were three keys. The first one was for Allenby's locker in the changing room. Myers would recognise one of those keys, with the square-shaped ring-hole, in the dark. The second was unmarked. But the third was clearly labelled 'Hard Copy Locker'. He remembered the term being used in a briefing. The digital files were soft copies and the paper files were hard copies. Hard copies were scanned and destroyed.

His hands were clammy and hot, and his heart was beating hard. For all Myers' inner thoughts and scalding mind, rarely had he ever actually gone out of his way to break the rules. If he were caught, there would be no talking his way of it.

He moved fast again, leaving the top drawer on Allenby's desk. The hard copy locker opened with ease, but the doors were made of aluminium and were loud when they opened. He was presented with three shelves, each of which stored three to four piles of paperwork eighteen inches high.

He began to rifle through them. He knew the file. It was blue with his doodles on the front. He checked every file on the top shelf and worked his way to the middle shelf. He was just halfway through when he heard a car door being closed outside. He considered going to the window to have a look, but he had found a system of searching and was moving fast.

It was the last file on the middle shelf that had doodles on. He ran to the window and looked down. Allenby's BMW was parked in her spot in the corner.

Damn it.

He ran back, pulled the file, and threw it onto his desk face down so the doodles weren't visible. He closed and locked the locker, ran to Allenby's office, and hung the key. He fought with the top drawer until it finally gave way and slid into its slot.

The office door banged closed.

He took a deep breath and left the little office, closing the door behind him as if he hadn't heard a thing.

"Myers?"

"Oh, there you are," he said, hearing the lie in his own voice. "I saw your car, but you weren't here."

"I've just arrived," she replied, and the distrust was clear. "What were you doing in my office?"

"Oh, like I said, I saw your car and just popped in to say hi."

"Right," she said.

"I've put the coffee on," he said, and then sat down at his desk, moving the file as if he was tidying up.

"I think we need to talk, Myers."

That was a new tone. There was something much more in what she had just said. Myers felt his heart jump into life.

"Sure. Here or..." He looked toward her office.

"I had a call an hour ago," she said.

Okay, so the chat had begun like a ball of snow at the top of a hill.

Myers said nothing. If it worked for the silent man, it would work for him.

"Rashid Al Sheikh."

She was waiting for him to speak or to defend himself. But he played the game, expressionless.

"You went to his house."

Sheikh was obviously hiding something if he made the call to Allenby.

"He's filing a complaint. It'll go above my head. I can't help you."

"I was just following up on-"

"You were harassing him. You were parked outside his house. Again."

Myers sucked in air and felt his chest swell beneath his shirt. He'd reacted. He was crap at the silent game. The snowball was picking up speed.

"Do you know what a harassment charge would do to your career?"

"It wasn't harassment."

"He's throwing in racism as well," said Allenby. "I won't let you bring me down. It's not just *your* career you're toying with, it's *mine* as well. If I'm seen to have condoned this type of behaviour, I'll be dragged into this. I warned you enough times, Myers."

"So, what was I supposed to do?" said Myers, his tone a little too brash. "Am I supposed to let him get away with it?"

"I'll remind you that I'm your superior, Detective Inspector Myers," said Allenby, and then she paused to let the air cool. "I know you've had it rough. Everyone knows. But I can't let this sort of behaviour carry on. You've been on the case for months and haven't got a single piece of evidence on the killer so you're looking to frame Sheikh. I know what you're doing. At this point, you're looking for a win. Any win. Your assignment was to track the killer, not harass government officials on a gut feeling that somehow they're involved."

"It wasn't harassment," he said, and his voice dropped. He knew what was coming.

"You were drunk," said Allenby. "You drove your car to his house and waited for him without talking to me. How does that make me look? I can't have my detectives sitting outside the house of a government official, drunk, on a whim and a prayer. I can smell it on you from here."

The snowball was out of control.

"Look, take a few days."

"I don't need a few days."

"Take a few days and spend some time with Harriet. Clear your head. There'll be an investigation if Rashid pursues the charge, in which case, I'll call you in for the interview."

"You're suspending me?" said Myers, but he could think of nothing to follow it.

Allenby stared at him as if she was analysing his expressions, his body language, and his emotions. But there was nothing he could do to emulate a calm man. He was raging inside.

"I'll call you in a day or so," she said, and she glanced at his desk then back at him. "Leave your files."

CHAPTER FORTY

The black Mercedes pulled out of the underground car park. It was the same black Mercedes he'd seen at the leather goods warehouse. Harvey watched through the first-floor window of the stairwell as it turned right. Then he ran.

If the car had turned left, it would be heading for the city. But it hadn't. It had turned right, which meant the driver was avoiding the one-way systems and security around Canary Wharf and was heading out of town.

He started his motorcycle and pulled on his helmet. He knew the route the car would take to leave the island, but he would have to ride fast to catch it to before it disappeared into the maze of East London and beyond.

The car would have to slow for the speed humps that plagued nearly every street on the island, but Harvey rode around them or between them. The driver would have to negotiate traffic lights and other drivers, which again, Harvey could drive around or circumnavigate.

He cut across the island, using the back streets to work his way around Millwall Dock, a large, man-made body of water that dominated the centre of the island. He came to a T-junction on the east side of the island and waited, wondering if he had been fast enough.

He didn't have to wait long for his answer. The black Mercedes rolled into view to his right and cruised along Manchester Road well within the speed limit. Three cars followed, each of them different and none of them opulent enough to be in the same party. They were just other road users stuck behind the slow Mercedes driver.

Harvey pulled out behind the last car. Three vehicles behind was a good distance from which to tail someone. The cars crossed the bridges and joined the large roundabout at

Blackwall. The summer sun was waning, and car headlights were on. Enough light remained for Harvey to keep well back and follow at a distance. They joined the A12 dual carriageway where lorries made tailing easier, but obscured Harvey's view. He remained in the left-hand slow lane watching the exits for the tell-tale, distinctive rear lights of the Mercedes. He saw them at the M11 exit and followed. But with no cars between them, the driver would easily identify the single headlight.

The car sped up.

Harvey followed suit.

They passed the speed limit of seventy miles per hour and the driver of the car weaved from lane to lane, meandering through the cars and using the power of the Mercedes V12 engine to his advantage. But there was no way of knowing if Harvey had been spotted. He hung back, allowing the distance to grow, and he saw the car leave the motorway at Chigwell. Harvey took the exit nearly thirty seconds later and turned off the headlight. He followed at a distance as the car passed through what used to be an old village but had developed into a thriving town. The car turned into Vicarage Lane, a road known for its affluence, demonstrated by expensive houses and a range of lavish vehicles.

It slowed then turned into the driveway of a large house. Harvey killed the engine and rolled to a stop a few hundred metres behind. The house was built to a classic Essex standard: old timbers with white render and neat brickwork with latticed windows. The entire property was ringed with wrought iron fencing and two pairs of electric double gates, one of which was closed. The other remained open.

He saw the driver emerge, unfold his huge frame from the car, and open the rear door. It was the younger of the females who climbed out first. Harvey was too far away, and the sun was too low for him to see any detail. But from her stance and posture, she seemed not to be afraid.

The older of the women followed. She let the driver close the door while she led the girl up the steps. Then she knocked and waited. She didn't look back or around her. She didn't even look back at the driver who had locked the car with a flash of lights and stood waiting to follow them inside.

The inside of the house was well-lit. Soft music came from one of the rooms. It wasn't the arrogant beat of modern music, but it was foreign to Harvey's ears. The door closed, cutting the music off, and Harvey moved forward for a better view. Opposite the house were fields with tall trees. It was the perfect house to watch, in Harvey's opinion. He jumped the ditch and waded through the long grass, then found cover behind a large oak with a fat trunk. From there, he surveyed the house.

The curtains downstairs were open, and he saw people inside moving around as if a party was in full flow. A window in the hallway gave him a commanding view of the stairwell. Two men wearing Asian clothing walked upstairs and then into a front bedroom. The curtains were closed but their silhouettes were clear. They made hand gestures as if they were in a heated debate. Then one turned to face the wall that was out of Harvey's view. He raised his hand above his head, and he struck out.

For a moment, Harvey doubted what he had seen, thinking it must have been a trick of the shadow. He watched and waited. The man stepped back and the second stepped forward. He too raised his hand, but instead of hitting out once, he struck out a few times, in a series of punches designed to maximise pain, each blow landing in the exact same spot as the last. Then he reached down and pulled the victim up with a handful of hair.

And Harvey knew.

He knew the shape of those feeble shoulders. He knew the weak chin and slender arms and he knew the way the victim held himself away from danger.

Like a coward.

Harvey jumped the ditch. He strode across the quiet lane and into the driveway. He knocked once, softly, to see if anyone was nearby. There was no answer. So, he stepped back and slammed the heel of his boot into the door, placing it beside the lock with maximum effect. The wood splintered and the door shot back, slamming against the wall.

Nobody ventured out to see what the commotion was about. Asian music filled the space. The quarter tones and metallic drums added confusion and the steady, incessant beat seemed to swell in his ears.

He moved up the stairs, checking behind him. There were raised voices upstairs. He pulled his knife from inside his jacket and, with his free hand, he nudged the bedroom door open.

The next few seconds were a blur. He stepped into the room. He froze at the sight of Donny and Julios tied to chairs in the corner, and Donny saw him. His eyes widened with hope then faded with despair. There was a rush of air and a grunt of exertion and Harvey turned too late. Something hard connected with his forehead and his world turned black.

CHAPTER FORTY-ONE

The ring of the doorbell was gentle and calm. Unlike Myers' racing pulse. He could feel his blood pressure rising, steady like the rising tide that licks the rocks before the angry waves crash against them.

There was a time when he could just open the door and be greeted by Alison. She would ask about his day and he would reply with anecdotes from the office, some of them fabricated to mask the loneliness. He would ask about her day and she would go into great detail about conversations she'd had with people he had never met, about topics that he neither knew about nor cared for. But he'd nod, smile, and tell her what she wanted to hear.

The door opened and Alison looked down at him. He held out the flowers he'd bought for her but couldn't bring himself to smile.

"Peace offering," he said. "Happy birthday, Alison."

She glanced up the street out of habit more than concern, then opened the door fully and stood back.

"Come through," she said, and walked to the kitchen.

All the things Myers hated about divorce and separation, he could detail in a comprehensive list. He could even order them from most annoying to mildly upsetting. Being asked to 'come through' in the home he'd paid for and had once loved was up there at around number seven. Maybe eight.

"Tea, coffee?" she asked. "Something stronger?"

"Coffee, please."

He wondered if she remembered how he liked his coffee. Or if she would make it another way just to displease him, to ruin his pleasure. She set the pot and hit the button for the percolator to do its thing, then pulled open a drawer and found some scissors.

"Where's..." Myers could remember the name of her new man. The man who saw her naked. The man who touched her body. And the man with whom she shared her deepest thoughts. But he couldn't bring himself to say it.

"Darren?" she prompted.

He nodded. "Sorry."

"He's taking a few of our friends home. Some people had a few too much to drink."

It was only then that Myers noticed the dirty wine glasses beside the sink. A few of the rims bore lipstick stains and among them were tall glasses with decaying slices of lemon curled up at the bottom.

"A few too many G and Ts?"

"Too many for some," she replied, and cut a diagonal line across one of the flower stems. "Not enough for others."

"I hope I didn't spoil your party."

"No, but your presence didn't go unnoticed." She cut another stem. "Raised a few eyebrows. Prompted some unwanted questions."

Snip.

He nodded.

"That was never my intention. I had actually forgot..."

He stopped himself from saying it, but he'd said too much.

"I can get you a spade from the shed, if you like?" she said. "You can dig yourself a deeper hole."

Snip.

"Do I need a spade?" he said, and he offered a tight-lipped smile that wasn't a smile.

"What is it you want, Matthew? Why are you really here?"

"To say sorry. To see you. To see Harriet."

Snip.

"A bunch of flowers from a petrol station doesn't really say sorry. Not in my books anyway. You of all people should know that."

"The flowers aren't the apology."

"So they're my birthday gift? Are you sure you don't want that spade?"

Snip.

"I've been suspended."

She softened. Her shoulders dropped and she adopted that sympathetic expression with her head cocked to one side that she had always done.

"Oh, Matthew-"

"I deserve it."

She stared at him from across the kitchen work surface.

"You're owning up to your own mistakes now?"

"Allenby said I should spend more time with Harriet. Sort myself out. You know?"

"Did Allenby say to come at eleven p.m. uninvited and with a cheap bunch of flowers?"

"I'm persistent. Too persistent."

"Like a dog with a bone," she said.

"That's why you married me, wasn't it?"

"Because you wouldn't give up? Because if I said no, you would have stalked me and hounded me?"

"I would have done whatever it took, Alison."

Snip.

"That ship has sailed."

Myers said nothing but felt the sharp end of her scissors in his chest.

"So, what are you going to do?"

"Sail after it," he said without hesitation, but he knew the wind was not in his favour.

Snip.

"With your time off, I meant. Are you going to see someone? Maybe get some help?"

"Some help? I don't need help. I just need to..."

She stopped snipping and leaned on the counter, her eyes wide and brows raised, waiting for his idea of therapy.

"I need to relax a little. That's all."

"Relax?" said Alison. "That's your answer?"

"I was hoping to spend some time with Harriet at least. It's the school holidays soon, isn't it?"

"Three weeks away."

"Oh. Does Darryl work?"

"It's Darren, Matthew. And yes, he does work, and no you can't hang around here. I'm trying to move on in case you hadn't noticed. The last thing I need is Darren thinking..."

She didn't need to say anymore. They both knew it.

"So it's not because you don't want me here, then?" he said, and smiled the first genuine smile he had in too long.

Snip.

"Take yourself away, Matthew. Find

somewhere to go. Explore. When was the last time you had a holiday?"

"The Seychelles. Three years ago. With my wife and daughter."

Snip.

"Darren will be home soon."

"I'd like to meet him."

"You'll be gone before he gets back."

Snip.

"How's the coffee doing?"

She sighed and dropped the flowers in a heap.

"One coffee then you go," she said, then turned and reached for a cup.

She looked good. Her waistline still was fine, and when she stretched for the cup, the outline of her bust was clear. He remembered the beach in the Seychelles. Harriet played in the ocean and he lay on a towel. Alison could never relax when Harriet wasn't by her side. She was sitting up with her knees drawn up to her chest.

It was the same view.

"Maybe I'll find myself a beach to lie on?"

"You should. It'll do you good."

"Allenby said there will be an investigation."

She poured the coffee with her back turned, said nothing, then walked to the fridge for milk. She stirred in the milk then turned and slid the cup across the kitchen surface, handle first. She had always done that. He'd never noticed before.

"Are you being charged?"

"I doubt it. But it'll go against me. Promotion might be a way off."

She collected the flowers and the scissors from the counter.

"Harassment," said Myers, answering the question she would ask next.

Alison shook her head. "Should I ask?"

"You wouldn't want to know the details."

"Have you finished your coffee yet?"

It was a prompt for him to hurry. He sipped at the drink. It was just how he liked his coffee. She stared at him, knowing the coffee was just right.

"I'll say hi to Harriet before I go."

If Myers could have stopped time and written down how he thought Alison would react to the statement, he would write something along the lines of, 'Alison will sigh. She will drop her head and close her eyes, then tell me to leave. I can see her tomorrow'.

She sighed and dropped her head.

"Be quick," she said.

Myers nearly coughed his coffee up. He waited for her to continue.

"Before I change my mind," added Alison.

"I'll be quick. I just want to say hi."

He crept up the stairs. He had to admit, he did like what she had done to the place. The colours were natural, and the light woods gave a sense of space. And the house smelled nice. Alison had always liked scents. Sandalwood was one of his favourites.

He knocked on Harriet's door and noted the sliver of light on the carpet that shone from inside. Three knocks, light but firm. There was no answer.

He glanced along the hallway to the bathroom. The door was open, and the light was off.

"Harriet?" he called. "It's me. Your dad."

He waited. No answer.

He opened the door. The lamp was on and her room was neat. Her large double bed was untouched.

He sensed rather than heard Alison behind him.

"What's wrong?" she asked. She must have read his body language.

He turned to face her and saw the horror sully her pretty eyes.

"She's not here."

CHAPTER FORTY-TWO

The sound of a man sobbing, Harvey considered to be as, if not more, disturbing than nails on a chalk board. It was the first sound he heard when he opened his eyes, and before he'd even worked out where he was, he knew that Donny was behind him.

Even with his hands tied behind his back and to the wooden chair, he could feel his own pulse in the swelling lump on the side of his head. A dull ache had formed while he'd been unconscious, and his eyesight had narrowed as if he was staring into a dark tunnel.

The room he found himself in was the front bedroom of the large house in Chigwell. That much he knew. Three of the walls were covered in a raised, floral wallpaper of white and green design, and the fourth wall was covered by a row of built-in wardrobes. Some of the doors were mirrored and he saw Donny watching him. His eyes were red and swollen and his face was bruised with traces of dried blood around his mouth and nose.

Beside him, Julios slept as peacefully as a bear in winter. The room was large. The three chairs that Harvey, Donny, and Julios occupied were on one side of a large double bed with plenty of extra space.

Harvey craned his neck to see behind him, but all he saw was a pair of dirty feet with cracked, brown skin in an old pair of sandals. He checked the mirror and leaned to one side to see who the feet belonged to.

"So, you're the man I've been looking for?" said the man's voice. He was Asian and if he was with the men Harvey had already encountered that day, it was a safe bet to assume he was of Pakistani origin.

Harvey didn't reply.

"My name is Rashid Al Sheikh. Perhaps you know of me?"

Harvey said nothing, and Rashid continued.

"We have a saying in my country. Retribution, though late, comes at last."

Again, Harvey didn't reply.

"So, you're the silent man, are you?" He laughed and muttered something unintelligible. "I wonder, was Asif as strong as you?" The man gave it some thought then drew his own conclusion. "I think Asif was stronger. Asif was a passionate man."

"Asif is dead," said Harvey.

"I know. He was my cousin. He never failed me. We both knew that one day he wouldn't return."

A hundred different things sprang to Harvey's mind. Verbal attacks that might provoke the man into venturing closer or that might aggravate him. With his hands tied, all Harvey had was his voice and his mind. The key to winning a verbal fight, according to John, was similar to winning a physical fight. Agitate them. Build the opponent up to a point where emotions take over. Make them lose control.

But somehow, even in his predicament, Harvey couldn't bring himself to say anything against Asif. He had taken his own life and had shown courage beyond which Harvey hadn't witnessed in a long time.

"Have you nothing to say?" asked Rashid.

Harvey didn't reply.

"You have killed many men. Good men. Loyal men. In my country, you would be treated with honour. With respect. But we are not in my country. We are in the free world. But, my friend, it is no longer free for you."

He stretched his feet on the bed and put his arms behind his head as if he was preparing for a nap. He found Harvey staring at him in the mirror.

"I've been looking for you for some time. I pictured somebody very different. I wondered what the man might look like who could do all those terrible things. Surely, he is a powerful man. Yet here you are. An ordinary man. There's nothing special about you. I wondered what kind of man could do those things. Faisal, Abdul, Amir, they all died at your hands, didn't they? Along with Hamid, Ghulam, and Ejaz."

Harvey didn't reply. He thought of their faces and remembered their cries.

"I know they did. I knew it the minute I laid eyes on you. Then there was Asif, my cousin, my best man, and closest friend. And Ismail, Farhad, and Fareed. Somebody has to stop you."

"Is it me that has to be stopped? Retribution, though late, comes at last," said Harvey, reciting the man's words that seemed so apt.

"Retribution," said the man, his accent thick and his R's rolling across his tongue, "retribution is for the worthy."

"What about all those girls? Aren't they worthy? Didn't their lives mean anything?"

The man laughed and snapped his fingers in the air. The tall man who had been driving the car earlier entered the room moments later. He dragged the young girl in by the wrist. Her face was sour, and her lip swollen. Her makeup was smudged, and her hair was a far cry from her earlier immaculate appearance.

"You mean girls like this?" said the man on the bed. "Farhad, show him what girls like this will do for a little money. Show him how little pride they have."

Without hesitation, the tall man pushed the girl onto the edge of the bed and bent to lift the hem of his kurta.

"Stop," said Harvey.

The girl, who seemed not to be able to focus, swayed where she sat. She gazed at Harvey as though she was drunk.

"Ah, I see," said Rashid. "I hope I made my point. Did you see her fight? No. Did you see her struggle? No. Did Farhad have to force her to do anything?" He paused to let the question sink in and Harvey searched for some kind of life in the girl's vacant eyes. "No," he finished.

"She's out of her mind."

"Yes, she is. But do you know what? Tomorrow she will return and tomorrow she will be out of her mind."

"You're grooming young girls. You're feeding them drugs in return for-"

"I'm giving them what they ask for. A good time."

"What about Jennifer Standing?"

"What about her?"

"The one that got away?"

He laughed again and swung his feet from the bed then stood behind Harvey. He stared at him in the mirror and Harvey tried to find a weakness in the rope. He found none.

"I don't like to hurt the girls. You have to

understand. But I am a powerful man. When the girls try to pull away, they threaten us with the police. It would destroy a man like me. But she hasn't said a thing to the police, has she? Jennifer will be back. She was a good girl. A *keeper*, as they say."

"You tried to kill her."

"*I* did no such thing."

"Faisal? I caught him. I slaughtered him and I pinned him to a tree."

The words hit home like a dagger to the man's heart. His tone shifted to a bitter and resentful scorn.

"Faisal was a sick man. He brought shame on us, but I loved him nonetheless for it. He always did have a soft spot for the younger girls. He didn't like to share."

"You're sick. She's a child."

"You, sir, will pay for what you have done to my friends and my family. As they say, retribution, though late, comes at last."

He began to walk away toward the door but stopped to rest his hand on the girl's head.

"What about Donny?" said Harvey, still working the ropes but finding no way out of them. "What about his wife? What did she do to deserve being killed?"

"Ah, young Julia," said Rashid, and he turned once more to face Harvey. "She was once like Harriet here, a sweet girl who would do anything for pleasure and without pride."

"You abused *her*?"

The comment riled the man, but he rose above the taunt and filled his chest with pride.

"I introduced them. A young runaway, she was. I gave her hope."

"You gave her drugs."

"I gave her opportunity."

"You took her life."

"She was a friend," said Rashid, and he leaned forward, lowering his voice to a whisper. "But she grew too old for the men in my circles. I thought I could trust her. But she opened her mouth. She told Donny far too much. Like I said, a man like me relies on reputation. But you have to admire Donny's spirit. Beneath that miserable wretch of a man are morals. Do you know what he did?"

"I'm working it out."

"Donny here was to supply my parties. You know? The good stuff. He didn't need to know what *happens* at my parties." His eyes widened and his tone was playful. Then it sank once more to the cruel and bitter bark of before. "But, as I understand it, Julia opened up to him, as a bride-to-be might. I imagine she told him things, things that should never pass a young girl's lips. Things that might have cast my parties in a less than favourable light. And this must have displeased him."

Harvey found Donny in the mirror. A steady drip of tears fell from his nose into his lap, and his eyes, reddened with sadness and fear, stared back at Harvey.

"So, he didn't know what Julia was before you introduced them?"

"I introduced her as an old friend. Where possible, I like to maintain friendships. A link to the Cartwright family could have been useful, you know?"

"But once he knew the truth, he stopped supplying your drugs?"

Harvey couldn't help but find pride in his foster-brother. It was the first time, that Harvey knew of, that Donny had done something honourable.

"Of course, he couldn't go to his father. Oh no. The great John Cartwright loathes drugs. He fears them."

"He fears nothing."

"He fears drugs because he doesn't understand them. He doesn't understand their power."

"Without your drugs, you're nobody. That's the only power you have. That's what you do, isn't it? You get people like Donny to bring you drink and drugs. You feed the drink to wealthy businessmen, and you feed the drugs to the girls. The men have a good time with the girls and the girls develop a habit. A habit that needs feeding. But when the girls refuse or when they threaten you with the police-"

"I warned Donny not to let me down. I told him there would be consequences."

"He gave the drugs to somebody else so that you couldn't get them."

"He betrayed me. They both betrayed me."

"So, you sent Asif to kill him and Julia? Well, let me tell you something about Asif," said Harvey. The time for honouring Asif had gone. The time for mutual respect had gone. It was time to bring down the man at the centre of the ring of abuse. And to do that, Harvey needed to play dirty. "Asif wasn't the man you thought he was. Did you ever see him cry?"

"Asif would never cry."

"He cried like a little girl, you sick son of a bitch. I had him strung up like a hog and I didn't even need to touch him before he pissed his pants."

"You mean like your friend here?" Rashid said, and he waved his hand at Donny, who gazed down into his lap when Harvey caught him once more in the mirror. "Asif wouldn't cry. He wasn't capable of tears. He was a *lion*. He was my friend."

Rashid clicked his fingers again and called out in a language beyond Harvey.

He heard her first and his senses placed the scent and the click of her heels before his mind had made the connection.

Pale and immaculate, in contrast to Rashid's dark and dirty skin, walked the girl who Harvey had nearly known. She was radiant. He remembered her as clear as day. He remembered her long legs and her passion. He remembered the heat of the moment and how close they had come before Asif's gunshot had sang through the sky.

He remembered her words. She had whispered them, and they had seemed out of place among the teasing, seductive tones.

A girl like me needs a man like you. Will you help me, Harvey Stone?

"Harvey," she said, but her charm had faded, and the connection clicked into place. Her confidence had gone, and in its place was shame.

"You supply this man with young girls?" said Harvey, ignoring Rashid and talking directly to the woman who was at the point of breaking down.

"Like I said, they'll do anything for the good stuff," said Rashid. "Samantha here supplies me with suitable girls in return for a nice apartment, an expensive car, and a lifestyle fit for a princess. I provide her everything she needs. You see, Harvey, the grooming, as you call it, is not in my hands. Farhad handles the drugs. All I do is host the parties and make sure people have a good time."

"You ruin lives," said Samantha, and all eyes fell on her. She raised her head, as if the words she had said gave her release. She exhaled loudly enough for Harvey to hear the compassion in her voice. "You destroy them. You break them. And when you're done with them, you give them to your reprobate family to do as they wish."

"Silence, Samantha," said Rashid, and he backhanded her hard enough to split her lip.

"No. No, not anymore. I can't do it anymore."

"You'll do as you're told, or you'll lose everything."

"Everything?" she said. "I *have* nothing. I have nothing but nightmares and an ache in my heart." She turned to Harvey. "I asked for help. I tried to tell you. But I had to trust you. Donny said you would help."

"It wasn't Julia who said too much. It wasn't Julia who told Donny about you. It was me."

Farhad forced her onto the bed and the girl, who had been swaying and staring into thin air, rolled off. She lay in a heap on the floor, her dress raised to reveal the track marks of injections on the inside of her thighs, where, Harvey assumed, her mother wouldn't notice.

Samantha screamed under Farhad's weight. He knelt on her spine and his broad hands encompassed her neck. But she fought. There was strength in her.

"It's over, Rashid," she hissed in a strange blend of tears and laughter.

"Nothing is over until I say," replied Rashid, and he nodded at Farhad to increase the pain.

Harvey pulled at the ropes that bound his wrists. He tried to stand and break the chair, but nothing gave.

"The girl..." said Samantha, and she waited for the right moment to finish.

Farhad looked up at Rashid, a questioning expression on his face, waiting for Rashid's decision.

"It's over, Rashid," Samantha continued. "She's your undoing. She's the one who will bring you down."

"Harriet?" said Rashid, not following what Samantha was saying. "She's as worthless as the rest of them."

"No," Samantha hissed, and there was a genuine smile of retribution on her face as it was pressed into the bed. "She's the policeman's daughter. She's Harriet Myers."

Even Harvey was taken back by the news. Rashid's expression morphed from the unstoppable sneer he had worn in the photos in Myers' file into a look of horror and realisation.

"It's over," said Samantha as Farhad's grip

released. "This house will destroy you. She will destroy you. I will destroy you. The police will come. They'll find the hairs of all those young, dead girls. They'll find the drugs. And all of it leads back to you, Rashid. You've been played. You'll pay for it-"

Her words were cut short by Farhad's grip. Her face was forced down and he used a pillow to smother her.

Harvey, incensed by it all, tried to stand, planning on smashing the chair against a wall. But with Farhad busy with Samantha, it fell on Rashid to strike out himself. He stepped over the young, unconscious girl and struck Harvey square in the jaw. He held his throat and gazed into Harvey's eyes.

"You're finished, Sheikh. One way or another. What are you going to do now? He'll hunt you down. He's onto you. I know he is."

"I'll start again somewhere else," he whispered. "Paris, New York, Amsterdam. It doesn't matter where. They'll come to me. They'll come to me like lambs to the slaughter."

The sneer broadened and his eyes narrowed, just as John's did when a plan formed that would increase his wealth and power. It was the hunger for power that drove men like him.

Samantha's bucking body stilled. The corners of Rashid's mouth curled, and that characteristic sneer returned to duty. Farhad held her a moment longer, then climbed off. There was no expression of distaste. There was no emotion whatsoever. He stood, dutiful, waiting for Rashid's next command.

"Men like me always find men like you," said Harvey.

Rashid replied with a whisper, his face so close to Harvey's that the lines around his eyes were like the Thames Estuary, deep and etched for eternity. "Retribution, though late, comes at last, my friend."

And although Rashid, who was calm in the face of disaster, peered into Harvey's eyes, he then spoke to Farhad, and gave a clear and final instruction.

"Burn the house to the ground."

CHAPTER FORTY-THREE

The unhurried tone of the phone seemed to tease at Myers. The spaces between the rings seemed to last twice as long as they should.

Clutching a cushion to her chest, Alison sat beside him on the bed she shared with Darren, filling those spaces with possibilities that they both knew were unlikely.

"Maybe I should call Tiffany's mum? She might have gone to her house."

Myers hung up the phone but picked it back up and dialled another number from memory, ignoring Alison's verbal thought process. He had no doubt where she was.

"Who are you calling? Are you calling the police?"

Thoughts raced through Myers' mind. Sick thoughts that he tried to banish. Thoughts of what had happened before and what might happen again. His daughter, and the faces of all those girls.

Once more, the lazy ring tone taunted him, and once more, Alison filled the spaces with her panic.

Three rings.

"Oh, Matthew, she's probably just with friends."

"Has she said anything unusual recently?"

Four rings.

"No. I don't think so. But she hasn't been herself. I'm not sure if there's a problem at school or if she has a boyfriend."

"Do you talk to her?"

Five rings.

"I try," she said, defending her custody. Then her tone softened. "She doesn't want to talk. She promised me she was okay."

"Has she ever sneaked out in the night before?"

Six rings.

Alison faltered and looked away.

"Alison? I need to know."

Seven rings.

"Once," she said. "That I know of."

"Alison, I need to know."

Eight rings.

"Then, yes. Yes, she has. I don't know how many times and I don't know where she goes."

The phone clicked and Myers heard an intake of breath.

"Allenby."

"Ma'am, it's Myers."

The inevitable exhale followed.

"I found the Rashid Al Sheikh file on your desk, Myers. What do you have to say?"

"I need help."

"Even if Sheikh doesn't press for an investigation, I'll have to act on this. You accessed confidential files. That's a gross misconduct charge, Myers. Do you know what that means? It means that's the end of your career, your job, your pension. It's all gone, Myers."

The words were like a kick to Myers' gut.

"Whatever you need to do, ma'am. I need your help. Please."

"I can't protect you, Myers. You got yourself into this. I can't be seen to condone harassment of-"

"Harriet is missing."

Allenby silenced.

"I think Sheikh has her."

He felt Alison stand from the bed, and in the corner of his eye, she covered her face with her hands. She spoke, but Myers was tuned into Allenby. He needed her now.

"You're right," said Allenby. "You do need help. This has gone far enough. You're a senior member of my team and you're like a dog with a bone, Myers. Get a grip."

"She's gone. I *know* he has her."

"How long has she been missing?"

He mouthed the question to Alison, who wiped her eyes and shrugged. "Two, three, maybe four hours? I don't know." Her voice was high with panic and thick with tears.

"Did you hear that, ma'am?"

"Was that Alison?"

"Yes, ma'am."

Allenby sighed and he heard the phone shift to her other hand. He pictured her perched on her desk the way he'd seen her a hundred times before. Maybe she was fiddling with the monkey pot? The distraction of thought was welcome, but brief.

"Tell her not to worry. Tell her Harriet

will be fine. Tell her that I said not to listen to you."

"Ma'am?"

"Pull yourself together, Myers. She's fifteen and you haven't seen her for a few hours. Don't you think you're overreacting?"

"No. No, as it happens, I do not."

"Well, you are. You're fixated on Sheikh and you're pulling people down with you. Get a grip, man."

"I just need some help. Can you get a unit to investigate the address in the file?"

"No, I cannot, Myers. She'll come back. Check her friends' houses. Check the local parks. You're her father. You must know where she'd be."

"Just a drive by, ma'am. That's all. Surely-"

"Surely nothing. You have no favours left and I'm not putting my reputation on the line any more for you."

She left a silence to let the words sink in.

"Look, if she's not back by the morning, give me a call. I'll see what I can do."

"The morning will be too late, ma'am."

"She'll be back. If I don't hear from you, I'll presume I'm right."

The call disconnected but Myers held it to his ear a while and stared at the wall. Alison waited anxiously. There was a battle taking place inside him. On one side, every face of every girl he'd seen lying on a slab enticed the fear from some place deep down inside him. The place only parents know exists, where others disbelieve.

On the other side of the battle, a rage was brewing. It was a rage that coursed through his body like a quake, trembling his fingers and watering his eyes.

"Matthew?" said Alison, and her voice was concern. "Matthew, what did she say?"

He stood and pushed past her. He wrenched open the door to the wardrobe and began pulling clothes out and throwing them onto the bed.

"What are you doing? That's Darren's things."

"The boxes, Alison. Where are my boxes?"

"What boxes?"

"The boxes I kept in here," said Myers, and dropped to his hands and knees to see further into the corner.

"You haven't got any boxes here. Stop that."

Myers stopped. He took a breath. "I kept two boxes here. I didn't take them with me when I left. Where are they, Alison?"

"Shoe boxes?"

"Yes, that's them."

"In the spare room, I think. Unless I threw them out."

Myers ran to the spare room. It was the only room in the house that hadn't been decorated since he'd left. It had the same old wallpaper on the walls and the same hideous light fitting he had always hated.

There was a pile of boxes on the bed and an old suitcase. Myers sifted through them with disregard for their contents.

"Matthew, if you tell me what you're looking for, I might be able to help."

He ignored her and pushed away two larger boxes that were in his way.

And there it was. The box he was looking for. He pulled off the lid and placed the shoe box on the bed. Inside was a small wooden box with his father's war medals. He opened and closed the box in one movement. It wasn't the time for nostalgia. Below the wooden box was a folded Union Jack. He pulled it out and laid it on the bed.

"What's that?"

He ignored her questions still. The scenes that were running through his mind were the type that a man should never speak of. This was true twice over for his ex-wife.

He unfolded the flag, feeling the reassuring weight of the contents.

He gripped the handle of the old Webley Mk VI revolver as if he were shaking the hand of his long dead father.

"Matthew, where on earth did you get that?"

Myers didn't reply.

"Has that been in this house all this time?"

He loaded the cylinder using the loose rounds that were inside the flag.

"Matthew, you can't," said Alison, but she cowered away when he moved toward her, and the road to redemption lay before him, as clear as ever it had been.

CHAPTER FORTY-FOUR

Samantha lay still.

Harvey sat helpless, staring at her body, the body he had known for the slightest of moments, and a mind that was swathed in shadow and lies.

The acrid smell that rose from below and poisoned the air had somehow overwhelmed Samantha's expensive perfume.

He shuffled in his chair until he could see Donny without using the mirror.

As expected, Donny was a snivelling mess. He had been stripped of his shirt, shoes, and socks and was tied in the same manner as Harvey. Julios had also been stripped of his shirt, shoes, and socks, but Rashid's man had gone to additional lengths to secure him. At least twice the amount of rope had been used and the rope around his feet had been tied to a wall-mounted pipe that fed the radiator.

And a swollen red lump on his arm matched the one on the girl's leg Harvey had seen before Farhad had carried her away.

"Harvey?" said Donny. He was breathless. His voice was broken and cracked like the old vinyl records that John listened to. "My feet."

Harvey had noticed Donny's feet were bruised from the beatings. His toes were swollen, some likely broken. But his feet appeared in far greater shape than the rest of him.

"You should be more concerned about your face, Donny," said Harvey. It was the first time the two of them had shared humour, though the sentiment was futile given the circumstance. Donny winced when he moved his mouth and to swallow appeared to be giving him some difficulty.

"Did they drug him?" asked Harvey, and he nodded at Julios. "Just nod. Don't speak."

Donny nodded, then spoke.

"Three times." He bared his bloodied

teeth then coughed and spat out a concoction of saliva and blood. "They couldn't put him out."

"Okay," said Harvey, trying to get him to rest his voice. "How are your hands? Can you move them? Just nod."

This time, Donny just nodded.

"Good. Can you shuffle around so we're back to back?"

During their lives, Donny had always been the spoiled only child of John Cartwright. He had developed into a snivelling, sly, and backstabbing wretch that Harvey despised. The man would go out of his way to see other people suffer. He had lied, cheated, and stolen, and made more enemies than friends.

It was no secret that he and Harvey didn't see eye to eye.

But right there, at that moment in time, Harvey would have gladly let bygones be bygones as Donny, with his bruised chest, began the monumental task of turning in his chair. He growled and cursed with every effort. He spat and moaned, and he cried with the agony of what Harvey was beginning to understand were several broken ribs.

"That's enough," said Harvey when Donny had completed ninety degrees.

His foster-brother let his head sink and he panted like a dog on a hot summer's day. It wasn't tears that dripped from his nose now; it was the sweat that only came with endured, excruciating pain.

"Rest," said Harvey, and he began to shuffle himself backwards to meet Donny back to back.

"Harvey?" said Donny when their hands touched. There was a moment of awkward insecurity. Then Harvey squeezed his hand as best he could. "I'm here, Donny. I'm going to get us out of this."

"My feet."

"I know, Donny. You've broken a toe or two. Just stay still."

"No," he said. "My feet. They're burning."

It took a few seconds for Donny's statement to register. But then Harvey thought of his bare feet on the carpeted floor. He smelled the acrid smell that had tainted the already polluted air.

"He's burning the house down," said Harvey. "Untie me."

"I can't, Harvey. I can't see what I'm doing."

"Try, Donny. Come on."

He felt Donny's weak fingers fingering the knot around Harvey's wrist. But the attempt was feeble.

"Donny, come on. Do it for John. Do it for your dad."

"I can't do it."

But no matter how many times Donny claimed not to be able to untie the knots, he still continued to try. He hadn't just given up as Harvey feared he might.

"Find the loose end, Donny. You can do it. I believe in you."

"I'm hurting, Harvey."

"I know you are, Donny. I'm with you. I'm not going to let anything happen to us. Just set me free."

"Oh, I wish Julios was awake. He could do this. He has strong hands."

It was true. Julios had hands like shovels. He could squeeze a man's head with one hand or break a man's hands without even trying.

"Well, Julios has spent his life protecting you and John. Now it's your turn to protect him. Get us out of here, Donny."

"I found it," he said. "I found the loose end."

"That's it, Donny. Now twist it. Twist until you can't twist it anymore."

"I am. I can feel where it goes. If I can just get my finger..."

His words were muffled by the damage to his jaw. He inhaled, long and deep, and exhaled juddering breaths as the sharp ends of his broken ribs found purchase in his soft flesh.

But he was doing it. Harvey could feel his fingers tracing the knot. He felt the loose end of the rope pass over his skin as Donny pictured the knot in his mind and worked blindly.

And then, like the release of water breaking through a dam, Harvey was able to move. He pulled the rope off his legs and stood, kicking the chair away from him.

He checked the door. On the wall of the stairs, an orange glow was growing stronger. He could hear the flames below as the old, wooden beams crackled and hissed.

"We don't have much time," he said to Donny, pulling his knife from his jacket. He bent and began to cut the rope.

"Harvey?" said Donny, then waited for him to stop and look at him. "Thank you, Harvey. I don't deserve this."

Harvey listened. He nodded, studying his foster-brother's face with its wounds and bruises. Harvey had borne similar bruises on many occasions, and he knew how much they hurt.

"Any other time and I might have agreed," said Harvey. "But from what I heard today, you deserve more than this."

He sliced through Donny's rope and pulled it free, tossing the rope to one side. He held his brother down before he could move by placing a hand on his shoulder.

"Stay. We'll all go together."

Donny nodded, and Harvey worked his way around the back of Julios.

"Harvey," said Donny.

"Wait, Donny."

He bent down to the big man's giant, bare feet and sliced through the rope.

"Harvey?"

"Donny, shut up."

He pulled at the lengths of rope and cast them aside, freeing one of Julios' massive limbs with each stroke of his blade.

"Harvey?"

Harvey sighed. He stopped what he was doing and looked across at Donny, who was staring at the door with wide eyes and the all-familiar fear etched into the lines of his face.

It was then that Harvey heard the tell-tale click of an old six-shooter revolver being cocked.

CHAPTER FORTY-FIVE

"You," he said, and the silent man turned to meet his stare. "It's you. I knew it was you."

The silent man was in the process of untying a man Myers recognised from John Cartwright's property, who was sleeping like a hibernating bear. It was then that the woman caught Myers' eye.

Keeping the gun on the silent man, Myers leaned forward to feel for a pulse.

"You don't want to do that," said the man, and for the first time, Myers heard the cold snarl in his voice.

They locked stares.

"It's not what it looks like."

Myers considered the woman, whose

deathly gaze betrayed an expression of content. He stepped away, suddenly unsure of the situation, and even more aware that Harriet was nowhere to be seen.

"Where is she?" asked Myers. "Where's my daughter?"

Behind him, smoke rolled through the doorway. He could hear the crackles and pops of the blaze and the silent man recognised that there was little time for conversation.

"Blonde. Five foot six. Slim. Pretty, but young," said the man.

Myers cocked his head but said nothing. He held the gun aimed at him and his hand trembled at Harriet's description.

"They took her."

"Who did?"

The man didn't reply. The knowledge was a bargaining chip that, he knew, once spent, left him worthless.

"Rashid Al Sheik?" said Myers, growing angrier by the second. "Was it? Tell me, damn it."

The man said nothing. His silence infuriated Myers even more. His hand shook and sweat trickled down the side of his face. He moved his aim to Donald Cartwright, who had beads of sweat on his forehead from the heat emanating from downstairs. A sheen of moisture across his bare and hairless chest along with the wounds on his scrawny body gave him the look of a beaten slave or a prisoner of war from one of the old wars films Myers' father used to enjoy. Myers moved the gun to the huge, sleeping bodyguard and back to the silent man, who, with the growing heat, had also developed a sheen, but with his strong mass and prominent brow, he appeared as the slave master. All he was missing was the whip.

"Are you going to kill us?" asked the silent man, who stood between the two bare-chested men dressed in cargo pants, boots, and a thick leather motorcycle jacket.

And Myers knew that jacket.

His voice conveyed no fear, and his face was as it had been that night in Myers' memories, cold and expressionless.

He shook his head. "No. No, just you. These two will go to prison."

"What about your daughter?"

"Where is she?"

"Close."

"You'll tell me," said Myers, and his hand

flexed involuntarily. The gun fired and a bullet buried itself into the lintel above the window behind the man.

"Further," said the man.

"Don't play games with me. I let you get away once. It won't happen again."

"Do you know who she is?" said the man, and he nodded at the woman who had found her peace. The woman who had escaped the terrible affair.

Myers stared at her, searching for pity. But no such pity remained in Myers' body. He would find his daughter, and nothing would stop him.

"She's the one who groomed your daughter, Detective Inspector Myers. *She's* the one who tricked your daughter into this. She's the one who knew you'd come running. She's the one who took her to Rashid Al Sheik to be drugged and-"

"Stop," said Myers. "I don't want to hear it." He let the gun fall to his side as he considered the acts he couldn't bear to hear.

"You don't want to hear what they did to her? You don't want to know the things they made her do and how they fed her with drugs to keep her coming back for more?"

"I said stop." He raised the gun once more. But this time, his hand was steady. He was focused. He was angry. His finger squeezed the trigger and the hammer began to move.

"I can get her back," said the man, watching the gun's hammer. There were fractions of an inch to play with. An old gun like the one Myers held was unpredictable. He knew that. The man knew that. But right there and then, Myers cared little for consequence.

It must have been the gas supply that caught the raging fire because, at that moment, the house shook, and beyond the door, the walls were bathed in a fervent orange glow. The fire was spreading fast, although the glow had retreated, the flames having devoured the flammable gas in the air. But Myers knew it wouldn't be long until they would be trapped on the first floor with no way out.

"We don't have much time," said the man, and he watched as Myers considered his options. His chest rose and fell with the calm confidence of a predator. Myers' heart beat like the drum of wild tribesman. It was the difference between a man like Myers and a stone-cold killer.

Time and exposure to the life had hardened the silent man to death. He appeared prepared for it. Ready to embrace his fate. Myers was not hardened to such a life. He may have stopped killers and imprisoned hundreds of villains in his career, but it was the first time he had held death in his hands. The man seemed to recognise the indecision in his eyes.

"I'm on your side, Myers. This time, I'm on your side. Let me get her back for you. I'm your only hope and you know it."

Rage and frustration boiled inside Myers. His entire body shook, and his face twisted as he agonised over his next move.

"I can get her. *I* know I can. *You* know I can. Let me go."

"You're a killer," said Myers, and the hammer teased its way back a little further.

"I'm your only hope. I'm the only one who can get her back. Think about Jennifer Standing and the others. Put the gun down, Myers. You're going to have to trust me."

An explosion of rage and fear and frustration spewed from Myers in the form of a roar so wild and raw that he felt the tears begin to stream down his cheeks.

He lowered the gun and Donald let his head fall back in relief. Myers stared at him, the bodyguard, and then at the silent man.

"Help me get them out," said the man. "We don't have long. This whole place is going up in flames. Help me get them out and I'll find Harriet."

Myers swayed on the decision. He could kill them all now. But what chance would he stand of finding Harriet alone?

It was Donald Cartwright who, from some place deep inside of him, found an inherent strength that belied Myers' opinion and everything he'd heard about the man.

"No," said Donald, speaking out for the first time. His feet were black, bruised, and swollen. His chest was marred with lashes and red sores from countless beatings. And his face was covered in a layer of thick, dried blood. With gritted teeth and animal-like tenacity, he pushed himself from the chair, holding onto the silent man for support. He sucked up the pain and grimaced with every move. But he stood defiant and turned to the silent man. "The detective and I will get

Julios out." He turned to the man who, until that point, Myers had referred to only as the silent man, and there was a connection between them that Myers couldn't place. "Go, Harvey. Go get her."

The silent man stepped forward.

"It's your call," he said to Myers. "You can either shoot me now and take your chances or let me get your daughter back."

And Myers nodded.

PART III

CHAPTER FORTY-SIX

The glorious summer sun that had shone upon Donny's wedding was warming the souls of people someplace far away. But in the distance, amid the midnight blues, was a fusion of oranges and reds, as if somebody had spread the colours across the horizon with a butter knife. In the wake of the sun, dark clouds had formed above the abattoir. It was the meeting place of two very different skies and two very different worlds. It was a place of death.

The first rain drops dotted the concrete and Harvey pulled his bike up beside an old, fat oak at the top of the drive and killed the engine. He removed his helmet and let the fat drops of rain wet his face.

He hung the helmet from the handlebars and stood before the abattoir and he let the wind carry Myers' file from his hand. The papers, the photos, and Myers' disjointed thoughts fluttered and flapped and were carried away.

"Like lambs to the slaughter," said Harvey, but his voice was lost to the wind.

The peaked roof and protruding dormers were black against the sky, tall and dominating in shape and size. A chorus of raindrops sung from the tiled rooftops and small puddles were already forming on the dry ground.

Harvey removed his jacket and laid it over the seat of his bike. He moved to the centre of the courtyard, stopped before the giant doors, and inhaled, long and slow. He closed his eyes and rolled his neck from side to side, stretching out the tight muscles, preparing his body for what was to come.

And he called out to announce his arrival. To enter the lion's den would be a foolish move. He would meet him outside, on equal terms. Somewhere in the pens that surrounded the building, an iron gate swung on a hinge and the deathly screech cut through the night until the gate slammed into the cage, steel on steel, and the percussive rattle of mesh faded.

"Rashid."

Harvey's voice returned from the far corners of the old buildings and he heard the taunt in his own voice. He was alive, and if Rashid Al Sheik had sense, he would be fearful.

"Rashid."

Harvey's shirt clung to his skin, and as the rain grew heavier, it found every inch of his body like the parched ground on which he stood.

A flash of lightning in the distance froze the scene in all its sombre glory on Harvey's retinas, then faded once more to the eerie shadows.

"Rashid."

A rumble of thunder growled high above. It seemed to roll across the sky like the snarl of a beast searching for a way through the dark and imperious clouds. Then, without warning, two large spotlights switched on, lighting the courtyard with bright, white light, semi-blinding Harvey. He raised a hand to block the light, squinting for better focus.

"Rashid," he called, as he searched for a sign of movement. He knew Rashid would be there. If Harriet were to die, it would be the perfect place.

Another flash of lightning lit the landscape and the old building, and as if on cue, the two huge barn doors swung open. There was a light on inside. Harvey saw a forklift truck and pens where livestock would be delivered. There were rows of butcher's hooks on a carousel and the wall was lined with tall livestock cages that disappeared into the darkness beyond. And there, silhouetted in the huge doorway, was a figure. It wasn't Rashid Al Sheik. The man was tall and lean, and he stood with a confidence that a man feels with unnatural power.

A length of chain dropped from his hand and rattled to the ground by his feet. He stared at Harvey from beneath his pronounced and foreboding brow.

"Where's Harriet, Farhad? Don't make this hard on yourself."

"You should learn to mind your own business," he replied. His accent was thicker than Rashid's, his voice was deeper, and the roll of his R's more pronounced. "Leave now."

Harvey didn't reply.

Farhad took the first step forward and Harvey remained where he was. He counted down the steps until Farhad was in range. And it would be then and only then that Harvey would strike.

Nine steps.

Farhad was a featureless puppet with the bright lights behind him. Even the whites of his large, brown eyes were masked in deep shadow. He took another step, trailing the chain behind him like the leash of some unseen beast.

Eight steps.

"I do this for Asif," said Farhad, though Harvey could see no expression on his face.

Harvey shook his head. "Asif was weak. He took his own life."

Seven steps.

"Asif would never. He and I endured a misery beyond anything you can imagine."

"He was tortured. He was strong."

"You saw the scars on his back?"

"He took his own life, Farhad. He knew

he would die anyway. You don't have to suffer the same fate as Asif."

"He was my brother," said Farhad, and there was an anger in his voice. "Together we played as children. Together we became men. Together we were lions. We should have died together."

Six steps.

"You don't need to die, Farhad. Not for Rashid. Look at you. You're not a lion. You're a puppet. The only thing you endure is the misery Rashid causes. Don't you see? You mean nothing to him. Where is he now? He's hiding. He's a coward."

A flash of lightning lit Farhad's face to reveal a grimace of fury etched in deep lines around his eyes and mouth.

"Rashid is our cousin. We are not like you. You may have broken Asif, but you will never break our bond. Not like I will break you."

In a rush of energy, Farhad whipped the chain over his head and slammed it into the concrete before Harvey. He dragged it back and Harvey was unmoved.

Five steps. He was one step from being close enough to strike Harvey with the chain.

The next attempt would be the beginning of the end, and for Harvey to survive, he would need to get close and personal to render the chain useless.

"You," said Farhad, "you are not like other men in this country."

Four steps.

"Like Asif, it is a pity to kill a lion such as you," said Farhad.

He dragged the chain back, triggering Harvey into action. He rushed at Farhad as he began to swing the chain and his shoulder found that sweet spot below the ribs and deflated him. Harvey drove forward with his legs until Farhad's great height toppled him and the two hit the ground with Harvey on top. Harvey managed to deliver a punch to the man's ribs, but it had little effect.

Farhad's strength was way beyond Harvey's. His free hand found Harvey's throat. His thumb jammed into his windpipe and his grip was like iron. He rolled, forcing Harvey off him, and tried to roll on top, but Harvey raised his leg, placed the flat of his boot against Farhad's gut, and launched the man backward. Harvey scrambled to his feet and felt a rush of wind as the chain soared past his head.

He staggered back to put some distance between them and, once more, the chain swung past his face. The momentum caused Farhad to half-turn with the chain. He prepared for another swing, leaving his flank exposed, and Harvey attacked with full throttle. But Farhad was fast. The chain found Harvey's arm and coiled around his bicep like a boa constrictor. Farhad moved quickly, pulling Harvey toward him with one strong arm then planted his other fist into Harvey's gut.

Harvey reeled, doubled over, and felt the hammer-like blows raining down on him. He drew his knife and fought to stay on his feet. Farhad, seeing Harvey in his weakened state, grabbed his throat and raised his head to meet him eye to eye. His hand seemed to tighten like a vice. His vile face contorted with pure hatred and his lips peeled to show yellow, tombstone-like teeth.

And Harvey thrust the blade upward, deep beneath the man's ribs. He watched as Farhad's expression turned from malice to disbelief. He straddled the line between life and death. Deep, red blood trickled from his thin lips and his grip on Harvey's throat waned.

Harvey gave the knife a final twist. Farhad's body, along with the chain, fell limp to the sodden ground, and, once more, Harvey stared up at the gnarly silhouette of the abattoir.

"Rashid," he called again, and he let the heavy rain wash the blood from his hands.

CHAPTER FORTY-SEVEN

The stairway was hidden beneath a fog of smoke by the time Myers and Donald had managed to get Julios on his feet. The big man stirred once he was upright but was feeling the groggy come down of whatever drug they had pumped him full of.

They each had one of his huge shoulders around their necks and bore much of the man's incredible weight. He was aware of himself enough only to stumble and they fell onto the stairs as a result of his loss of balance and bulk.

But surprising at it may have been, it was Donald Cartwright who stopped them all from tumbling down and breaking their necks. He dug in his heels and planted his back against the big man, while Myers at the top tried to pull him upright. And it was in that manner they descended one step at a time, coughing and choking on the fumes and turning their heads from the insufferable heat as the fire that had burst through from the lounge licked at the hallway walls and the wooden banister. Then the hungry flames settled to feed on the hallway floor at the foot of the stairs, and the road ahead was blocked.

"Hurry, Donald," shouted Myers over the din of the blaze. "I'm not sure how much longer I can hold him."

"We'll have to jump the flames before the fire gets too big."

Donald descended two more stairs.

"I can't hold him, Donald."

The ceiling in the hallway crashed down in a shower of dust and smoke, and the flames reached up to feast on the new, clean air. They spread across the banister and torched the skin on Myers' fingers. He let go. It was just a reaction, and if he had known what would happen, he might have suffered the pain. Julios' weight carried him forward and, in that split second, no matter how hard he tried to find a footing, gravity had other plans for them all.

They tumbled. It was a slow fall at first, but as soon as Donald had fallen beneath Julios, and his huge mass had rolled on top of him, Myers was flung over the top. He landed on the lower stairs and rolled to the floor where the flames were encroaching. He stopped with his face just inches from the fire and he rolled again, patting his skin and his hair with frantic slaps. He staggered to his feet, surprised not to discover broken bones.

"I can't get through," said Donald. He was at the base of the stairs with Julios, who had regained some consciousness during the fall. He flinched at the heat and seemed to be aware of the position he was in, but his body was yet to catch up with his mind.

Myers ripped down the lime green curtains from the front window and began to beat the flames, but it was useless. The curtains began to burn and his already singed hand blistered.

"I need help," said Donald.

It was then that Carver's words repeated in Myers' mind.

They all deserve to die.

But they were two men. Two living souls just five steps away, and between them and safety was a wall of raging fire that was spreading with every second that passed. He had to do something.

"Jump," he screamed.

But the two men were forced back by the heat. Donald climbed back up two steps, dragging the big man's bulk. Their options were running out.

"Go," said Julios. His voice sounded drunk and lazy, but it was deep and carried over the crackles and hisses of the fire as a cannon might bellow above the sound of small arms. He tore his arm from Donald's grip. "Leave me."

Donald, more defiant than ever, began to drag Julios back up the stairs to the relative safety. But it was certain death and they all knew it.

"No," said Myers. He pulled off his jacket and began to beat the flames.

It was at that point that the ceiling at the top of the stairs crashed down above them. The hot and unbearable air was filled with dust, and burning timbers blocked their upward escape.

Myers beat with everything he had. He beat so hard his arms ached, but his mind seemed to ignore the pain.

"Go now," he screamed at them. They were two men. Barefoot and bare-chested. They had endured God knows what torture and suffering and their bodies bore the bruises, the abrasions, and the breaks with tenacious pride. He beat again, finding success with bursts of three. The flames retreated enough for a man to pass.

But they lingered, doubtful of their escape, and the flames returned. More of the ceiling behind them gave way and burning debris tumbled down the stairs. A wooden beam swung from its fixture in an arc. It all happened in slow motion. Donald saw the blazing beam. He raised his hands, but he was weak with fatigue.

The beam caught him square and he tumbled down in a ragged heap.

It was Julios, with quite possibly the largest shoulders Myers had ever seen, who bent, collected Donald onto his shoulder in a fireman's carry, and, in his drunken state, descended. Myers saw the move. It was brave and it was noble, but one mistake could kill them both. He beat again, three times, harder than before. Then again, and again, beating the flames back for a momentary space, a narrow path on which their lives depended.

The smell of burning skin was a smell that Myers could identify blindfolded. It was a smell that would never leave him. Julios growled and moaned with the first step and Myers stepped back, ready to help them through, just as Fox burst through the door in a stream of water. She held a fire extinguisher and, taking a few short moments to read the scene, she soaked Julios' feet as he walked.

Fox backed out of the door, followed by Julios and Donald. Myers followed and felt the cool air lick at his skin. Together, Fox and Myers helped Donald down, and Julios, dazed, limped in a tight circle fighting the agony of the charred and blistered soles of his feet.

"The fire brigade is on its way," said Fox, as she put the empty fire extinguisher down. "Standard police issue kit, sir."

Myers nodded, grateful for her obedience to all the rules. She was in full control of the situation and, in that moment, he admired her. She would do well in the force. She had something that Myers could never find within himself.

"I also called an ambulance. In the meantime, I suggest we all move away from the house. Is there anybody else inside?"

The woman.

Myers pictured her content expression as she lay on the bed. He heard the words of the silent man.

She's the one you want, Detective Inspector Myers. She's the one who tricked your daughter into this.

"Sir?" said Fox, her voice loud, clear, and in control. "Tell me. Is anyone still in there?"

He glanced at Donald Cartwright, who lay motionless, and Julios, who said nothing.

"Sir?"

"No," said Myers. He shook his head. "No. Not anymore."

"Are you sure? You don't seem so sure about that."

"There's nobody left," Myers snapped. "Nobody alive anyway."

A fire engine rounded the corner at the end of the street and Fox led Myers away from Julios and Donald.

"Sir, there's no easy way to say this," she

began. Her face was that of a stoic professional, solemn and focused. "I'm under orders to arrest you, sir."

"Arrest me? I just helped two men from a burning building."

"There have been claims of harassment and Allenby has added gross misconduct. She didn't give me the details, sir."

Myers turned away from her and swept his hair from his forehead. The fire engine stopped with a hiss of airbrakes, but the sirens continued. Myers guessed they were ambulances and police cars. The whole street would be awash with uniforms soon.

"I thought you might appreciate an opportunity to say something before I arrest you, sir."

There was a hidden meaning in her words. Some message that lay beneath the formalities.

"Did Allenby tell you about Harriet?"

Fox nodded.

"She thinks you're losing it, sir."

"I'm not losing it. She's out there. Rashid Al Sheik has her."

Fox bore that tight-lipped smile again. It was anything but a smile.

"You don't believe me either."

She said nothing and Myers could see her searching for the kindest words to say.

"I need time, Fox."

"Sir, I can't-"

"It was you that told me to trust my gut. I know he has her. I know we can get her back."

"We?" Her expression altered and that wall of right and wrong began to rise. "Sir, I can't-"

"Not you," he said, and nodded toward the two charred men. "Them."

It was a huge ask. He knew it and she knew it. He was not only asking her to disobey a direct order, but he was asking her to forget about two key witnesses and potential suspects.

"They aren't the suspects here, Fox. They're just two men who escaped a house fire. My daughter is the victim."

The light of the fire cast an orange glow on one side of her face. The other side lay in shadow. She had the favour of youth and beauty on her side. Her flawless skin was almost doll-like. Her wide eyes were pure and honest, and her slender frame, though agile and lithe, was upright with the confidence of integrity. An integrity he was asking her to break.

The first drops of rain began to fall, adding insult to injury. Fox appeared not even to register the rain. She was deep in her own battle of moralities. Flashing blue lights turned the corner at the end of the road. It was an ambulance followed by two police cars.

A flash of lightning lit the scene like a photograph embossing the moment in time on a roll of film for eternity.

"Fox? The clock is ticking," said Myers, and the convoy of emergency vehicles drew closer.

"Do you know where she is?"

"I'll find her."

She said nothing but nodded once. She turned away and closed her eyes to her decision.

"I won't let you regret this," he said, and he stepped away from her, pulling his keys from his pocket.

"Sir?" called Fox, and she walked toward her car. She opened the door and reached inside, then emerged, unsure of her actions.

"You told me once that this wasn't a nine-to-five job."

"I did," said Myers with his hand on the car door. He glanced once at the two men, then approached her.

"You might need this."

She handed him a blue file. There was a doodle on the front and Myers opened it to find Rashid Al Sheikh's report, and the addresses of his businesses.

The girl he had belittled, ignored, and distrusted had not only disobeyed a direct order and let two witnesses leave a crime scene, but she had incriminated herself by giving him a head start.

"Seems like a likely place, sir," she said, and she stepped out into the road to flag down the first of the squad cars, turning her back on Myers and the two men.

CHAPTER FORTY-EIGHT

"Rashid."

Harvey's voice, hoarse with rage and fury, broke.

He could shout no more.

He would face the lion in his den.

The entrance to the abattoir was filled with the sickly and sweet cold smell of death. There was a carousel to his right that continued into the next part of the building, disappearing through a curtain of clear PVC strips to keep the air inside cool for the lamb carcasses that hung from S-shaped butcher's hooks. To his left was a row of offices. The doors were open, and the lights were off. But his eyes were drawn to those curtains and the light beyond.

Outside, thunder grumbled like a slumbering beast and he thought of Julios, drugged and benign. He surprised himself by not only hoping that Julios had gotten out, but that Donny had too. He wondered if that hope was borne of what John's reaction would be or if there was a genuine concern for his foster-brother's wellbeing. But his thoughts were overshadowed by what he imagined he would find beyond the strip curtains.

His curiosity was further teased by a loud click, which was immediately followed by the whir of an electric motor. The carousel jumped into life and each of the lambs swayed with the motion. Then it stopped, and a loud buzz filled the huge space. The carousel began again with a click and the carcasses danced in unison.

Click. Whir. Click. Buzz.

One by one, they disappeared through the curtains, releasing small clouds of frost into the warm, stormy air. But for each of those empty hooks that disappeared from view, another appeared on the far side, laden with the burden of some poor headless and trussed beast.

The rain dripped from Harvey's wet skin onto the concrete floor and his boots oozed water with every slow and cautious step he took. He pulled back the strip curtain and bracing, cold air found his wet clothes, prickled his skin, and tightened his tired muscles. He had been on the move for an entire day and his body was telling him that the ordeal had taken its toll.

He pushed through into the cold space.

Click. Whir. Click. Buzz.

There was a network of beams and chains to move the carcasses that hung from the huge hooks. The row of cages along the wall were like small prison cells with a torturous view of the tiled space where animals were hung by their feet to be killed. It was the halal way of slaughtering an animal and had been, in one form or another, done that way for centuries. The animals were stunned to keep them subdued and to calm them. Then their jugulars were sliced, and the animals were left to bleed out. The meat was deemed permissible to eat by Islamic law.

At the end of the carousel, where the

hooks turned on themselves to continue their endless cycle, was a tiled space with a hook on a chain that hung from a beam high above. But it wasn't the hook or the chain that caught Harvey's attention. Nor was it the flash of spark from the stun gun that was positioned to find the soft fleshy rumps as each lamb reached the end of the carousel.

It was Rashid Al Sheik. He stood there, fearless with privilege and arrogant with sanctimony.

Click. Whir. Click. Buzz.

"You're on your own now, Rashid," said Harvey, raising his voice above the monotonous thrum of the carousel. "There's nobody left to save you."

Rashid's face twitched as he thought of Farhad.

"He didn't die like a lion. I thought you'd like to know." said Harvey, and he gestured at the laden hooks that passed by in a slow and tedious cycle. "Like a lamb to the slaughter, Rashid."

"Who are you?"

Click. Whir. Click. Buzz.

"Where's Harriet?"

Both questions went unanswered.

"In my country, halal meat is law," said Rashid. "It is a kind method of killing the animal."

"Where's Harriet, Rashid?"

Click. Whir. Click. Buzz.

"Did you know that when an animal is killed in the halal way, we hide the blade until the very last moment, so the animal is not frightened?"

Harvey didn't reply.

"We respect the animal."

"Where's Harriet?"

"We respect life."

Rashid stood with his hands folded behind his back. He began to pace the tiled floor and listened to the rain on the roof high above.

"Harriet deserves respect. She deserves kindness."

"But you, you are a savage. You are no killer of lions. You hide in the shadows."

"I'm not hiding now," said Harvey, and he stepped forward. In his right hand, he held his knife. The handle was sticky with Farhad's blood. With every step he took, Rashid's face grew clearer and that part of Harvey that knew no limits grew agitated.

"Who do you want? Me or the girl?"

"I came for the girl."

"But you want me too?" Rashid smiled. "You can't help yourself, can you? Maybe it's the smell of blood in the air?"

Click. Whir. Click. Buzz.

Harvey moved forward again. His pace quickened, closing the distance with long strides.

It was Rashid's laughter that slowed him. He stopped. And something beside him seemed out of symmetry with the surroundings. Among the pairs of trussed hooves on the far side of the carousel was a pair of human feet. They were still, pale, and rocked only with the movement of the carcasses on either side.

Harriet.

Harvey tried to run between the great chunks of meat, but the movement and their weight pushed him away.

"You coward," Harvey shouted. "You couldn't do it yourself, could you? There's nobody left to do it for you."

Click. Whir. Click. Buzz.

The stun gun would merely subdue a beast, but for a young girl, the bolt of electricity that passed through her body would be fatal.

"Leave her. It's the kindest thing for her," said Rashid, seeing Harvey fight his way through the already slaughtered beasts. His voice boomed in that terrible space. "It's over for her now. Stop."

Harvey searched the carousel to find her bare feet among the pairs of hooves, but as he turned, he saw movement. The huge hook that had hung beside Rashid was swinging towards him. It caught him in his chest, knocking him off his feet. He rolled and fought for breath, clutching his ribs.

The hook began its return swing and Harvey followed its course.

Rashid was gone.

Click. Whir. Click. Buzz.

He climbed to his feet and retrieved his knife just as the lights went out.

Guided only by the flash of sparks as the automated stun gun found its mark, Harvey felt his way along the line of carcasses. Their skin was cold and hard to the touch. He followed the line round by the slaughter station where Rashid had been standing. He felt every animal and every leg, feeling for the warm and hairless skin of Harriet's legs.

Click. Whir. Click. Buzz.

And he found her.

He tried to raise her up and unhook her legs, but she was too heavy.

Click. Whir. Click. Buzz.

Blind to the world save for the intermittent shower of sparks and deafened by the rain on the roof and the thunder of blood in his ears, he reached down and held her in both arms, cradling her limp body. But the hook from which she hung was reaching the end of the line.

Click. Whir. Click. Buzz.

With everything he had left, he pulled her to his chest, moving with her and swaying with the carcasses as another passed through the deadly stun gun, and he sliced through the rope that bound her legs.

Click. Whir. Click. Buzz.

The animal before her swayed then stilled and the stun gun found its mark.

Click. Whir.

Harvey reached up to her feet with his bloodied knife in his hand and held her tight against his chest with the other.

Click.

He sliced and they fell together. He cradled her head and rolled to protect her.

Buzz.

A shower of sparks fell on them and Harvey held her face to his chest.

He held her there for a moment to regain his breath and as more beasts passed above them and more sparks fell, he found himself holding her head and stroking her hair. She was just a girl. A young, innocent girl. His fingers found the soft part of her neck and he felt the faint but steady beat of her pulse.

He held her in his arms and sat upright. Then he climbed to his feet and cradled her as if she were his own. He used the flash of light to find his way and he stumbled with her in his arms through the curtains of death. Outside, the rain hammered down and, in the distance, Farhad's body was an island in a shimmering sea of rainwater.

Harvey walked and Harriet hung limp and heavy in his tired arms. His body ached. His mind was racing. All he had to do was get her to a hospital and find Donny. He stepped outside into the rain and once more relished the cold, fresh feeling as the day washed his tired face.

She stirred.

It was just a little but enough for Harvey to know she was coming round. He laid her down on the sodden concrete and smoothed her hair from her face to reveal her young and perfect skin.

It was a side of death Harvey knew little about. His experiences had always brought him closer to the darker side where recovery and resuscitation were not the desired outcome.

He felt as if he should say something. Like he should be calling her name to bring her back. To let her know she was safe.

But he didn't know what to say.

He held her hand.

But it was in that moment that two headlights shone, bright and cavalier. He turned to face the black Mercedes. The headlights lit the rain and the puddles, and steam rose from its bonnet. It was fifty metres away, parked in the darkest of corners.

The engine revved once, loud and raw.

Harvey rested the girl's head on the ground, and he stood.

The engine revved once more, this time louder and for longer, as Rashid's sandaled foot planted into the thick, lavish carpet.

And Harvey stepped forward, placing himself between the car and the girl.

Then the tyres spun on the wet ground. The gears crunched into place and the headlights rose as the car lurched forward.

Harvey bent and picked up Harriet from the ground. He held her in his arms, swearing to protect her, swearing that she would be okay.

Rashid found second gear and the car gained speed, closing the distance fast. Harvey prepared to absorb the impact. He cradled Harriet close to his body and raised her as high as he could.

He braced for the collision.

Then three gunshots rang out from nowhere.

The car swerved and Harvey felt the rush of air as it passed him with inches to spare and crashed into the abattoir. The front of the car crumpled with the metallic scream of twisted steel. A hiss of hot steam sprayed, and the horn blared as Rashid's body slumped over the wheel.

Harvey dropped to his knees, still cradling Harriet in his arms. He let his head fall back and closed his eyes to savour the rain and the cool air.

He knew he was there. He felt his presence but heard no footsteps.

He opened his eyes.

Myers stood looking down at him. His face had softened, and though Harvey had never known his own parents, he knew the expression to be that of paternal love. Myers let the gun slip from his hand. And Harvey raised her up for him to take.

Two strong arms pulled Harvey to his feet. Two arms with such strength that they could belong to only one man.

Harvey didn't turn to see him. Nor did he search for Donny, who he knew would be close by. He stared at Myers and studied the expression of relief on his face.

"I can't thank you enough," said Myers, his voice whispered so as not to disturb his little girl.

Harvey didn't reply.

It was the convoy of flashing blue lights that streamed along the lane in the distance that killed the moment. But it was a moment

Harvey would never forget. And he was sure that Myers too would remember it always.

"Go," he said, and he looked up from his daughter's face. "Go now. Be quick."

"Someone has to pay for this," said Harvey. "You know how it works."

Myers nodded and offered one of those smiles that wasn't a smile.

"Yes," said Myers, and he turned his attention back to his daughter's sleeping face. "Yes, they do."

CHAPTER FORTY-NINE

King George Hospital, Chadwell Heath, in the early hours of Sunday morning was a quiet place. Patients slept in the wings and nurses moved from room to room in practised near silence.

Two uniformed police officers were standing guard outside one particular recovery room. Inside, two parents sat either side of their daughter's bed. The mother held her daughter's hand. The father hung his head.

"You had no choice, Matthew," whispered Alison, and he nodded. "Look what you did. You got our little girl back. You saved her."

"I killed a man."

Alison sighed and her eyes flicked to her daughter's.

"You don't have to hide it, Mum. I know what he did." Her voice was cracked and slurred, like that of a sobering drunk, and her eyelids were lazy as sleep beckoned.

"You should sleep, Harriet." Alison's motherly tone was calm, quiet, and strong. "I'll be here when you wake up. I'm not going anywhere."

"What about Dad?" said Harriet.

Myers stared up at her. He offered a smile that wasn't a smile at first, but when he saw her beautiful eyes staring back at him, it was.

"Anything you need, you just ask. I'll make it happen."

"I need *you*, Dad."

"How's your head?" said Myers, moving the subject on. Time was running out.

She gave him a disappointed look and reached for his hand.

"Do you know what I really want? What would really make me happy?" she asked.

Myers knew what she was going to say, and he had a good idea Alison knew it too. But there was no room to manoeuvre and no time to deflect it.

"I want us to be a family again."

"Oh, Harriet-"

"I'm sorry, Mum. I love Darren. He's a kind man, but..."

"We *are* a family," said Myers, and he offered her his hand. She took it and he reached across to Alison who, after a moment of doubt, took it so that the three of them were united in a circle. "Nothing will ever break us. We'll get over this. Your mum and I will always be your parents and we'll always be with you."

"Always?" she asked.

"As often as we can," said Myers, and he squeezed their hands, savouring Alison's touch. He knew those fingers so well and he was sure he could feel the indent where her wedding and engagement rings had been. He wondered if she wore them in secret, but then doubted the notion.

"Do you remember when you lost me?" said Harriet. She held their hands tight but stared ahead, recalling the time. She had been just a child, dizzied by fear, and she remembered the moment when she had seen their faces. "That's how I feel now."

"I think you'll find that *we* remember that

time better than you do," said Alison. "One day you'll understand, when you have children of your own. Do you agree, Matthew?"

He laughed once as a response and nodded. But it wasn't a laugh. It was more of a breath with a smile that wasn't really a smile. "I remember when you fell and hit your head and we had to bring you here. When you trapped your finger in the door jamb and your fingers swelled like big, fat sausages. When you choked in the swimming pool and I had to drag you out of the water. I remember all those moments, Harriet. We both do."

"Will you remember this time like all those others?" she asked.

He would. He knew he would, and Alison would too. She wouldn't be able to help but remember it. He imagined that Alison would take Harriet home when the nurses gave the all-clear, and she would put her to bed. And Myers wouldn't be there. That would be a time he wouldn't remember.

"No," he said. "No, some times are meant to be forgotten."

She nodded.

"Sir?" said Fox from where she was standing by the door. He'd been so engrossed in his own family that he'd forgotten she was there. "It's time."

Harriet's hand tightened and Myers' heart felt like it would split in two. But then Alison squeezed too, and she stared at him from across the bed.

He swallowed and fought to control his voice, and he stood. He let their hands slip from his and held them both in his gaze for a moment, capturing a memory that would see him through.

"I love you both so very much," he said, and he leaned over to kiss Harriet on the cheek.

Then he felt Alison's warmth sidle up beside him and they hugged as a family. A unit. Unbreakable. A loving family. Just as Harriet wanted.

"Dad, no," cried Harriet, but Fox was professional. She moved fast and didn't hesitate as she pushed the cuffs onto his wrists. At least she allowed him the dignity of hanging his jacket over his arms to hide the restraints. Alison was a picture of strength, but he knew that face like he knew his own. She was fighting back the tears.

He tried to say something but found no

words. Instead, he just smiled at them. And this time, it was a smile. It was the smile he wore the day he married Alison and saw her face as she peeled back her veil. It was the smile he wore when the nurse handed Harriet to him as a new-born. It was the smile he saved for special occasions. He just didn't know where he kept it.

He turned by the door to steal one more mental picture that nobody could take from him.

"I'll be back before you know it," he said, and Fox nudged him through the door.

The corridor was a blur. Knowing faces watched him pass and muttered to their friends. The automatic doors opened with a hiss and he stopped to breathe the fresh air one last time.

"Thank you, Fox," he said. "Thank you for making this happen."

"Come on, now, sir," she said. "I had no part in this. Remember?"

There were two armed police standing beside a police van. There were no flashing lights. No drama. Just a police van escorting a man from the hospital. Allenby was there wearing her dark-blue skirt suit. She watched as Fox led him to the rear of the van and the officer stepped to one side.

"I'll do what I can, Myers," said Allenby. "If not for you, for your family."

He nodded but said nothing.

"Six months to a year," she said. "Parole in three to six months. I'll to see it the judge has all the relevant facts."

Again, he nodded and searched for the window of Harriet's room before the rear doors were closed and locked and he was alone.

He felt eyes on him, and he found them through the tinted rear window, cold and fierce. The man was standing beside the entrance with his hands in his jacket pockets.

And Myers felt him.

Just a ripple.

"That's what it is," he said to the man, though he wouldn't hear the words, and he thought of himself in a parallel life. One where Harriet was a memory and every day was steeped in shadow. "It's just a ripple."

CHAPTER FIFTY

The van doors closed with a boom that was final.

The woman in the blue skirt suit shook the younger girl's hand and said something that made her smile. It was a proud smile and her eyes shone.

They climbed into a BMW and waited for the van to leave, then, after a few short moments of reflection, they followed with the armed police car behind.

Harvey sighed.

It had been close. As close as he'd ever been. The blood on his hands would never wash away and that shadow he lived in was, for a while, lit for all the world to see.

But he could trust that man. The man that, only twenty-four hours before, had breathed in his face and vented his fury from the far side of the interview room. He could trust him not to breathe a word. They had shared something. Something that neither Harvey nor Detective Myers could ever articulate.

Myers owed Harvey his daughter's life, and, in return, Harvey was free.

A pale, blue sky hung over London and the air bore that clean, natural scent that follows in the wake of a storm. That same clean air carried the smell of cigar smoke and expensive cologne and roused Harvey from his musings. John's presence darkened the shadow that Harvey had found.

He wore his long, formal jacket over an immaculate white shirt with black trousers, and the wooden heels of his shoes clicked on the pavement. The steps were unhurried. He would be thinking of what he might say.

There was always a plan. Always a strategy of some kind.

He said nothing at first.

He stood beside Harvey and his arm grazed Harvey's as he too found the lining of his pockets a welcome distraction. A cloud of cigar smoke washed over Harvey, then dispersed, leaving only a bitter taste in his mouth.

"He'll be okay," said John.

Harvey didn't reply.

"The doctors are treating his burns and his feet are in casts. Broken toes."

Harvey didn't reply.

"I should thank you, Harvey," said John. "I should thank you for bringing him home. I should thank you for what you did. Whatever it was."

It was John's way of asking Harvey what exactly had happened.

"Do you mind if I spare you the detail, John?"

"I should thank you for doing as I asked. You took care of your brother, Harvey. You did what I asked. I know he doesn't deserve it, but..."

"You're wrong," said Harvey, and he heard the words, alien and in contrast to anything he had said before. "You're wrong. He does deserve it, John. And I don't need you to ask me to look after him. Believe me, there were times when all I was doing was hunting for Julios, but..."

"But what?"

"But I learned things, John. I learned things that I think Donny would prefer me not to say. But, trust me, when times were tough, Donny stood tall. And when things had to be done that should never have had to be done, Donny did them."

Harvey paused, leaving John to wrestle with the ambiguity.

"He did you proud, John. He's a Cartwright."

John cleared his throat and looked away.

"That's the nicest thing you ever said about him."

"Well, his heart was in the right place. He might be the spoiled, arrogant only child of a wealthy businessman, John, but he meant well, and he did the right thing. If he didn't, I..."

Harvey stopped himself from saying it.

"You would have what?" said John, catching the scent of the bone that Harvey had offered.

"I would have killed him myself."

Harvey took a few steps and opened the

back box on his motorcycle. He retrieved his helmet and noted the scrapes from the dock-side slide.

He fingered the flakes of paint and the small dent and made a mental note to repair them.

"He'll be home in a few days," said John, as Harvey climbed on the bike. "I doubt he'll be in the mood for a party, but I was thinking we could do a little something, you know, to remember Julia. It might give him a chance to say goodbye."

Harvey started the engine. It was a nice idea, and he told him so.

"Maybe I'll have Sergio arrange something. Just us. You, me, Julios, Donny, and Sergio. What do you think?"

"I think you should ask Donny what he wants, John," said Harvey, and he flipped his visor down to stare at his foster-father through the darkened tint.

John was very much like Rashid, he thought. He was capable and intelligent beyond words. He was a man that moved mountains to get what he wanted. But he was unable to do anything himself.

He was a powerful man. He was a good

man at heart and Harvey could only be grateful he wasn't a monster like Rashid.

"Come to think of it," said John, his face adopting a confused expression. "Where is Sergio? Have you seen him?"

Harvey didn't reply.

The End.

Also by J.D. Weston

J.D. Weston is the award-winning author and creator of Harvey Stone and Frankie Black. He was born in London, England, and after more than a decade in the Middle East, now enjoys a tranquil life in Lincolnshire with his wife.

The Harvey Stone series is a prequel series set ten years before The Stone Cold Thriller series.

With more than twenty novels to his name, the Harvey Stone series is the result of many years of storytelling, and is his finest work to date. You can find more about J.D. Weston at www.jdweston.com.

Turn the page to see his other books.

THE HARVEY STONE SERIES

Free Novella

A terrible moment in time, captured in blood.

See www.jdweston.com for details.

The Silent Man

To find the killer, he must lose his mind...

See www.jdweston.com for details.

The Spider's Web

To enter the spider's web, he must become the fly...

See www.jdweston.com for details.

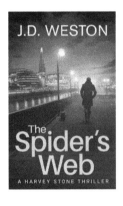

The Mercy Kill

To light the way, he must burn his past...

See www.jdweston.com for details.

The Savage Few

Coming March 2021

Join the J.D. Weston Reader Group to stay up to date on new releases, receive discounts, and get three free eBooks.

See www.jdweston.com for details.

THE STONE COLD THRILLER SERIES

The Stone Cold Thriller Series

Stone Cold

Stone Fury

Stone Fall

Stone Rage

Stone Free

Stone Rush

Stone Game

Stone Raid

Stone Deep

Stone Fist

Stone Army

Stone Face

The Stone Cold Box Sets

Boxset One

Boxset Two

Boxset Three

Boxset Four

Visit www.jdweston.com for details.

THE FRANKIE BLACK FILES

The Frankie Black Files

Torn in Two

Her Only Hope

Black Blood

The Frankie Black Files Boxset

Visit www.jdweston.com for details.

Copyright © 2020 by J.D. Weston

All rights reserved.

The moral right of J.D. Weston to be identified as the author of this work has been asserted by him in accordance with the Copyright, Designs and Patents act 1988.

All the characters in this book are fictitious, and any resemblance to actual persons living or dead is purely coincidental.

All rights reserved. No part of this publication may be reproduced, stored in a retrieval system or transmitted in any form or by any means, without the prior permission in writing of the publisher, nor to be otherwise circulated in any form of binding or cover other than that in which it is published without a similar condition, including this condition, being imposed on the subsequent purchaser.